EmERalds and Envy

JUNKIN' JEWELRY MYSTERIES: BOOK 1

ANGELA MCRAE

Emeralds and Envy

Junkin' Jewelry Mysteries™

Red Adept Publishing, LLC

104 Bugenfield Court

Garner, NC 27529

http://RedAdeptPublishing.com/

For Madison Horton

Chapter One

My foot slammed on the brakes. As the tires squealed, my huge tan leather purse flew to the floor with a thud. Pens spilled, and a lipstick bounced neatly into the passenger-side door pocket like the prize-winning beanbag in a game of vehicle cornhole. I quickly looked in the rearview mirror. Thank goodness it was early morning and there were no witnesses to my less-than-spectacular driving.

I was lucky another car wasn't behind me. Despite the hot-pink I Brake for Garage Sales decal in my rear window, I knew sudden stops were risky. My foot, however, seemed to have a mind of its own.

My livelihood depended on successful treasure hunting at garage sales, so my heart fluttered wildly at the sight of a scalloped-edge paper-plate sign nailed to a utility pole. Someone had written "Moving Sale, Friday & Saturday, 7 Till?" in big black Magic Marker.

I put my car in reverse and backed up so I could read the address scrawled across the bottom of the makeshift sign—23 Wilson Avenue. A chunky scribbled arrow pointed right, so I turned, gunned the engine, and zoomed up Wilson.

My antiques-loving mother had taught me years ago that if I saw a professionally printed sign advertising a garage sale, I needn't bother stopping. They'd spent too much money on marketing, and their junk would be overpriced. The Paper Plate School of Advertising meant the seller was having a last-minute sale and needed some fast cash. I counted on those sales to make a living.

Ever since leaving my job as a newspaper reporter two years ago to launch my own home-based business, I'd been making a name for myself by creating my own line of handcrafted jewelry, Emma Madison Designs. Most of my jewelry bits and baubles came from garage sales, and the early bird really did get the jeweled worm.

That Friday morning, I was out and about early because I'd run out of hazelnut creamer and craved some with my caffeine fix for the day, so I was on my way to the grocery store. The Wilson Avenue garage sale hadn't been advertised in the newspaper or on the town's *Thrifty Shopper* Facebook page, so I was extra lucky to have stumbled across it.

A glance at the dashboard clock told me it was only a few minutes past seven. I couldn't believe it, but I was apparently the first customer to arrive. After parking my cherry-red Ford Fusion along the street, I headed up the driveway of the small beige brick house. A young couple was hard at work behind a table loaded with coffee mugs, CDs, old cell phone chargers, and a laptop computer missing its battery cover.

"Good morning," the blonde said. She stepped out from behind a large box that had once held a flat-screen TV, and the likely reason for their move was clear—she was great with child. "We're still getting set up, but feel free to go ahead and browse if you like." She paused to rub the small of her back. "Looking for anything in particular?"

"I like old costume jewelry." I glanced around with a practiced casual air. "Will you have any of that today?"

She nodded. "There's a metal tin around here somewhere that's got some old jewelry that belonged to my grandmother." She blew a stray wisp of hair out of her eyes. "It's mostly gaudy old rhinestone stuff, not really anything I'd ever wear."

No surprise there. The woman's only jewelry was a plain gold wedding band and tiny gold stud earrings.

She turned her attention to the goateed man who had just finished wrestling a dusty ficus tree out of the garage. "Dave, have you seen that tin of junk jewelry?"

"Huh?" He ran his fingers through his dark hair then headed over to the woman and slurped from his Dunkin' Donuts cup. The man appeared to have just gotten out of bed. He looked toward the garage and pointed at several large cardboard boxes labeled Housewares. "If you don't mind going through the boxes"—he gave me an apologetic look—"I think it might have landed over there somewhere."

"No problem," I said. "I don't mind a little digging." I made a beeline for the carport and started removing items from the first overflowing box. On top were old blue jeans and T-shirts. If the jeans were truly vintage and collectible, they could easily be worth a few hundred bucks. But upon closer inspection of the faded knees and broken zippers, I realized they were just old and tattered.

Pawing through a pile of T-shirts, I was slightly troubled by the growing family's college football loyalties as evidenced by their cast-off clothing. The large red sweatshirts—probably his—depicted the Georgia Bulldogs. The smaller yellow-and-black T-shirts—probably hers—represented Georgia Tech. *A house divided? That poor baby. What will he or she do during college football season?*

Remembering not to get distracted, I moved on to the next box. On top were some unfortunate orange polka-dotted place mats that still had the Target price tags on them. They were probably a wedding gift the couple didn't like. *I don't blame you. I wouldn't have used those either. Good call.*

Beneath the place mats, the late Diana, Princess of Wales, peered up at me from the cover of a dog-eared *People* magazine. The issue was dated 1997, the year she died in a tragic car wreck in Paris. I flipped through the magazine, wistful. I was just a teenager when the princess died, and I recalled how my mother and grandmother had been obsessed with the news coverage of her death. They'd even gotten up before dawn the morning of her funeral to watch it live on TV.

Then it hit me—those magazines must have belonged to the grandmother, not the young couple. No one in their twenties owned Princess Diana magazines.

Flinging the poor princess aside, I was hopeful that the tin of jewelry was nearby. I returned to my digging and soon unearthed a rusty, rose-patterned round tin that screamed "Grandma." The lid was on tight, but I knew from years of experience that prying up one side at a time would get the job done. I lifted the lid and held my breath. *Pay dirt!*

My heart skipped a beat. An ornate piece with tiny seed pearls was almost certainly a Miriam Haskell brooch. I gently set it aside, my eyes widening as I uncovered a bracelet made of chunky blocks of candy-colored Lucite. It was probably one of those magnificent old Coro beauties.

I reached in my purse in search of the small magnifying glass I kept on my key ring. I had to flip past a few other trinkets to find it since my key ring was equipped with all of the single woman's essentials—car keys, a canister of pepper spray shaped like a tube of lipstick, and a heavy-duty whistle. After I flipped to the magnifying glass, I quickly checked the bracelet's clasp and confirmed that the piece was indeed Coro.

A glance over my shoulder confirmed that I wasn't being watched. The man I now knew as Dave was busy adding two old coffee makers to the moving sale's growing electronics department. His wife guzzled what looked like ice water from a gigantic plastic mug.

Sifting through the tin, I came across a rhinestone bow pin that was missing one small clear crystal, which could easily be replaced. *Be still my heart! Is that one of Delizza and Elster's coveted rhinestone bracelets, the ones nicknamed Juliana jewelry?* With trembling fingers,

I turned it over and counted the rectangular links. One, two, three, four, five. *Bingo!* No stones were missing, and even the safety chain was in perfect condition. I was already more than a little enamored with the old tin of jewelry, and I hoped the price would be reasonable.

That one stash of valuable costume jewelry could be the big break I'd been looking for. Instead of merely meeting expenses for another month, I might actually make a tidy profit that I could use to help grow my jewelry business. And the family and friends who'd doubted I could make a living as a jewelry designer and seller? I'd prove them all wrong.

"Excuse me, but I see a few things here that I'm interested in," I called to the mom-to-be. "Are you selling it by the piece, or would you give me a price on the whole tin?"

She turned to Dave and tapped him on the arm. "Honey, what do you think?"

He looked at her and shrugged. "I don't care. It's *your* grandmother's. I just want to get rid of this stuff before the movers come."

The wife turned to me and chewed her lip, appearing to consider the price. I waited with what I hoped was my best I-can-take-it-or-leave-it look, glancing around as if the tin of junk jewelry were no big deal.

"We're about to move to a new house before the baby gets here, so I really need to clean out some things," she said. "How about ten dollars for everything? Is that too much?"

I thought I would choke. "No, no. Ten sounds fair, and—"

"Hi there, Emma! I hope you've found some nice treasures this morning!"

I cringed. Harriet Harris's chirpy voice was not what I wanted to hear at that precise moment. A retired schoolteacher, Harriet had decided to open an antiques shop as her second-act career. She was constantly on the prowl for items for her Making Memories Antique Mall. She also had a reputation as the stingiest woman in town. Whether she was or not, her near-constant presence on the local garage sale scene was a thorn in my entrepreneurial side.

Before Harriet could sabotage my good deal on the jewelry, I rooted around in my purse for a ten-dollar bill and forked it over to the expectant mom. "Here you go. Good luck with your sale." I nodded at her belly. "And your baby."

"Thanks," she said. "We'll need it."

Harriet sidled up beside me and jutted her chin at my floral tin. "So, did you find anything good this morning?" She was clearly engrossed by the container tucked securely under my arm. She reached out and gave the tin two strong taps. "Let's see what you've found."

Clearly, the woman had boundary issues, and some common sense issues for that matter.

I wasn't about to let Harriet know what I'd found, so I gave her a wink. "It's only some of that old junk jewelry I like. And the funny thing was, I was out running errands this morning when I stumbled across this sale. But hey, good luck going through the rest of their things." I breezed past a gaping Harriet and returned to my car. I should have been ashamed of myself for taking such pleasure in having outscored Harriet, but I wasn't.

Like a triumphant junk-hoarding queen, she reigned over the garage sale scene in Roseland. Ever since opening her antique mall, Harriet had become famous for her wheeling and dealing. Many local residents remembered her from their school days, back when she taught kindergarten and her husband, Hubert, was the principal. Perhaps it was for sentimental reasons that they let her browse their castoffs before they held a garage sale. It was rare that anyone ever learned about a sale before Harriet.

I relished the thought that, for once, I had actually beaten her to a sale. And in an even rarer bit of luck, I'd managed to nab a few treasures before they ended up in a case of overpriced jewelry at Making Memories.

Suddenly, that hazelnut creamer I'd been so set on picking up at the grocery store could wait. I headed back to my cozy Craftsman bungalow on Buchanan Street, pulled up beside the small English rose bushes that were just beginning to leaf out, and hurried inside the house to explore my new jewels. *Ten dollars? Score!* I could hardly believe the treasure chest I'd just purchased—a find I probably wouldn't have gotten if Harriet had arrived five minutes earlier.

In the kitchen, I opened a cupboard door and grabbed the powdered coffee creamer I kept on hand for emergency use. I poured some into a vintage Pyrex mug and added the coffee that had been brewing for the past thirty minutes. Dollar signs flashed before my eyes as I fantasized about how much the Delizza and Elster bracelet might fetch—at least a few hundred if the eBay sales I religiously monitored were any indication. Maybe I would be able to boost my savings account again after investing so much money in the launch of my jewelry business. If I were really lucky, some of the other pieces would bring top dollar as well.

I decided to microwave a bowl of instant oatmeal, and while it cooked, I plucked one of my jewelry identification guides from a crowded bookshelf in the living room. When the oatmeal was ready, I plopped it on the kitchen table and spooned away as I eagerly flipped through the glossy pages of a price guide. A swish of fur brushed against my leg.

"Good morning, Miriam Haskell. Guess what?" I asked, looking down. My Siamese kitty flicked her tail. "I might have found a brooch made by your namesake this morning."

Miriam meowed her approval. My Meezer was such a sweet girl.

When I found her at the animal shelter last year, I'd immediately fallen in love with the distinctive band of white around her face. It contrasted sharply with the dark gray of the rest of her coat. She'd reminded me of a gracious gray-haired lady wearing a strand of pearls, so I named her for one of the designers I most associated with the creamy white jewelry. Miriam lay at my feet and playfully teased my tennis shoe laces as I pored over the pages of the jewelry book.

Not all of my friends could understand my passion for finding a great deal on costume jewelry, but I knew one who would. I reached for my cell phone and gave her a call. Carleen Wood owned a high-end antiques shop downtown, the Silver Squirrel, and she also shared my affection for old costume jewelry. She picked up on the second ring.

"Good morning, Emma. What has you up so early?"

I laughed. "The steal of the century."

"Oh? Tell me more."

That was all the encouragement I needed. I described my morning, from digging through the boxes to finding the tin of the grandmother's jewelry to the discovery of all those fantastic pieces inside. I ended by telling her about my close call with Harriet Harris.

"Sounds like you got there just in time," Carleen said. "Harriet can sniff out a treasure like nobody's business, but I'm glad you're the one who hit the costume jewelry jackpot this time."

"That's exactly what it was. And now I have a favor to ask you."

"Let's hear it."

"I've been sitting here looking through one of my jewelry guidebooks. While this brooch with the seed pearls sure looks like Miriam Haskell, it isn't marked. Didn't you once tell me you've got some costume jewelry books I can borrow?"

"Do I ever," Carleen said. "My office is running over with them, in fact."

"Do you mind if I stop by and take a look?"

Carleen said she was heading to her shop in about fifteen minutes and told me I was welcome to stop by. I promised to see her within the hour.

After I finished my breakfast and washed a few dishes, I changed clothes. Old jeans, a plain T-shirt, and my favorite tennis shoes were fine for an early-morning run to the grocery store—or in my case, an unexpected garage sale. But if I was going to be out and about downtown, I needed to look more polished. Since I made my living in the jewelry world, I was trying to cultivate an image as a casual chic dresser who never left home without a few well-chosen accessories. I slipped into my favorite floral blouse, navy cotton slacks, and a pair of silver flats. I wore one of my own navy-blue beaded necklace designs then added a few silver wire bangle bracelets and my grandmother's white-gold filigree cocktail ring.

Carefully, I tucked the possible Miriam Haskell brooch into a small cloth bag. After saying goodbye to the feline Miriam, I climbed into my car for the second time that morning and headed to the Silver Squirrel.

Carleen had been in business for nearly twenty years, and she was a fixture of the Roseland business community. I valued her friendship as well as her jewelry expertise. If the pin was Haskell, Carleen would know, even if it wasn't shown in one of her jewelry guides.

I wheeled into the lot behind her shop, and as my tires crunched on the gravel drive, I was stunned to see three police cars and an ambulance nearby. The back door of the Silver Squirrel was standing wide open.

"Oh no!" I whipped into the closest parking space, jerked the car into Park, and quickly got out. My heart was in my throat as I rushed to the door. A Roseland police officer surveyed the back-alley lot and eyed me warily.

"Officer, what's going on? Is something wrong with Carleen?" My eyes darted back and forth between the officer and the open door of the Silver Squirrel. I hoped something terrible hadn't happened to my friend.

"Ma'am, I'm going to have to ask you to step back," he said. "We've got a situation here, and I'm afraid we don't need any bystanders getting in our way."

"Can't you at least tell me if everything's okay in there?"

The officer shook his head and said more firmly, "Ma'am, please..."

I backed away and stood near a corner of the neighboring building, terrified. I feared I was about to be sick.

Not thirty minutes before, I was on the phone with Carleen. Now I was left to wonder what on earth had happened.

Chapter Two

"**E**mma!" Carleen stepped out of her shop, weeping.

Officer or no officer, I ran forward and grabbed her hand. "Thank goodness you're okay!" Relief swept over me but only for a moment.

Carleen swiped at the tears streaming down her cheeks. "It's Tina. When I arrived this morning, I found her on the floor right here, just inside the door, and she wasn't breathing. I can't believe I'm even saying this, but... but... she's been murdered!"

"Are you sure?" I stole a peek inside the door. All I could see was an arm that apparently belonged to Tina LeMann, Carleen's assistant at the shop, and a small bloodstain on the rug near the threshold. Before I could look any farther inside, I felt a firm tug on my arm from a man in a navy suit. He identified himself as Detective Alan Shelton of the Roseland Police Department.

"Ma'am, again, we really must ask you to step back. This is an active crime scene now. Maybe you and your friend could step over there for a few minutes." He gestured toward one of the three patrol cars parked behind the shop.

Carleen's eyes darted back and forth between the detective and me. "Am I being taken in?"

"No, ma'am," the man said. "But we can't let you back into your shop while we're processing the scene. And we're going to need to get a statement from you when we're done. So if you'll just have a seat in the car over there"—he pointed at the police vehicle farthest from the shop—"that would probably be best for everyone."

Carleen seemed shaken, so I draped an arm over her shoulder and walked her to the car. A bald man in a blue uniform stood there, holding the door open, and he waved Carleen inside.

From my not-so-long-ago reporter days, I remembered that the local officers were always diligent in making sure that no one contaminated their crime scene. At that moment, however, I was more concerned about Carleen's well-being than police protocol.

As she wept softly, I leaned down into the car's back seat and gave Carleen a hug. She was clearly distraught, and I wasn't doing so well either. Tina had been Carleen's sole employee at the store and her very dear friend.

"They're taking her away," Carleen said, her voice cracking. A gurney was heading toward the ramp of an ambulance. We watched as the sheet-covered body rolled up the ramp and the vehicle's doors slammed shut with a thud of finality.

Carleen looked toward the ambulance as it prepared to exit the lot. Its sad exit was marked by the ten o'clock chiming of the courthouse clock. Then the vehicle's red light slowly revolved as it pulled away. The scene was surreal. A few tears slipped down my cheeks.

"Ma'am, like I told you, we've got an investigation to conduct here, and we need to talk to Ms. Wood alone, if you don't mind." This Shelton person had a scowl on his face that didn't sit well with me.

"Certainly, Detective." I held his gaze long enough for him to realize that I didn't appreciate his stern tone at such a sad time. I let go of my friend and patted her on the back.

"Emma, can you please wait for me?" Carleen asked, her eyes pleading.

"I'll be right here." I reached into my purse and handed her a tissue. "Try not to worry. I know the police will do everything they can to find out who did this." I nodded toward the detective and fervently hoped that was the truth.

I walked over to my car and waited in the front seat, where I tried unsuccessfully to corral my racing thoughts. Tina was dead—murdered, according to Carleen—and Carleen was being questioned by police. Someone I'd called a friend had gone to work that morning and had her life suddenly cut short.

Gripping and ungripping the steering wheel, I eyeballed the dashboard clock, impatient to talk with Carleen. Then I tried to distract myself by checking email on my phone, but that was pointless. I had little interest in the junk mail offers clogging my in-box and finally realized there was nothing I could do except wait.

Meanwhile, one devastating question kept running through my mind. Who in our sweet little town would have wanted to murder a kind person like Tina?

CARLEEN LOOKED UP AT me, and her normally clear blue eyes were bloodshot. "It was absolutely the most awful thing I've ever witnessed in my life." She sniffed into a tissue I'd given her. After first offering the tissues one by one, I had finally just handed over the entire pocket-sized pack.

Her interview with Detective Alan Shelton was finally over, and she and I were seated at a back table at the Cupcake Café, which was located a few doors down from the Silver Squirrel. Even though it was almost lunchtime, Carleen wasn't interested in ordering a meal. Instead, we sipped hot chai lattes and nibbled on dark-chocolate-fudge cupcakes. At least I was nibbling. Carleen merely picked at hers.

"I knew something was wrong when I got to work this morning and the door was ajar," Carleen said. "Tina always found it so unbearably hot in these old buildings, even in early spring, that she was careful not to waste any of our precious air-conditioning. When I opened the door and was about to step into the hallway, she was ly-ing there on the floor next to the old telephone bench. And that's where... that's where I found her." Her tears started flowing. Impulsively, I reached for Carleen's hand and gave it a gentle squeeze. "That antique sterling candelabra, the one I've had on a shelf in the hallway for a while, was mere inches from the back of her head. I'm sure that's what they used to murder her."

"Murder?" I asked. "You used that word earlier too, but you're sure the candelabra wasn't up on the shelf and simply got knocked off accidentally? Couldn't it have simply fallen on her?" Carleen was clearly upset. It was possible she wasn't thinking rationally.

She shook her head. "That piece was sitting on the desk in my office when I left the shop last night. I'm sure of it. I noticed it was looking tarnished, and I put it on my desk so I'd remember to get Tina to polish it when she got a chance today. Of course now..." Carleen looked positively forlorn. "I can't believe someone used that candelabra to kill Tina. And yes, I'm absolutely positive there's no way that candelabra was up on the shelf this morning."

I hated to keep pressing, but I needed to know more. "Did the police agree with you about her death being a homicide and not an accident?"

Carleen's eyes watered again. "Yes, and they did say not to talk to anyone about the crime scene, but..." She looked around then whispered, "They said she was definitely struck in the back of her head and that there was no way this was an accident."

Mavis Eastwood, the sixty-something owner of the Cupcake Café, walked up and frowned upon seeing our still-full snack plates. "My cupcakes aren't doing the trick today, ladies?"

One of downtown's most beloved merchants, Mavis owned the bakery and lunch spot that had been a gathering place in Roseland since before I was born. If customers didn't leave with their stomachs full and their hearts fuller, Mavis took it personally. I couldn't help admiring her protective hairnet. It covered what was surely one of the world's last authentic beehive hairdos.

"It's delicious as always, Mavis, but I'm afraid I just don't have much of an appetite right now." Carleen placed her plastic fork and paper napkin atop her dissected cupcake and handed it off.

Mavis accepted the plate and patted Carleen on the back. "After what you've been through today, hon, I don't blame you one little bit. Now listen, I've got to go put the layers in the oven for a wedding cake, but you two holler if you need anything. Anything at all, you hear?"

Carleen nodded, seeming to appreciate Mavis's concern. She took a sip of her chai latte, but I could tell she was merely going through the motions and didn't have much interest in her drink.

Lowering my voice, I turned the conversation back to the murder. "I've got to ask you, who would have wanted to kill Tina?" I looked around to make sure we weren't being overheard. "Was anything going on in her personal life? Did she have any enemies?"

Carleen teared up again. Immediately, I regretted jumping right into the unpleasant topic. My big mouth had always been my downfall. *Way to go, Emma.*

"I'm so sorry," I said. "I shouldn't be pressing you about this when you've obviously had such a horrible day already."

"It's okay." Carleen smiled for the first time in hours. "Once a reporter, always a reporter, right?"

I wanted to say no. I had been out of the newspaper business for two years, but many of those in town—including friends like Carleen—still associated me with my old job.

"That's not being a reporter," I said. "That's merely asking what your average *Law and Order* viewer would want to know. Besides, I left the *Daily Tribune* more than two years ago, so I hardly qualify as a reporter anymore. And you haven't answered my question."

Carleen looked as though she might cry again, but she pursed her lips, swallowed, and continued. "Enemies, huh? I simply can't imagine Tina having any. Since she was a young woman with no children, she spent a lot of her free time volunteering with the Humane Society, and—" Carleen raised a finger and stabbed the air. "Oh yes, I remember now. She had just finished serving her first year on the library board." She sighed. "We always loved to come in to work and tell each other about whatever best seller we had just finished reading."

I smiled, not at all surprised that Carleen would treasure a friend who loved books. I felt the same way.

"Did she belong to any groups, then? Like a book group, maybe? Have any social connections she might have mentioned?"

Carleen toyed with a strand of her sleek gray bob and looked away as though she were deep in thought. "I do know that she often went to visit her elderly mother, who lives on the outskirts of town. We didn't socialize much outside of work, but the few times I went to Tina's house, it seemed she lived a nice, quiet life. I truly can't picture her having any enemies."

I thought about that as I broke off a small piece of cupcake and took a bite. "Mm-hmm." I was starving, and the dark-chocolate-fudge frosting was melting into delicious little puddles in my mouth. Carleen might have lost her appetite, but I most assuredly had not. I scarfed down a few bites of the cupcake and quickly got back to business.

"Then I've got to ask the obvious." I dabbed at the corners of my mouth with a napkin. "If this wasn't a personal attack on Tina, robbery is the only other motive I can think of. Was anything taken from your shop?"

"Nothing I'm aware of. No silver, no jewelry, and it doesn't look like anyone tried to get into the safe either. Maybe it was a thief who got scared and ran off when Tina arrived. I just don't think Tina was a target. Everyone in town thought so highly of her."

Everyone except her killer.

"Whether the act was premeditated or not, we've got to find out who did this and what he or she was doing at your shop this morning," I said.

Carleen straightened in her seat, her eyes widening. "I know! Do you think you can get the *Daily Tribune* to help us? Ask people to come forward if they saw anything unusual downtown this morning? What if I offered a reward? I'll be happy to offer a cash reward to anyone who helps us find out who did this." She was practically manic and suddenly more energetic than she'd been all day. Perhaps Carleen felt responsible since Tina had died in her shop.

For once, I paused to think before I spoke. After leaving the newspaper business, I'd vowed never to impose on my reporter friends. These days, they had a hard enough time trying to keep up with readers' dwindling attention spans and competition from the internet without being hit up for favors by old colleagues. But my best friend still worked there, and I knew I could count on her help if I asked for it.

I took a deep breath. "Now you know I can't promise anything since I don't actually work at the newspaper anymore, but I'll get in touch with my old editor friend and see what she recommends. Why don't you head home and try to get some rest?"

Carleen looked as though she were about to weep again. I was afraid she would have a full-blown crying jag if she didn't go home soon.

I patted her on the arm. "I'll call my friend and see what we can do. Then I'll stop by your shop tomorrow morning, and we'll come up with a plan."

Carleen inclined her head. She seemed to be moving in slow motion again. "I don't think I'd have made it through this day without you, Emma," she said as she rose from her seat.

I smiled and tried to look more confident than I felt, but my insides were churning. Maybe I could help Carleen without pestering my friend at the newspaper. All I knew was that I had to try.

The two of us walked to our cars, which were still parked in the lot behind her shop. I was afraid that the memories of the morning's horrific scene might come racing back to her, so I kept up a constant stream of chatter, babbling about how much jewelry I needed to finish making that afternoon. "Now please don't make yourself sick over this." I patted her arm. "I don't care how long it takes, we'll find out who killed Tina and make them pay for what they did. I promise you that."

When we got to the lot, I gave Carleen a hug as we said our good-byes.

Only a few hours earlier, I'd been celebrating a great garage sale find and innocently planning to stop by to share the news with a friend. Around that same time, Tina had arrived at work, probably expecting to have an uneventful day filled with the usual retail activity. Surely she'd had no idea it would be her last hour on earth. Because for whatever reason, someone had decided to snuff out her life.

Driving home after the emotionally exhausting day, I realized I was holding my steering wheel in a death grip. When I got to a stop sign, I hit the brakes so hard that my car squealed to a stop, earning me an angry look from the two gray-haired ladies walking their dogs. I knew that I needed to get it together despite the emotions roiling within.

Whoever had been at Carleen's shop that morning had, for the moment at least, gotten away with murder. With one evil act, they had deprived us of Tina's friendship. Carleen and I would miss her, and so would her family and friends. She would no longer be around to serve in the humane society or on the library board. She would no longer be there to help her aging mother either.

It was so unfair, and someone needed to pay for that crime.

When I got home, the first thing I did was call Jen Davis, my best friend and the newly promoted editor of the newspaper. She picked up on the first ring, and I got straight to the point. "Are you by any chance available for dinner this evening?"

"Yep," she said. "And listen, I don't know if you've heard, but a dead body was found today at—"

"That's what I want to talk to you about," I said. "She was a friend of mine."

"Really?" Jen's voice went up an octave, the way it always did when she got excited about a story. "How'd you know her?"

"Just from stopping by to see my friend Carleen at the Silver Squirrel. But I'd gotten to know Tina pretty well, and I've promised Carleen I'll help with the investigation. I thought you might give me some advice."

"Wow," Jen said. "I don't have a clue where to start, but I'll come up with a few ideas before dinner. Sombrero at five thirty okay with you?"

I agreed to meet her at our favorite Mexican restaurant, pleased that I didn't have to wait long to keep my promise to Carleen. Hopefully, Jen would assign one of her reporters to write a sidebar to the murder story and mention that a reward was being offered for any information leading to the arrest of the killer. That would at least help keep the investigative ball rolling.

After I relaxed with a long, hot shower, I ate some peach yogurt to tide me over until dinner. Then I checked email to see whether any new jewelry orders had come in from my website. With all that had gone on that day, I was glad I'd remembered to look. A returning customer wanted eight beaded bracelets for her book club. I loved my customers, and I especially loved the ones who liked my work well enough to make repeat purchases.

The jewelry wouldn't take long to whip out, so I decided to get going on it. My jewelry supplies sat on open shelves in the kitchen. Since the kitchen table was my favorite workstation, it made sense to store the supplies where they were easy to access.

I pulled out several plastic boxes of beads and charms. As I flipped through carefully organized bins of beads, it dawned on me that my early-morning jewelry bonanza had been eclipsed by the day's events. The garage sale finds that had seemed so exciting a few hours ago hardly seemed important in light of the morning's tragedy. I was grateful for a task to take my mind off Tina's murder as I waited for dinner with Jen.

My customer had ordered simple stretch bracelets with royal-blue beads and pearls. I plucked one more plastic box from the shelf and located a small bag of beautiful blue beads that mimicked lapis lazuli, and they were the first ones I strung on my beading needle. Then I added some vintage silver beads I'd been saving for just the right project, making the pieces "simple but elegant," as my customers liked to say. The bracelets were suitable for dressy occasions as well as everyday wear. In just over an hour and a half, I had completed all eight pieces and packaged them up for a drop-off at the post office.

With a look up at my kitchen's silver-and-red sunburst wall clock, I realized it was time to head downtown for dinner, so I made haste to the bathroom, where I freshened my makeup. Then I dashed to my bedroom's overflowing jewelry armoire and added a chunky cuff to the thin bangle bracelets I was already wearing. If I hadn't been strapped for time, I would have switched out the silver hoop earrings I'd worn all day. Earrings were my jewelry passion-slash-obsession, and I owned far too many of them.

My thoughts kept returning to the day's tragedy, and I wondered whether Tina's killer was long gone or still wandering around Roseland. I made a mental note to be extra vigilant as I was out for the evening.

The wind was whipping up outside, and a few tree branches scraped the glass of my bedroom window. Standing before my jewelry armoire, I had just clasped my honey-blond hair into a simple ponytail when a noise startled me and caused me to drop my brush. Miriam, clearly sensing that I needed some extra affection, purred at my feet. "Aren't you a sweetheart?" I stroked her sleek coat. "Thanks for looking out for me. I'll be fine."

After making sure Miriam had fresh water and a bowlful of shrimp-flavored cat food, I gathered my jewelry package and headed downtown.

Normally I loved spending an evening in the historic downtown square, but Tina's murder had set my nerves on edge. *What if the killer is still around? What if robbery really was the motive and the killer is targeting the next victim?*

As I got into my car and prepared to start the engine, I checked my key chain and fingered the whistle and canister of pepper spray. I was probably being paranoid. Still, it couldn't hurt to pay attention to my surroundings and remain cautious.

On the way to the post office, I looked out the window of my car and sighed. My lovely little town had experienced its first homicide in years, and I wondered how long it would be before I truly felt safe again.

Chapter Three

Our new brick post office—one of the few nods to modernity downtown—had closed for the day, so I circled around to the big blue drop-off mailbox and slipped my jewelry package inside. I hoped the bracelets would arrive quickly and safely, satisfying my customer and resulting in even more sales down the road.

It still amazed me that I'd taken the leap of faith from journalist to jewelry designer. Yearning to make a career move, I had ditched the news deadlines and jumped headlong into jewelry making. While I didn't miss the pressures of my old job at the *Daily Tribune*, I sure did miss some of my old colleagues. My closest friend on the staff was Jen, and I was eager to see her at dinner. As a result of early retirements and more than a few cutbacks, most of the older staffers had gone on to other pursuits, so Jen had gotten tapped for the top spot in the newsroom. Whenever we were together, she loved to talk shop. Jen said she liked to discuss the news business with someone who could relate, and it helped that I had a new career and could view my old one with fresh eyes.

At 5:20 p.m., I circled the courthouse and parked in a spot across from Sombrero, a popular Mexican restaurant that would be jam-packed in another hour. I was headed across the street when I heard someone call out. "Hey, Emma, wait up!"

I glanced over my shoulder and spotted two friends and fellow artists, sisters Savannah Rogers and Augusta Townsend. I would have known those two anywhere simply by what they were wearing. Savannah had on a slim-fitting black shift and lightweight yellow sweater, a wise choice for Georgia's unpredictable springtime weather. As usual, her sleek black hair was meticulous and looked as if she'd just had a fresh blowout at the salon. Savannah and I had gotten to know each other well through our work on the local arts council, and she had become a good friend. I wasn't as close to her younger sister, Augusta, whom her friends called "Gus," but I liked her and was always intrigued by her style. Today, she wore her signature overly feminine attire—a bell-sleeved ivory lace blouse, matching gauzy skirt, and pastel-pink ankle boots. The two sisters were hurrying to catch up with me.

"Hi there," I said. "Are you ladies going to Sombrero? I'm meeting another friend there for dinner."

"No. We're headed over to do some work at the gallery," Savannah said. The Foothills Gallery, which featured the work of artists and craftsmen throughout the foothills of the North Georgia Mountains, was owned and operated by the Ross County Arts Council, and all three of us had work for sale in the gallery.

Gus wagged her head, her lush strawberry-blond curls gleaming in the late-afternoon sunlight. "A few of our volunteers are coming over with ladders and hammers and nails, and we're hanging some of my new pieces while no one's around. You know how it is. You finish some art, and you're so excited about it that you can't wait for everyone to see it."

Gus created large-scale collages and assemblages on culturally relevant, sometimes controversial themes. Her work had been getting a lot of press, and her pieces were displayed in prestigious galleries throughout the Southeast.

"I can see why the early evening would be a great time to do that," I said. Getting my jewelry in and out of the shop was a breeze, but swapping out six-foot-by-six-foot artwork was another matter entirely.

Savannah patted me on the arm. "Listen, I heard what happened at Carleen's shop today. I'm so sorry you had to be there for that."

Her comment surprised me. "Oh? You've heard already?"

Savannah raised her eyebrows and gave me a skeptical look. "This is Roseland, remember? Word gets around quickly. I'd already heard about it from some friends who were downtown this morning, plus I saw Carleen at the grocery store this afternoon. She was on her way home from the shop and told me what a horrible day it had been."

I nodded. "It definitely was. You can't imagine how shocked I was to pull up behind the Silver Squirrel and find an ambulance there picking up Tina's body. She and I had become friends over the past couple of years, and I still can't believe she's gone. Did you know her?"

Savannah shook her head. "Not really. I saw her a couple of times when I went by the shop to deliver some of my watercolor note cards to Carleen. She seemed nice, though."

Gus, suddenly much less animated than she'd been only moments before, had an odd look on her face.

"Did you know Tina?" I asked, studying her expression.

"No, not well." She bit her lip and stared absentmindedly across the street. "She was on one of the local boards I sit on, but I never really got to know her. Still, I was sorry to hear about the way she died."

Gus was holding something back. I was sure of it. Her reaction to my mention of Tina was definitely odd. I would have to tuck that away to explore later.

"So I guess you're excited about installing your new artwork in the gallery tonight," I told her.

Gus's curls bobbed, and her face brightened. "Sure am. I've been working on new pieces that make a statement about our use of social media, and I can't wait to see what sort of reaction they get."

I smiled. "Could be dangerous, you know."

"Oh, I hope so." Her mischievous streak on full display, Gus bounced ever so slightly in her ankle boots. She was clearly eager to have her new work installed, but I found it strange that she didn't seem overly concerned about the murder we'd had downtown that morning.

Savannah glanced at her watch. "Is your friend waiting for you? It's almost five thirty."

"Yes, she is, and thanks for the reminder. I'd better run." After telling the sisters goodbye, I headed to Sombrero. As I walked over, I thought about how Savannah had seemed troubled by Tina's death but Gus hadn't wanted to talk about it. I couldn't put my finger on it, but something about her reaction troubled me.

I decided to put that thought on hold for an hour and focus on enjoying some time with Jen. As I entered the restaurant, I recognized a few couples and young families who were having an early dinner, but the largest dining room appeared completely empty. As my eyes adjusted to the dim interior, I looked around.

"Emma!" Jen waved to me from a booth in the far corner. "I'm back here." Jen liked to arrive first and claim what she called "the power seat," the spot where she could see who was coming and going. She always said she didn't want to be overheard when talking about work.

Jen paused from munching her chips and salsa as I walked up. "How's the jewelry empire coming along?"

"Today? Better than I could have dreamed." I slid into the booth, stashed my oversized purse out of the way, and poured some more salsa from the glass bottle into the small beige plastic bowl. Even after eating that fudge cupcake and peach yogurt earlier, I was famished. And Sombrero's homemade salsa was fantastic, brimming with fresh herbs and chunks of tomato.

"And exactly what"—Jen stabbed the air with a tortilla chip—"makes today so special?"

I savored a bite of zesty salsa before licking my lips and answering. "This morning, I scored some costume jewelry worth hundreds of dollars for the princely sum of ten bucks. So it looks like I'll be able to pay the bills for at least one more month before I have to move in with you and Todd."

Jen grinned. She and Todd, the real estate agent who had sold her on a house then sold her on himself, were newlyweds of just eight months. There was little chance of them inviting anyone else into their love nest, unless a baby came along at some point.

"I know you didn't ask me to dinner tonight just to talk about jewelry, though." Jen leaned forward and looked me in the eye. "This morning, you said something about wanting some advice regarding that murder at your friend's shop. What did you have in mind?"

"Any advice you can offer about how to find a killer is most welcome," I said. "I have no idea where to even begin. And I wanted to mention a few things that might be of interest to both of us."

"Such as?"

"Such as... wouldn't the *Daily Tribune* like to announce there's a reward for information leading to an arrest in the murder of Tina Le-Mann? A reward being offered by Roseland business owner Carleen Wood?"

"Okay, now I'm interested. Will she talk to us?" Jen crooked a finger in the air, signaled our waiter, and asked him to bring more chips. She might have been a five-foot-two waif, but she could sure put away some food.

"She will if I ask her to," I said. "But I decided I wouldn't even mention it to Carleen unless you thought it was doable. So you're willing to run something?"

"Are you kidding? Of course I am. The police don't seem to have any leads in this case. A reward is bound to help keep the story in readers' minds."

That was just what I had hoped Jen would say. "Great." I pulled out a piece of paper I'd stashed in my purse. "I took the liberty of writing down Carleen's number for you so you can have someone call her." When Carleen got a call, she would at least know that something productive was happening with the investigation. If we were lucky, the article might help produce a few leads in the case.

A fresh basket of chips and more salsa arrived, and our waiter asked whether we were ready to order. Jen chose her usual—a beef burrito, refried beans, and rice—while I ordered the fish tacos with lettuce and guacamole. I planned to eat only half and take the rest home. Perhaps by consuming some fish and veggies, I could make up for that fudge cupcake I'd indulged in earlier.

"So I guess the question remains, if it wasn't a robbery—and Carleen doesn't think it was—who would have wanted to kill Tina?" I asked. "Since she was single and has no relatives here, except for an elderly mother who lives close by, there don't seem to be any obvious suspects."

Jen lowered her voice and brushed her wayward brown bangs out of her eyes. "Yeah, and it doesn't sound like her ex had any axes to grind either."

"Her ex? Her ex-what?" I asked, puzzled.

"Ex-husband, of course." Jen looked around then whispered, "Do you mean to tell me that you didn't know Tina had been married before?"

I set my red plastic water glass on the table. "No, I didn't know that. She never mentioned it, and neither, for that matter, did Carleen. How did you find out? The police?" I found it more than a little strange that Tina had never revealed she'd been married.

Jen finished a sip of her Diet Coke. "I'm on pretty good terms with Alan Shelton, one of the newer detectives here, and—"

"Shelton?" I slapped the table. "That man was so rude to me this morning. I can't believe he was actually helpful to you."

Jen seemed surprised by my reaction. "Maybe you have to get to know him first." She shrugged. "So anyway, I asked him if there were any persons of interest. He said no, that even her ex-husband had on-

ly nice things to say about her. The ex is remarried now and was in
Gatlinburg with the wife and kid around the time Tina was killed, so
he's in the clear."

Jen's ever-present cell phone lit up on the table. She'd apparently
gotten a text, and she paused to read it. I was glad for the interrup-
tion because it gave me time to absorb what I'd just learned. Finding out that Tina had an ex-husband didn't bother me, but somehow,
her silence on the matter did. Apparently, she had been more private
than I'd realized. We hadn't been the closest of friends, but I thought
I'd known her well enough to be trusted with the news that she had
been married before.

After Jen finished reading her text, she tapped out a quick reply
and set her cell phone down as our steaming platters of food arrived.
I was still puzzling over the news that Tina had been married, but Jen
was eager to share the latest office gossip. She was excited about her
new responsibilities as news editor, but she didn't like all the extra
hours she had found herself putting in, and a couple of her staffers
were doggedly refusing to meet their deadlines. That was the nature
of the news business, though, and we both knew it.

Our discussion was interrupted once again by Jen's phone, which
started ringing. "Dang it!" Jen glanced at the screen and quickly
scarfed down a big bite of burrito. "Okay if I take this call?"

I nodded, not that it would have mattered.

"This is Jennifer," she said. Then I heard a lot of "uh-huh" and "I
see" before Jen ended the call by saying, "Okay, I'll be there in five
minutes." With a roll of her eyes, she dropped her phone into her
purse and got up, obviously preparing to leave. "Our stringer hasn't
shown up to cover the high school baseball playoff game, and the
new sports editor somehow managed to lose his big feature for tomorrow's paper and has to start over from scratch." She heaved a
great sigh. "And if all that weren't enough, the intern in the ad department misspelled 'Roseland' in the full-page ad promoting the

next Gallery Stroll. What happens in advertising isn't my fault, but I'll be the one getting calls about it all day tomorrow if I don't get it corrected. It's gonna be a long night."

"I'll get this," I said, waving a hand over the remains of our meals. "You run on, and you can pay next time."

She pointed at me. "Deal."

"And Jen," I added to be sure she didn't forget my request. "Thanks for agreeing to help find out who killed Tina LeMann."

Chapter Four

Boom!
A clap of thunder shook the house, and I sat up in bed, my heart racing and Miriam Haskell clinging to my side. I hadn't bothered to watch the local news before I'd gone to sleep, so I'd had no idea that severe thunderstorms were moving into town. Both mentally and physically exhausted, I'd come home from my dinner with Jen, mindlessly watched a few Netflix shows, and gone to bed.

Most Saturday mornings found me prowling garage sales and estate sales in and around Roseland in pursuit of vintage jewelry for my business. In some ways, Saturday was one of the most important days of my workweek. Had I watched the evening news, however, I would have known that all the weather forecasters had been predicting violent thunderstorms.

Clearly, there wouldn't be any outdoor sales in the torrential rain pounding on my roof. So around seven o'clock, instead of filling my travel mug with coffee and heading out as usual, I decided to settle in and take advantage of an unexpected Saturday morning off. I made a huge pot of coffee, pulled one of my mom's homemade tea breads out of the freezer, and popped it in the oven. Soon, the warm, comforting scents of coffee and hot blueberries filled the air.

On the bright side, the unexpected day off from garage sale shopping would give me a chance to tackle one of my least favorite but most necessary tasks—sorting the junk jewelry I'd already purchased. I didn't fancy spending the morning alone, though, so I tapped out a text to Savannah. *Have hot coffee and hot blueberry tea bread to share. Interested?*

The reply came quickly. *Yes!!! Be there in 15 min.*

I tucked a leg under me as I sat at the kitchen table, the tin of jewelry and a Pyrex mug of coffee sitting before me. My retro kitchen with its red-and-aqua decor was the most colorful room in the house. I collected vintage Pyrex in all the red and aqua patterns, and seeing it on my open kitchen shelves made me happy. The kitchen also had the benefit of a large bay window that was great for letting the sunshine stream through—on brighter days, anyway. That morning, the window revealed only angry clouds and rain.

I walked to the front porch and retrieved the *Daily Tribune*. It was a little thicker than usual for a Saturday paper, which probably meant that some new advertising inserts were inside, ads critical to helping a newspaper stay afloat these days. *Good for them.*

After returning to the kitchen with the day's edition, I pulled off the protective wrap and dropped the plastic into the trash can. As I had expected, Tina's death was the lead story. The *Trib* had included an old picture of her at a library board meeting. The only photo from Friday's tragedy was of crime scene tape stretched across the back door of the Silver Squirrel. I finished the story, skimmed the rest of the paper, and tossed it in the recycling pile in my laundry room.

Still savoring the unexpected morning at home, I finished a second cup of coffee and was debating whether to have a third when my phone rang. It was probably Savannah calling to ask if she could bring anything when she came over, but when I glanced at the screen, I saw Jen was calling. "Hey. What's up?" I asked.

"Just one thing that may or may not be important." That was Jen. No intro, no chitchat.

"And that is?" I asked.

"Did you know Tina's home was for sale? One of the gals who does the real estate ads noticed the address of the deceased woman was the same as the address in a real estate listing she typed up for to-day's paper. She wondered whether we should keep running the ad."

"I didn't know Tina's home was for sale, but that doesn't neces-sarily mean anything," I said. "Maybe she was buying another house. Maybe she was moving into a townhome or—"

"Yeah, I know. It could be nothing, but I guess it could mean *something* too," Jen said. "I just wanted you to know."

I thanked her before she quickly clicked off the call, then I re-trieved the paper from the laundry room and searched for that real estate listing. I Googled the address on my cell phone, just to be cer-tain, and sure enough, the home belonged to Tina LeMann.

I went back to my jewelry sorting, but my mind was swirling. I wondered why Tina had been selling her home and if it was signifi-cant or had something to do with her death. Maybe she was having financial trouble and needed to sell the house and move somewhere more economical.

On the other hand, I'd always gotten the impression that she was fairly well off. She had often joked about using half her paycheck to purchase some of the more irresistible antiques for sale at the Sil-ver Squirrel, so I assumed she had some discretionary income. She'd worked for Carleen for at least ten years. Maybe Carleen would be able to shed some light on Tina's finances when I spoke to her later.

Another clap of thunder made me jump in my seat. Grateful to be snuggled indoors with Miriam and my jewelry stash, I continued to riffle through the tin of junk jewelry while I waited for Savannah to arrive. I couldn't help smiling as I gently poked around the mound of glittering jewels.

A pair of iridescent red rhinestone earrings marked "Beau Jew-els" caught my eye, and I set them aside for my mom. The maker was listed in my price guide, and the earrings were yet another great find from the previous day's sale. With her love of sparkly red jewelry, Mom would definitely be getting those for Christmas.

A knock at the kitchen door interrupted my adventures in jewelry excavation. Savannah had arrived and was trying mightily to stay dry beneath an umbrella featuring the polyester version of Van Gogh's *Starry Night*. It was too bad he didn't have a painting called *Stormy Morning*.

The rain was deafening when I opened the door. "Come in, come in." I held out my hand to take the umbrella while Savannah stepped inside.

"It's dripping wet."

"No problem. Let's put it right here by the door, and this"—I quickly slipped a terry cloth kitchen towel out of a cabinet drawer—"can soak up some of the water. Your umbrella will be good to go by the time you leave."

Savannah sniffed the air. "Mmm. With those scents, I may never leave."

I laughed as I pulled down a turquoise Pyrex mug and handed it to her.

Savannah studied the design. "Foulard pattern?"

"Very good," I said. "Clearly, you've been paying attention."

"And you're still looking for more of them?"

"Always." I sighed. "Like everything else in the world of vintage, the old Pyrex keeps getting more and more expensive. But grab a slice of that hot blueberry tea bread and join me at the table. I can't wait for you to see the treasures I found at a sale yesterday."

Savannah visited often enough that she knew where I kept the plates and flatware, and I was glad. I loved having my friends over and wanted them to feel at home. She pulled out one of the chrome chairs from my fifties-style dinette set and tucked into her coffee and tea bread.

I had placed the lid back on the jewelry tin, and Savannah eyed it with a smile. "Okay, I'm ready for the big reveal," she said. "I gather that whatever you found must be pretty special."

"Oh, just you wait." I removed the lid with a flourish and pushed the tin her way. "Take a look."

Savannah put down her coffee mug long enough to gently poke around in the jewelry tin. She carefully fingered the brooches, bracelets, necklaces, and stray charms. Her oohs and aahs were exactly what I'd expected. Then she lifted a tiny gray velvet pouch that was buried underneath some other jewelry. "What's this?"

"Open it," I said, eager to see her reaction.

She tugged on the drawstring, turned the pouch upside down, and out slipped a child-sized silver charm bracelet. "It's darling!"

"Isn't it? Carleen almost always buys my sterling charm bracelets for the Silver Squirrel because she says charm bracelets never go out of style. I mean to show this one to her once..." I bit my lip.

"Once things die down?" Savannah's hand flew to her mouth. "Oops, I didn't mean—"

"It's okay," I said. "There's no easy way to talk about something like this, but I guess we can't help thinking about the murder yesterday."

Savannah shook her head. "It doesn't make any sense to me. The newspaper article said it didn't appear that robbery was a motive, but isn't it odd that the murder took place at the back door of a high-end antiques shop? That can't be a coincidence, can it?"

"Who knows? Carleen said nothing was missing, and the police didn't seem to have very many leads to check out."

Savannah frowned. "There's got to be someone who knows something about this."

"That's what I think," I said. "The killer knows, obviously, but I'll bet someone else does too. Unfortunately, when I asked Carleen for a list of anyone who might have wanted to hurt Tina, she said Tina spent most of her time caring for her aging mother and volunteering. It doesn't sound like she had too many opportunities to make any enemies."

Savannah drained the last of her coffee and set down the mug. "I don't know about that."

"What do you mean?"

"The few times I was around her, I thought Tina was a nice person, but she and Gus had a few run-ins on the library board."

"What on earth about?" I asked.

"You know how Gus is about her work," Savannah said with a wry smile. "Not everyone is a fan of socially relevant artwork. At a library board meeting last year, Tina asked whether Gus's art was appropriate for a display designed for children."

I folded my arms across my chest and sat back in my chair. "You have to admit that some of Gus's work can be a little edgy, so that doesn't sound like an entirely unreasonable concern."

"No," Savannah said. "But for whatever reason, Tina seemed to get pretty worked up about it, and Gus took it personally."

I raised an eyebrow. "How personally?"

"Oh, for goodness' sake, Emma. Not personally enough to kill her or anything ridiculous like that, but personally enough that it became a thing on the library board. And you know how this town is when something becomes a *thing*."

I knew what she meant. Roseland's gossip mill ran just as efficiently as that in any other small town. One misspoken word, one thoughtless slight, and someone could suddenly find herself on the outs with half the town. That was one of the few downsides to small-town life.

Thinking back to the previous evening, I remembered the odd look on Gus's face when I mentioned Tina. "So did Gus say anything to you last night about who might have wanted to kill Tina?"

Savannah shook her head. "But she did say she wondered if Tina had ticked off someone who wasn't quite as good at tuning out the criticism." Savannah looked at her watch. "Oh dear, I need to run. Paul and I are supposed to have a late lunch with his parents, and I promised him I'd make something for dessert. But listen, thanks for the coffee and blueberry bread. Delicious as always."

I followed Savannah to the door, handed her the no-longer-dripping umbrella, and waved her off into the still-pouring rain. Returning to the jewelry sorting I'd started earlier, I studied the Juliana bracelet with the colorful pastel rhinestones. With a soft cloth, I wiped away some dust, careful not to disturb the prongs holding the stones in place. I snapped a few photos with my iPhone and quickly uploaded them to an online auction site popular with jewelry lovers. I listed the bracelet with a starting price of $299 and hoped for success.

Another rumble of thunder caused me to look up from my rhinestone reverie. The skies were growing darker, and rain arrived in increasingly louder splats at the kitchen window.

But after nearly an hour of separating the jeweled wheat from the chaff, I was starting to get a little stir-crazy. Rain or no rain, I would run a few errands to get out of the house for a while.

As I showered, I thought about Jen's earlier phone call. She had called with news about the real estate ad before I could even read it in the newspaper, and I hoped that was an indication the *Daily Tribune* would remain focused on the case. She hadn't mentioned the story on the reward Carleen was offering, but I was sure something would run soon.

What should I wear on such a dreary morning? The slouchy sweats I'd had on during Savannah's visit weren't suitable for going out in public. Hot pink was always my go-to color. If I looked cheerful, maybe I would begin to feel more cheerful too. I paired a simple fuchsia blouse with my black slacks and black clogs.

I looked longingly at the new white girlfriend jeans sitting in my closet and the white strappy sandals I'd caught on sale at the end of last summer. But the sandals weren't a practical choice on a rainy day. And no matter what the fashion bloggers proclaimed about white being a year-round color, I simply couldn't forsake the famous fashion rule—no wearing white before Easter and after Labor Day. And Easter was still a few weeks away.

Instead of wearing white clothes, I accessorized with white jewelry, one of my pearl choker-and-earring sets. As usual, I strapped on my late grandmother's tank-style watch with its simple brown leather band.

After checking my purse to be sure the possible Haskell brooch was still inside, I locked the front door, held on to my umbrella for dear life, and raced to the car. After checking my hair and makeup in the rearview mirror, I headed downtown.

Carleen and I needed to talk about some unpleasant things, but I also hoped the moment would be right for me to get her expertise on the brooch. I wanted to list the brooch for sale online as soon as possible.

I wiped a few raindrops from the face of my watch, which showed that it was fifteen minutes later than I'd thought. I'd chewed the fat with Savannah longer than I'd intended. Now that I ran my own home-based business, I valued time more than ever. Somehow, though, I would have to balance my normal workload with the new job that I had volunteered for—helping to find Tina's killer. But a quick run by Carleen's shop wouldn't take up that much of my Saturday. And I wanted to show her that Haskell-looking brooch, anyway.

I was still spooked by the scene at the Silver Squirrel's back door the previous morning, so I retrieved my umbrella from the passenger-side floorboard, parked in front of the shop, and quickly got out of the car. I clicked open the umbrella and somehow got to the shop fast enough to avoid becoming drenched.

Two customers were inside when I entered the store. From what I could overhear, they were conferring with Carleen about some nineteenth-century German silver napkin rings. It sounded as though my friend were about to make a sale, so I pretended to be interested in the case of costume jewelry. Ironically, the first items I spotted had originally belonged to me.

"I can't believe you actually had four of these gorgeous napkin rings," a brunette in a cropped black denim jacket and white skinny jeans told Carleen. "My sister and I have been trying to collect a dozen each to use at Thanksgiving. We alternate hosting each year, you see. To find even one of these napkin rings is such a rarity. Would you mind wrapping them for me?"

"I'd be happy to." Carleen swiftly placed the napkin rings atop a stack of tissue paper and returned the padded black velvet display board to its usual spot beneath the glass case. "What brings you two ladies to rainy Roseland today?" Carleen asked as she carefully wrapped the napkin rings. The deluge had stopped, but a steady trickle of rain lingered.

The blond sister said, "We decided to come up from Atlanta for the day and check out some of your cute shops we keep hearing about. And I must say that despite the weather, your town did not disappoint."

Carleen smiled. "I'm glad to hear it." Carleen was a whiz at gift wrapping. In minutes, she handed the woman an elegant black gift bag with an embossed silver foil sticker bearing the store's name and signature squirrel logo. Sheets of scalloped silver tissue paper spilled out of the top, and the customer beamed when Carleen handed over the luxurious bag.

The women were headed out of the store when the brunette said, "Oh my, Ellen. Look at this bracelet!" Her sister came over to join her at the jewelry case, and the two women peered inside. "It's just like that Eisenberg Ice bracelet I saw that time in Albuquerque. I could still kick myself for not buying it."

Carleen smiled as she slipped behind the counter. "Let me pull the bracelet out for you."

I glanced over, but I already knew which bracelet was causing the commotion, and it was a stunner.

"Here, try it on." Carleen gently clasped the glittering bracelet around the brunette's wrist.

The woman sighed, or maybe purred. "I saw one of these a few years ago and didn't get it, afraid I'd see something I liked better while we were on vacation. I didn't know at the time how rare it was to find a bracelet like this in mint condition, so I'm getting this one."

"Terrific. I'll package it up for you." Soon, Carleen was handing over a second Silver Squirrel gift bag.

Once the store's gentle chime confirmed that the two sisters had left, I stepped away from the jewelry case. "I'm surprised you haven't sold that Eisenberg Ice bracelet before today." I'd admired how the bracelet's clear, bright stones were simply luminous. Even the tiny rhinestones in the clasp were intact.

"Harriet Harris at one time wanted it so badly she couldn't see straight," Carleen said. "She kept thinking I'd trade it for something of hers. I told her at least a half dozen times that I don't believe in trades. I've worked too hard to develop a reputation as a fair seller, and if I have a price on an item, it's a fair price, not a bartering tool."

I tsk-tsked. "Harriet should have known better. And with all the money she's said to have, I find it odd that she didn't just spring for it."

Carleen grinned. "Maybe she's one of those women who likes to hang on to her money for a rainy day." She looked out her shop's windows, apparently taking in the traffic—or lack thereof—up and down the street. "Hardly anyone else is out this morning, thanks to the storm. Let's go talk in my office, and we'll come back out if I hear the chime."

I followed her down the hallway and paused to admire a framed print. "A new addition to your collection of vintage botanicals?"

"That's a print Tina gave me for Christmas a few years ago." A sad look clouded Carleen's tired face. "I've had it hanging in my study at home, but I decided to bring it to the shop this morning. A tribute to Tina, I guess." As we entered her office, she motioned for me to sit on the white slipcovered sofa near her desk, and she sat in her black-and-white toile-upholstered desk chair nearby.

"I didn't learn until yesterday that Tina was divorced," I said. "I assume you knew."

Carleen looked thoughtful. "That happened years ago. She married young and divorced young. From what little she told me, she and her ex were both immature when they wed. They had what she referred to as a rather friendly divorce, if there is such a thing."

I tucked a small needlepoint pillow behind my back and snuggled into the soft sofa cushions. "I was a little surprised I'd never heard about it. It's fine, really, but I did consider Tina a friend, you know."

Carleen was starting to look glassy-eyed, so I resolved to tread lightly.

"Tina was a very private person." Carleen reached for a tissue from a box on her desk. "But she loved to talk about antiques, and even about our high-maintenance customers sometimes, yet she rarely talked about herself. My sense was that she'd been hurt in the past and didn't want to risk getting too close to someone again."

I pondered whether it was the right time to bring up the news about Tina's house. It weighed on my mind, so I knew I might as well get it out there. "Did you know her home had just been listed for sale? It's in the newspaper today."

"What? Oh, that can't be true. I would have known about that." Carleen dismissed the idea with a flick of her well-manicured hand. "She adored that little cottage on Cedar Lane."

I bit my lip, wondering whether I should tell Carleen what I'd learned from Jen—and the *Daily Tribune*—about Tina's home being for sale.

"What is it?" Carleen asked. "Something's on your mind. I can tell."

"Don't you subscribe to the *Daily Tribune*?"

Carleen confirmed that she did.

"Have you looked at today's issue yet?"

"No, but if you'll wait a sec, I'll go get it from the mail receptacle out front."

Carleen stepped into the hallway, and I heard the clack of her heels as she walked out the front door then back inside. Coming into the office, she shook a few drops of rain off the plastic bag protecting the latest edition of our town's newspaper. "And can I assume one of your friends at the paper told you this news about Tina's house?"

I nodded. "Look at the real estate ads, near the back of the B section."

Carleen quickly turned there. Her eyes scanned the page, focusing on one spot before her expression turned quizzical. "You're right. And it also says the house at 87 Cedar Lane is a new listing."

"Isn't that the side street off Lunsford Drive?"

"Yes, it is. Tina's lived there as long as I've known her. In fact, it used to be her parents' home, so I'm rather surprised she'd even consider selling it. Hmm..."

"Hmm what?" I didn't like the sound of that *hmm*.

"The listing is with Harris Realty." Carleen made a clucking sound. "Hubert Harris is the Realtor selling Tina's house. And how very odd since..."

"Since what?"

Carleen cleared her throat. "Tina often found our customers amusing, and there was rarely anyone she couldn't get along with, but she absolutely detested Harriet Harris. She said Harriet overestimated her importance in this town, and she hated seeing Harriet come into the store. Tina also knew about Hubert's infamous womanizing and said he'd tried to hit on her a time or two. She chose to simply ignore him and stay out of his path. Isn't it strange, then, that Harriet's husband was selling Tina's house?"

I couldn't argue with that. "And stranger still that you didn't know about it."

Carleen agreed it was all quite unusual, and I knew then that the relationship between this particular Realtor and client was worth exploring.

"You know, as much as I love hanging out here, I believe I need to take a quick run over to see our friend Harriet at Making Memories."

Chapter Five

H arriet Harris was not exactly an unattractive woman. She had short wash-and-wear gray hair and a ready smile that could almost pass for friendly. I couldn't always tell whether her smile was sincere, though, and for some reason, I kept Harriet at a distance. I didn't dislike Harriet, but I didn't exactly like her either.

Harriet's antiques business, the Making Memories Antique Mall, was located in one of the town's former big-box stores. It had plenty of parking and happened to be located next door to Craft World, a popular crafts supply store, so I was over there at least once or twice every week. The mall's location made it convenient for me to shop for old and new jewelry-making supplies in one stop.

The cowbell on the door made its customary clanging sound as I entered, and I got a nice whiff of Eau De Musty Antique Mall as I stepped inside. Harriet looked up from reading a country-decorating magazine. She peered at me over her funky reading glasses, which were black with lime-green polka dots. Harriet owned some nice jewelry—I'd seen her wear it plenty of times—yet she rarely wore any jewelry at the mall. I got the impression she aimed to dress down when working there.

"Well, if it's not the bling girl," Harriet said. "Good timing too. That booth you like at the back is moving out in a few days. She's offering at least twenty-five percent off everything, including her good costume jewelry."

"I'll be sure to take a look." I glanced at the latest jewels beneath the checkout counter. "Now that I've started getting more custom jewelry orders online, I'm on the lookout for inexpensive bags of broken jewelry too, not just the good stuff. In fact, those junk bags have resulted in some of my best one-of-a-kind creations. The customers love those."

"The junk ought to be pretty easy to spot," Harriet said. "I'm sure I don't have to tell you that it's getting increasingly difficult to put my hands on the good stuff. For some reason, all the high-end pieces seem to land at the Silver Squirrel instead of here. And I still don't know what *you* scooped me out of at that yard sale yesterday, you know."

I bristled at her comment but tried to hide my annoyance. "Oh, Harriet, like I told you, it was just some of that old junk jewelry I like. A few nice pieces but a lot of odds and ends, really."

It was no mystery to me why people preferred to sell their best pieces to the Silver Squirrel rather than Making Memories. Carleen paid solid, fair prices for the items she bought for her shop. Harriet, according to the local sellers I'd talked with, always wanted to buy low and sell outrageously high. Serious collectors and sellers in town knew to visit Carleen first.

"Funny you'd mention the Silver Squirrel," I said. "I just came from there."

One eyebrow shot up over the top of Harriet's readers, as if she suspected I was up to something.

"I wanted to"—I looked down and gave a sad shrug—"offer a little support to Carleen after Tina's tragic death yesterday."

Harriet nodded sympathetically. "Tina was a nice girl. It's ironic that she died right before her house was listed for sale in the paper, which I'm sure you know about with all of your friends in the newspaper business. It's a shame she ended up having to sell that house. She must have really wanted to keep her mother in that pricey assisted-living place."

Aha. Now we're getting somewhere. I leaned in. "I didn't know much about Tina's personal life, but Carleen told me she was devoted to her mother. So Tina was paying for her mother's assisted-living care?"

Harriet propped a hand on her hip. "She sure was, and there was some flap about it with her siblings too." She tossed the decorating magazine aside and let her reading glasses drop to the beaded chain around her neck. "She gave Hubert and me all the details the night we met with her about listing her house with us." She jutted her chin as if to emphasize that she and Hubert had the inside scoop.

"So you're in real estate too? Not just Hubert?" I couldn't help being curious. Now that I was a businesswoman, I was learning that the women of Roseland had their fingers in quite a few entrepreneurial pies, even if they weren't always very vocal about it.

"We own a number of those little houses up and down Tina's street. Rental property used to be a good investment back before the economy tanked and the riffraff started tearing up the places they live in. So we went back to buying houses to flip. Plus, once I retired, we needed to find something to get Hubert out of the house more often."

I nearly choked because rumor had it that Hubert had no problem wandering away from home. Quite the opposite, in fact. But I wasn't about to stop her since she was on a roll.

The cowbell clanged again, and Harriet's eyes darted to the front door. "Hi, Janet. Come on in. There's some new Roseville and Mc-Coy pottery in that booth you like on aisle two. Be sure to check it out."

Harriet paused, appearing to wait only long enough to make sure the new customer couldn't hear us. "As I was about to say, when Tina's father died a few years ago, the family sold the house to pay for her mother's new apartment at Magnolia Manor. Tina wanted to keep the house for herself, but she couldn't afford it, so she sold it to us. Then during the recession a few years back, we couldn't move anything on that street. We let her rent it for a few years, and she must have done a good job of saving her money because eventually she offered to buy it back."

After standing there for so long, I shifted my heavy purse to the other shoulder to relieve my aching arm. "So if Tina worked so hard to buy the house back, and her mother had been in the assisted-living place for years by that point, why would she have the house for sale again?"

Harriet smiled. "You haven't ever had to deal with aging parents, have you, dear?"

I shook my head. I hadn't, and I was grateful for that. My parents were still in their early sixties, and so far, both of them were enjoying excellent health. When Dad retired the previous year, he and Mom bought an RV and hit the road. I had a hard time keeping up with them and their travels.

Harriet steepled her fingers in a pose that I imagined she'd once used with schoolchildren. Then she pointed at me and continued. "Tina didn't want Carleen to know, but Magnolia Manor had increased their fees significantly since her mother moved in, and there was some trouble among Tina and her siblings about paying for their mother's care. Tina said most of the financial responsibility fell on her, and she simply couldn't afford that on a salesclerk's salary. She didn't want to uproot her mother again, but she was too proud to ask Carleen for a raise. Said she'd been thinking that one of the local townhomes was more her style, anyway."

It was a lot to take in. "I can't believe Tina didn't at least talk to Carleen about the situation."

"Sad, isn't it? But that Tina was a trouper. I'll tell you that." Harriet looked around the store and lowered her voice even though no customers were in sight. "Some folks get mad when they have to leave a place, but Tina had that house in tip-top shape by the time she asked us to list it. In fact, she was boxing things up and preparing to move into her new townhome at the time of her death. She wasn't bitter about it, just resolved, I guess. We hated to see her sell the house again, but once she told us about her mother, we understood why she needed to."

"Any idea why she chose to list with you and Hubert?" I asked with as much innocence as I could muster. I knew better than to add, "since she didn't even like you very much."

Harriet narrowed her eyes at me. "Obviously, it was the same reason anyone chooses a real estate agent to list their home—our reputation." Her tone was a tad too defensive. "Or..."

"Yes?" I tried to seem interested but not overly curious.

"Maybe she felt she owed us since we bought the house from her the first time. I guess she trusted us to handle it again. Either that or we just happened to be in the right place at the right time."

I nodded. "I see." *It was probably the former reason and not the latter.*

"It's really a shame," Harriet said. "Now we need to find out if anybody in Tina's family will come and claim all those things she'd been boxing up to get ready for the move. Clothes and books, mostly, but she did have a few nice antiques, like some old family china and a set of sterling silver. I offered to help her when we were there one day, but she only let me help pack a few boxes. Seemed bent on doing it all herself."

So nosy Harriet hadn't been able to resist stealing a peek at Tina's things. Although, now that I thought about it, I had to admit I was a bit of a nosy Rosy too.

Not wanting to let on that I'd really stopped by merely to snoop, I changed the subject. "Listen, later today, I've got to work on designing some new necklaces for the Gallery Stroll this Thursday. If you know of anyone with junk jewelry pieces for sale, holler, but otherwise, I'm going to buzz through here and see if I can find any big bags of broken jewelry."

"Honey, I don't pretend to know everything that's in all the nooks and crannies of this antique mall, so have at it is all I can tell you." After waving me off, Harriet perched her polka-dotted reading glasses back on her nose and turned to the laptop on the counter. She was probably checking eBay. Harriet either didn't know or didn't care, but many of my fellow antiques lovers in town were well aware that she often listed her best inventory online first. I'd heard the gripes. Frankly, I was too busy managing my own growing business to give much thought to how Harriet managed hers.

Whether the antiques lovers and sellers in Roseland personally cared for Harriet or not, she had done a terrific job of getting the new antique mall up and running. With so many vendors in one location, the mall had become a hot spot for antiques lovers and junkers. The Harrises even advertised the store on a flashy digital billboard out on the interstate, and that brought in some tourist traffic too, especially when the leaves started to turn in the fall.

As usual, I started on the right-hand side of the antique mall and sprinted up and down the aisles. At the end of aisle three was the sale booth Harriet had mentioned. Strips of paper bearing the booth number and the words "Twenty-five percent off" were hanging there, available for the taking. I liked the new trend of having discount coupons right there at the booth. In a large antique mall like Harriet's, it kept the cashier from having to flip through a notebook in search of each seller's discount.

A small handwritten sign caught my eye. All Christmas Tree Pins, Half Off. That was a good deal. I shopped for vintage rhinestone Christmas tree pins all year long. When the holidays approached, all the last-minute lookers suddenly decided they simply had to have a new Christmas tree pin. I could almost name my price, especially for the hard-to-find signed pieces.

The glass jewelry case was locked, so I walked up front and asked Harriet to send someone to open it for me. A college student who occasionally helped out brought the key ring and waited as I made my selections. I chose two Trifari pins, one Cristobal, one Hollycraft, and a particularly stunning all-red-rhinestone Christmas tree pin that was unsigned but probably Austrian. I would have about fifty dollars invested in the pins. At those prices, I could easily triple or even quadruple my investment come Christmas.

The college girl placed the pins on a black velvet display board and said she would follow me to the checkout counter. As we were about to head that way, she stumbled on an electrical cord duct-taped across the tile floor. She tipped the board and dropped the Hollycraft pin. I cringed as I heard the sound of metal pinging against the floor.

"Oh no!" She scrambled to retrieve the pin from beneath the table where the jewelry cases were displayed. "I'm such a klutz. I'm so sorry."

"Happens to the best of us." I smiled, secretly hoping she hadn't caused any damage. "Do you mind if I check it to be sure all the stones are still intact?"

She handed over the pin. "Sure. No problem."

I wasn't trying to make her feel bad, but a bargain piece of jewelry wasn't a bargain if stones were missing. All the stones appeared to be securely in place, and we made our way to the checkout without any further mishaps.

Harriet quickly turned her laptop from view as we approached the counter. "I had a feeling you'd leave with a few treasures. Good for you. You know, I was thinking about all of that pretty vintage costume jewelry you like so much, and I've decided to finally go get that Eisenberg bracelet your friend Carleen's had in her jewelry case forever."

"Do you mean the Eisenberg Ice bracelet with the pretty horseshoe-shaped accents near the clasp?" I asked.

She furrowed her brow. "Yes, that's the one. Why?"

"I hate to tell you this, Harriet, but Carleen sold that to a woman from Atlanta when I was in there earlier today."

Harriet looked crestfallen. "You win some, you lose some," she said with a sigh.

For once, I almost felt sorry for her.

***

DESPITE MY UNPLANNED day off from treasure hunting, I had a busy and productive Saturday. After leaving Harriet's shop, I spent a good hour and a half at Craft World, where I stocked up on beading wire, some pretty new toggle clasps, and a few strands of beads that were on sale. Once I returned home, I checked email and found I'd sold some of the vintage jewelry I'd listed online earlier in the week. Those pieces needed to go in the mail first thing Monday morning, so I got busy packaging the jewelry into sturdy cardboard boxes and padded mailers. I also photographed a couple of the unsigned brooches I'd purchased on Friday, as well as that Coro bracelet, then quickly listed them on eBay. I started the bracelet at thirty-nine dollars, and it quickly got a bid. It was nice to know my ten-dollar investment was paying off so handsomely.

Almost the moment the jewelry listings were taken care of, my stomach let out a hearty growl. I was famished but not in the mood to cook. Since the rain had finally stopped, I decided to call in an order of my favorite fast food, moo goo gai pan from Little China, a takeout restaurant only a few miles from my home. After picking up the order, I came home and ate it straight out of the container while snuggled under a lightweight quilt on the living room sofa. A happy Miriam Haskell sat contentedly at my side, languidly flicking her tail.

It had been a good day on some fronts, but I was also disappointed to realize I had made zero progress on the investigation into Tina's murder. So I did what I always did when I felt overwhelmed by a problem—I whipped out a yellow legal pad and made some notes.

At the top of the first page, I wrote *What we know*. My bullet points covered only the undisputed facts. Tina was killed before Carleen arrived at work. Investigators said Tina died of blunt force trauma. And finally, Tina was in the process of selling her home.

At the top of the next page, I wrote the word *Suspects*. Tapping my pen on the legal pad, I had to admit I didn't have any. That was a real problem.

I flipped to a third sheet of paper and made another list, titled *Questions*. I had no shortage of those. Who were Tina's enemies? Why was she the child most responsible for her mother's care? Why didn't her siblings feel obligated to help? And why hadn't she told Carleen about selling her house? Could there have been some friction there? Some embarrassment, maybe?

Thanks to Harriet, at least I knew why Hubert Harris was selling Tina's home, the home that had meant so much to her family and to her. What a sacrifice it must have been for her, yet I could understand why Tina had wanted to help with her mother's assisted-living expenses. Since she'd rented the house from the Harrises then later bought it back from them, perhaps Tina had felt she owed it to them to let them list the house.

In between my list making, I ate about half of the Chinese food and realized I was mindlessly stabbing at the rest. I closed the takeout container and put it in the refrigerator before turning on the stovetop teakettle. I loved the ritual of preparing my nightly mug of herbal tea. Soon, the water had boiled, and I was inhaling the cozy, comforting scent of chamomile tea as I sipped my favorite nighttime beverage.

I was about to call it a night and head to bed with a new novel when I remembered that I hadn't updated my records with the jewelry I'd purchased at Making Memories earlier that day. Record keeping was such an important part of my business that I never let it slide, and that day was no exception. The antique mall's no-frills brown paper bag was on a counter in the kitchen. I carried the bag to the table and sat down to record the purchases in my expense ledger.

Unwrapping the Trifari Christmas tree pins, I thought of how lucky I was to have invested in Christmas jewelry that would pay off handsomely in a few months. The pins were such a good buy, but the Hollycraft pin was the one I was most excited about. I unfolded the tissue surrounding the pin. Squinting, I tried to make sure my eyes weren't going wonky on me. But no, one of the clear baguette rhinestones was missing from the base of the tree.

How odd. It was the same Christmas tree pin that the college girl at the antique mall had dropped, but all the stones had been there. I'd examined it carefully.

I checked the back of the pin to be sure a loose stone hadn't lodged itself in the pin back or clasp. No luck there. I checked the tissue. I even checked the plastic bags containing the other Christmas tree pins, but no loose stone turned up.

I had been in a whirl that afternoon when I bought the pins, and I'd certainly been distracted by the events of the past twenty-four hours. Maybe I hadn't been that attentive when inspecting the pin after all.

Some rhinestones could be hard to match, and I hated to think I was stuck with a bum pin. But there certainly wasn't anything I could do about it late on a Saturday night.

It was a long shot, but the stone might still be on the floor at that seller's booth. After church the next morning, I would run by the mall to see if I could find it. I had nothing to lose. If I found the missing rhinestone, I could easily replace it.

With my mind still reeling from my busy day, I sighed and stroked Miriam. "I say we call it a night, little friend. Do you agree?"

Miriam quietly meowed, and I knew I had my answer. We would both feel more refreshed in the morning.

Chapter Six

Sunday dawned bright and breezy. I was glad I'd grabbed a light sweater to wear over the simple periwinkle shift I'd quickly pulled on for church. I'd hit the snooze button too many times and almost missed the service, but I managed to slip into a back pew at the last minute. The pastor's hopeful message about the coming of Easter was exactly what I needed to hear. With the sorrow of Tina's death fresh on my mind, I latched on to that message. I also said a prayer for Tina's family. Sadly, they were probably busy planning her funeral.

As I was about to leave the church, Michele Fairchild, whose gift shop, the Feathered Nest, was just a few doors down from the Silver Squirrel, grabbed my arm. "Hey, are you doing okay after what happened Friday?"

"What? Oh yes, I'm fine, but—"

"But I imagine Carleen's pretty shaken up." Michele dropped her hand. "Is she?"

"I think we all felt a little on edge on Friday. It's frightening, to say the least, to think that it could have been any one of us."

"I hear ya," Michele said. "I've got a security firm coming out tomorrow to upgrade my alarm system. I mean, I know Tina had a few enemies in town and all, but—"

"Mom, can we go home now? I'm hungry." A cute little tow-headed boy pulled on her sweater.

"What? Oh, sorry, son. I know you're hungry. I told you to eat your pancakes this morning, didn't I? Listen, I'll catch you later, Emma!"

Tina had a few enemies? Really? I would have to contact Michele later and see what she meant by that.

After I got home from church, I changed into jeans and a light-weight aqua knit top. Then I ate a grilled cheese sandwich and some wheat crackers before heading to Making Memories on a rhinestone-recovery expedition.

Harriet's daughter, Holly Harris Burke, a twentysomething mother of twin boys, was minding the counter when I arrived, if her halfhearted attempt at work could be called "minding." She looked up from the teen vampire novel she was reading only long enough to offer a bored nod in my direction. That was fine by me. I wanted to get my business done and get out. Heading directly to the booth where I'd bought the Christmas tree pins, I was surprised to look down the aisle and see that the seller appeared to be there. An attractive blonde in her early-to-mid-forties, she wore her long hair tied in a loose ponytail. Her pale-blue T-shirt had black smudges on it, probably from all the newspaper she'd been using to wrap the small glass-topped jewelry cases she was packing up.

"Moving day?" I asked.

"I'm afraid so," the woman said. "Sales have been slow, so I'm moving to another antique mall where the rent and commission aren't so expensive."

"Anyplace I'd know?" I was always on the lookout for a new honey hole for costume jewelry.

The woman nodded. "A new antique mall is opening on the bypass, part of that building where the old Piggly Wiggly used to be. The owner, Teri LeMann, said she's thrilled to have found the space and hopes to fill the whole building in time."

Another antique mall? Harriet wasn't going to like that. But the owner's name was what really caught my attention. "Teri LeMann? Do you happen to know if she's related to the LeMann woman who was killed in town two days ago, Tina LeMann?"

"That was Teri's sister," the woman said with a frown. She paused long enough to wipe her hands on a paper towel. "She was going to let the sellers in early this week to start setting up our booths. Then yesterday, she sent an email blast saying there'd been a tragedy in her family and she wouldn't be able to have us in until next week. She didn't actually tell us that it was her sister, but when I read the obituary in the newspaper this morning, I saw Teri's name listed among the survivors."

I could have kicked myself. I had worked at that newspaper for eight years and some change, yet I'd forgotten to look at the Sunday obits. When I got home, I would be reading Tina's, pronto.

The seller returned to the task of breaking down her costume jewelry displays and said, "I'm sorry. I've been so busy packing that I didn't even ask if there was something I could help you with. I'm Cindy. And until the end of the day, at least, I'm still a seller here."

"Thanks, Cindy. I'm Emma. And this is going to sound strange, but I need to crawl under your table for a minute." I pulled out the pin that was missing a stone. "I bought some of your Christmas tree pins yesterday, and the girl who got them out of the case for me accidentally dropped this one. When I got home with it, I discovered a stone was missing."

"Sure thing." Cindy stepped back into a corner of her booth. "Let me know if I'm in the way."

I fished around in my purse, pulled out my iPhone, and turned on its flashlight app. "If you don't mind my crawling around here for just a moment, I'm usually pretty good at finding wayward stones."

"Be my guest." Cindy had an amused look on her face, so even if she thought I was a weirdo, at least she didn't have a problem with letting me search.

Down on my hands and knees, I swept the phone's light slowly back and forth and was rewarded with not one but two glittering rhinestones. "Found it." I stood up and dusted a hand off on my jeans. "There's a second one too, but the clear one is my match." I reached into my purse and pulled out the plastic bag with the Hollycraft Christmas tree pin. "See? Perfect fit and perfect color. And here's the other one." I handed her the tiny ruby-colored stone.

"Take it if you'd like," Cindy said. "With your sharp eyes, you'll have more use for it than I ever will."

"Thanks. I'll do that. And I hope to see you around sometime at the new antique mall." I tucked the pin and stones back into my purse and turned to leave. As I walked past the front counter, Harriet's daughter still had her nose stuck in her vampire book. This time, she had the book propped in one hand while she used the other to fish Cheetos out of a bag on the counter. She didn't bother saying goodbye.

Finding the missing rhinestone was a small victory, and I was gratified to be leaving with the item I'd been searching for. But I couldn't help thinking I was leaving with something much more valuable than a stray rhinestone—the news that Tina's sister was opening a new antique mall in town.

THE SUN WAS STILL OUT when I got home. Miriam complained loudly when I walked into the living room, no doubt telling me that she didn't appreciate being left alone once again. I gave her a hug, pulled aside the living room curtains, then slid the ottoman close to the window so she could watch the birds flitting about on the lawn. Miriam took the bait and seemed happy to watch the goings-on from her favorite perch.

I put away my newly rescued rhinestones and headed to the foyer to retrieve the Sunday edition of the *Daily Tribune*. After turning to page six, the usual home of the obits, I scanned the names and found the announcement for Tina:

LEMANN, TINA RENEE: Tina Renee LeMann, 35, of Rose-land, passed away suddenly on Friday. Ms. LeMann was the daughter of Mrs. Etta LeMann and the late Mr. Anthony LeMann Jr. of Atlanta. A graduate of the University of Georgia with a degree in art history, Ms. LeMann was assistant manager of the Silver Squirrel, an antiques shop in Roseland. In addition to her mother, she is survived by a brother, Anthony LeMann III, of Atlanta, and a sister, Teri LeMann, of Marietta. The funeral will be Monday at 11 a.m. at McKinsey and Sons Funeral Home in Roseland. In lieu of flowers, the family has requested that memorial donations be made to the Foothills Humane Society.

Huh. I never knew that Tina was officially the assistant manager of the Silver Squirrel. I was also intrigued to learn that both her brother and sister lived fairly close to Roseland.

I walked into the kitchen and opened my laptop, which was still sitting on the dinette table where I'd left it the night before after checking for new jewelry orders. I opened the browser window and typed "Anthony LeMann III" into the search field. Up came listing after listing for LeMann, Mason & Lee in Atlanta. The law firm had received numerous five-star ratings and accolades for its up-and-coming young lawyers, including Anthony. The company website proudly noted that he had just been named to the 40 Under 40 list in a popular Atlanta magazine.

But if Anthony was an attorney—and he was obviously a successful one—I wondered why he wouldn't have helped with the assisted-living expenses for his mother. *Why did that responsibility fall to Tina?*

Then I Googled "Teri LeMann" and "Marietta." Her name popped up on a number of websites for design firms and antiques shops in the town, and she'd been named to the Best of Marietta list for several years running, mainly for her upholstery and design work. A high-end lifestyle magazine had run a brief profile of her, and it mentioned that Teri's design business had grown so much that she'd had to hire two assistants. Unlike the articles I'd found on Tony, though, Teri's didn't include a photo. I wondered if she looked at all like her sister, who'd had gorgeous auburn hair.

But as with Tony, I wondered why Teri hadn't been able to help Tina if her design business was doing so well. Surely a woman who could afford to buy the old Piggly Wiggly building was financially secure enough to help make sure her mother was able to stay in her assisted-living facility.

Shaking my head, I reminded myself that families had all kinds of complicated relationships and situations I knew nothing about. Besides, I knew better than to make snap judgments regarding someone I'd never met. For all I knew, Anthony and Teri *had* helped. Perhaps that help still wasn't enough to cover Mrs. LeMann's daily living expenses.

According to Tina's obituary, the funeral was coming up sooner than I'd expected, early Monday. I figured I'd better make plans to attend. I scrolled through my phone's contact list for Carleen's number and tapped the call icon. She picked up on the second ring. "You busy?" I asked.

"Not at all," Carleen said. "I was sitting here reading a new book about eighteenth-century silver hallmarks. I hoped something arcane would help take my mind off..."

"I know," I said. "Keeping your mind occupied is good. And listen, have you read the newspaper today?"

Carleen sighed. "I have. I guess you saw that Tina's funeral is coming up tomorrow morning."

"That's what I wanted to ask you about. I'm planning to go, and I'm assuming you are too. Do you want to go together?"

"I'd like that. Where should we meet?"

"At your shop at ten thirty? How does that sound?"

Carleen agreed on the meeting time, and I said I'd see her in the morning then clicked off the call.

THAT NIGHT, I LAY IN bed with Miriam Haskell curled up beside me and attempted to read a new mystery. I ended up skipping entire paragraphs as I mulled over the past few days. I debated whether it was too late on a Sunday night to make a call. Finally, I picked up my cell phone, but I looked at the hour and placed the phone back on the nightstand. Then I couldn't stand it anymore and called Jen's number. When she picked up, I asked, "Are you at home or at the office?"

"The office, unfortunately," she said. "I was trying to get a jump on some things before our Monday morning meeting. But the servers are down for some reason, so I can't get to the stories I wanted to check on. And since it's a Sunday night, there's no one up here who can do anything about it. Right now, I'm waiting on the IT guy to get here. He said it'll be at least thirty minutes before he arrives, so please, distract me."

"Good," I said. "Well, not 'good,' but—"

"What is it, Emma? Something's up, or you wouldn't have called me at... good grief, it's ten twenty-seven already. It'll be midnight before I get home."

"You know Harriet Harris, right?"

"That old grump who used to be a teacher at Maple Street Elementary?"

"Right."

"Yeah, I know her. Or at least I know of her. She used to call up here and complain if we didn't get the kindergarten class's Jell-O day feature in the newspaper fast enough for her. Did she die?"

"No, no." I snorted. Jen had a wicked sense of humor, and she always made me laugh, often inappropriately. "I was at her antique mall today, and one of her vendors told me something interesting. It seems that Tina LeMann, the murdered woman, has a sister who's opening an antique mall of her own out on the bypass."

"Is that what's going in the old Piggy Wiggly building?"

"Yep. It seems that Teri, the sister, sent an email telling her vendors there had been a tragedy in her family. She said the sellers wouldn't be able to move in as soon as she'd hoped. And when I looked her up online this afternoon, I found out she's been selling her custom vintage furniture in Marietta. She's even been written up in a few of the lifestyle magazines there because of her work. She got all five-star reviews on her business page on Facebook, and apparently, her customers adore her furniture designs."

"With your curiosity, you'd make a great newspaper reporter, you know that?" Jen teased.

I ignored my wisecracking friend and continued. "So I was wondering, has the *Trib* heard anything about a Teri LeMann opening an antique mall here in Roseland? Has she contacted you about a feature story or a business brief yet?"

"Doesn't ring a bell," Jen said.

"I was afraid that would be the case, but on the other hand, if a feature was coming out about her, you'd know, right?"

"Yeah, I would. And that last name would've definitely jumped out at me because of Tina's death. In the morning, I'll see if the features editor has come across that name in any of her calendar listings in recent weeks. And I'll be sure to talk to the cop reporter about it tomorrow to see if he's heard anything new on the murder. Speaking of murder, I'm going to kill that Alan Shelton you're so fond of. I had one of the reporters call him yesterday morning. We heard something on the scanner about a person of interest being served with papers and then leading police on a wild-goose chase. Shelton wouldn't say who it was or what it was about, but I can guarantee you he knew who it was, and—"

A muffled conversation ensued on her end of the call.

"You still there?" I asked after a too-long pause.

"Listen, Emma, my IT wizard has arrived, and I need to get busy here. I'll call you in the morning, okay?"

I was about to tell her that that would be fine, but I looked down at my cell phone and realized my friend was no longer on the line. At least I knew not to take it personally.

Chapter Seven

The funeral for Tina LeMann would be held in the chapel at McKinsey and Sons Funeral Home. I planned to go out of respect for Tina, whom I had considered a friend, but I also wanted to be there to support Carleen. She was clearly still shaken by the murder, and I couldn't blame her. It was always sad to lose a friend or family member, but it was absolutely unnerving when that loss was the result of murder, especially one that remained unsolved.

I woke early and read the morning's newspaper while drinking a large mug of hazelnut-flavored coffee. On the front page, a below-the-fold story told about the reward fund Carleen had sponsored: Local Shop Owner Pledges $1,000 for Info Leading to Arrest of Killer. The story recapped what had happened on Friday and gave a police department tip line number for readers to call if they had any information that might help lead investigators to Tina's killer.

Miriam was content to play at my feet, and I let her paw at the fuzzy bedroom slippers I was wearing. A little fun never hurt anyone. Then I typed a quick text to Jen: *Nice article on the reward fund today. Thanks for getting that in!*

After a light breakfast of fat-free Greek yogurt with some granola sprinkled on top, I showered and dressed for the funeral. It was another beautiful spring day outside, yet I felt a sense of gloom. I dreaded going to the funeral, but then I supposed no one ever *liked* going to a funeral. I chose a simple outfit consisting of a classic black-and-white geometric print blouse paired with black slacks and black pumps. I debated whether a long strand of vintage jet beads might be too much but finally decided to wear them. Funeral or no funeral, my outfit needed a little pizzazz.

Shortly before time to go, I opened a can of Miriam's favorite cat food, the shrimp flavor. When she finished eating and wandered into the living room, I gave her sleek coat a quick finger brushing. I was about to head out the door when I remembered I'd never shown that possible Miriam Haskell brooch to Carleen for her appraisal. I retrieved the piece from the small antique oak cabinet in the living room, where I stashed my "For Sale" jewelry, and tucked it into my purse just in case the topic came up later that afternoon.

Since Carleen and I had decided to meet at the Silver Squirrel before the service and walk over to the funeral home together, I knew we would arrive in plenty of time. The funeral home was located only a couple of blocks off Main Street.

I drove downtown and found it unusually busy for a Monday morning. Cars filled all the spaces in front of the stores, so I pulled around back to see if any parking was available there. A few spaces behind Carleen's shop remained empty, so I pulled in and parked. As I walked past the corner of the building and headed around front to the Silver Squirrel—the idea of entering through the back spooked me—a sparkle on the ground near the shop's back door caught my eye.

I paused to be sure I wasn't simply seeing a reflection off a piece of broken glass. A glint was definitely coming off something on the ground. I walked over then reached down and picked up what appeared to be a grimy, mud-covered stone. *Probably just a shard of broken green glass.* I rubbed the surface of it, and even more of a bright-green color shone through. Its oval shape convinced me I wasn't looking at glass. *A vintage rhinestone, maybe?* I'd rarely seen a green one that large. Maybe someone had stopped by to sell some jewelry to Carleen and dropped it along the way.

I reached into my purse for a tissue and wrapped the stone, knowing that Carleen would likely tell me that I'd found a lovely piece of green glass and nothing more. Determined to avoid the stark reminder of my visit to the shop's back door on Friday, I entered through the front door, and its electronic chime signaled my arrival.

"Emma, I'm glad you're here," Carleen said as I walked in. She had a plastic container of glass-cleaner wipes in one hand and was using the other to swish one of the cleaning cloths across the top of a glass counter. "Tina used to take care of this for me each Monday, along with a hundred other little things I never thought about until she was no longer here to do them. I knew I was going to miss her as a friend, but I'm starting to realize how much I'm going to miss her as a coworker too." She sighed. "If you know of anyone dependable who's looking for a job, will you let me know?"

I assured her I would. "It's not going to be the same around here. That's for sure." Then I reached into my purse. "And here. I brought you a present."

Carleen looked puzzled as I handed over the tissue bearing the dingy stone. She opened the tissue and examined the object inside. "Where did you find it?"

"Almost at your back door. I thought maybe a customer dropped it or something."

"It seems awfully heavy for an old rhinestone, but I'll give it a look later if that's okay."

I shrugged. "Sure. And feel free to toss it if you find out it's trash. I just wanted to be sure it wasn't something important that fell out of a piece of old jewelry that was on its way here."

"I doubt that's the case," Carleen said. "But I'm glad you're here early so we can head over to the funeral home. And to be honest with you, I'm a little nervous about going to this funeral."

"Nervous? Why?"

"They always say that a killer returns to the scene of the crime, and that person sometimes goes to the funeral. What if the killer's there today? It jangles my nerves to think we might be sitting in a funeral service with a murderer."

I saw no need to tell her that the same thought had crossed my mind. "Even if the killer is there, which I seriously doubt, he—or she—probably won't be killing too many of the attendees. Too many witnesses, you know."

"You're right. I'm sure I'm just being ridiculous." Carleen flicked a piece of lint off her navy linen blazer with a small cameo on one lapel. "It's just so hard to act like everything is normal when I have a murdered friend and there's still no clue about who might have killed her. Or at least I'm assuming there's not since you haven't shared any news with me."

"No, but I hope you saw that the *Daily Trib* has the article about the reward fund in today's paper. That's bound to help." I perked up when I realized I did have one new piece of information I could share with Carleen. "Now I can't promise you that this means anything, but I learned from a vendor at Making Memories yesterday that Tina's sister, Teri, has moved to town. She's opening a new antique mall out on the bypass. Did she ever mention her sister to you?"

Carleen tilted her head. "A few times. Her sister had gotten in financial trouble some years back as I recall. She was trying to get some money from her mother to pay off a business loan. The brother had plenty of money, I gathered, but he was too busy grabbing the brass ring and made it clear he didn't have any interest in bailing Teri out. Tina gave what funds she could afford at the time, but I got the impression that she lost touch with Teri after that. I never sensed any ill will, though. Just one of those sad cases of a family member making poor decisions then drifting away from everyone back home."

"It doesn't sound as if she would have had anything to do with Tina's death, then. I suppose she could have hoped to knock Tina off and inherit her sister's estate in order to help launch the new antiques business, but..."

Carleen visibly cringed at my poor choice of words. For the millionth time, I wished I could superglue my lips shut.

"Yes, that would seem a bit far-fetched for someone who hasn't even known what Tina was up to for the past few years," Carleen said.

I shrugged. My friend was right, and I hated that my big lead wasn't actually leading us anywhere.

"Have you had any more visits or calls from the police?" I asked. "Maybe there's something going on behind the scenes that we don't know about."

Carleen shook her head. "I've thought of that, but I can't bring myself to call up and check on their investigation. Besides, if I appear too interested, that might make *me* look like a suspect."

I couldn't imagine Carleen as a killer. "I don't think you have anything to worry about there."

She glanced at her sleek gold watch for the second time in as many minutes, so I knew we'd stalled long enough.

"Why don't we go ahead and walk over to McKinsey and Sons?" I tipped my head toward the door. "We'll be there a little early, but it could be interesting to arrive in time to see who attends."

"And who doesn't," Carleen said, a thoughtful expression on her face.

"What do you mean?"

"What if her family doesn't come?" Carleen looked worried. "That would be incredibly sad. And I've got to tell you, I'm not going to be very happy if there's not a good turnout of our fellow merchants at the funeral today. Tina was always a supportive member of the downtown business community, and she deserves a proper show of respect."

I could only hope she would get one.

AFTER A BRISK WALK up a few blocks, we arrived at McKinsey and Sons Funeral Home. The elegant white-columned antebellum home had been in the McKinsey family for years before it began to serve as the town's only funeral home back in the late sixties. Ward McKinsey and his four sons were well respected in Roseland for offering tasteful, distinguished funerals that ministered to the families and honored the deceased.

Carleen and I approached the entrance to the funeral home, and a petite elderly woman with a walker was being helped up the ramp and past the double doors that opened to an expansive foyer. She wore a simple black skirt and a pink sweater set that looked a size too large. At her elbow was another petite woman, who had hair in an impossible-to-ignore shade of orangey red. She appeared to be in her early thirties. The younger woman wore a bright fuchsia blouse and a colorful skirt, unusual choices for a funeral. Like a lot of Southern women, I'd been raised to believe that black and navy were the only acceptable colors for such an occasion.

As I studied the sartorial choices of the two women who had just entered the funeral home, Carleen lightly touched the sleeve of my blouse. "Do you think that's—"

"Yes, I do," I stage whispered. "That's got to be Tina's mother and sister, and I want to watch their body language. Maybe we can get a sense of how she and her mother interact. And holler if you see someone who looks like he might be the brother."

"Emma, please!" Carleen hissed. "We shouldn't be investigating while we're at a funeral."

"Don't 'Emma, please' me. This is a prime snooping opportunity, and there's no sense in letting it go to waste."

Before I could follow the women, one of the McKinsey sons—I could never tell them apart—gently tapped me on the arm and pointed at the lectern holding the guest register. "Ladies, the book is this way."

I'd been in that funeral home enough times to know where the guest book was located, but I simply smiled and pretended that I didn't understand him as I continued to walk toward the chapel. Unfortunately, two more of the interchangeable McKinsey sons were standing at the doors and gently led away the two women I'd planned to follow in.

Near the vestibule was a short line of visitors waiting to sign the guest book. Since there had been no viewing as there usually was at Roseland funerals, I definitely wanted to sign the book. It was important that the family see that Tina's friends had shown up to pay our respects. And if I was being honest, I also wanted to see who else had already signed the book.

"Help me out here," I whispered to Carleen. "I'm going to scan all the names in the guest book real quick. Strike up a conversation with anyone who comes in behind you and cover for me for a few minutes, okay?"

Before she had time to protest, I grabbed the pen and pretended to sign the guest book.

I heard Carleen say, "Well, hello there," so I knew I had a few minutes. I plopped my huge purse on the lectern holding the book to shield it from anyone who might wonder what was taking me so long.

The guest book was standard funeral home fare, cream-colored leatherette with a pearlescent long-stemmed pink rose on the cover. Three full pages were filled with names already, so we hadn't arrived that early after all.

As I scanned the list, I saw that the only two LeManns listed were Harold and Grace LeMann, obviously a married couple. I imagined they were Tina's aunt and uncle since the names Harold and Grace didn't sound young enough to be cousins. Other close family members could have failed to sign the book, so I didn't know how many other LeManns might be inside, waiting on the service to begin.

Tina's obituary had mentioned no graveside service, only the funeral at McKinsey and Sons. Like so many others these days, Tina was probably being cremated. I, on the other hand, fully intended to be pushing up daisies when my time rolled around.

Carleen loudly cleared her throat, and I knew my snooping time was up. I turned to her with what I hoped was my most apologetic look. "I'm sorry that took so long. Their pen ran out of ink, and I've been looking for one here in this bottomless purse."

I rooted around in my black tote that doubled as a purse and finally came up with a fluorescent-orange pen from the gas company. It wasn't the most dignified color choice for a funeral home pen, but it would have to do. I turned back to the lectern bearing the book, quickly added my John Hancock, then stepped aside while Carleen signed.

We finally entered the beautiful, quaint chapel. After walking past doors of gleaming polished oak, we headed up the aisle between two rows of padded pews. The vintage wooden benches had been refurbished over the years, most recently updated with simple teal-cushioned seats. Carleen was heading farther up the aisle when I gently tugged the hem of her blazer.

"We'll have a better view of everyone if we stay closer to the back," I whispered.

She widened her eyes, clearly understanding my meaning. We slipped into seats three rows from the back on the right side, far enough in to see almost everyone who entered.

As we were seated, the McKinsey sons handed each of us a small funeral service program bearing Tina's photo and the dates of her birth and death. The picture looked about a decade old—the young Tina sported a Jennifer Aniston hairstyle—and I wondered who had provided it. Most likely, it was her mother or sister.

After settling in our seats and tucking our purses beneath the pew ahead, Carleen and I began reading.

"I never knew that Tina was born here in Roseland," I whispered. "For some reason, I assumed she was a transplant like me."

Carleen nodded. "She dearly loved this town, and she actually knew a lot about Ross County history. I can't believe that never came up in any of your conversations with her."

The organist played a selection of traditional hymns. The soft melodies were soothing. I quieted my mind and reflected on the all-too-brief life of the woman who had been my friend.

I was relieved to see so many others at the funeral. Quite a few of the downtown merchants filled the pews. Mavis was there from the bakery and café, seated beside Michele from the Feathered Nest. Perhaps I could catch a few minutes with Michele after the service to ask her about the comment she'd made at church the previous day regarding Tina's "enemies."

I felt a hand on my shoulder and turned to see Harriet Harris. She and Hubert had slipped in behind Carleen and me. That detective who had been so testy on Friday, Alan Shelton, sat alone on the pew behind the Harrises. Funeral duty was probably a part of his job.

At eleven o'clock sharp, the minister asked us all to stand, and the elderly woman I had seen earlier shuffled up the aisle and took her place on the front pew. The flaming-haired woman in the colorful outfit was at her side every step of the way. About a dozen others took their seats in the family pews up front, but I didn't see anyone who looked as if he might be Tina's brother.

The program identified the minister as Reverend Joshua Smith of the First Methodist Church in the neighboring town of Hudson. A short, bald man with a gray beard, he was older than I had expected. Just as the minister took to the podium, a tall man with sandy-blond hair, whom I immediately recognized from my internet research as Tony LeMann, dashed down the center aisle and made a great show of claiming a seat on the other side of his mother.

"I'm so pleased her brother could make it," Carleen whispered with a look of disapproval.

The minister seemed unperturbed by the tardy mourner and smiled as if he had all the time in the world to conduct the service. "Dearly beloved," he said, "we are gathered here today to celebrate and remember the life of our wonderful friend and family member, Tina Renee LeMann." He paused and looked out on the family, smiling kindly toward them all. "To her mother, Mrs. Etta, her brother, Tony, and sister, Teri, we extend our deepest sympathies and our prayers for your peace and comfort in the days ahead."

The pastor explained that he was a longtime friend of the LeMann family, and he lightened the mood by sharing some humorous memories of Tina. He recalled the time five-year-old Tina had tried to rescue a kitten that had gotten stuck in a tree. The fire department had to come rescue both of them, then that same kitten got stuck up in another tree a few houses down and had to be rescued again. Tina had cried and cried until the kitten was safe once more. Tina had been a huge animal lover, so that was no surprise.

Reverend Smith went on to say that Tina had also been a gifted singer and had sung solos in the youth choir as a young girl.

"I didn't know Tina sang," I whispered to Carleen.

"Me neither," she said.

I was beginning to wonder what else we didn't know about Tina.

The minister did an admirable job of reaching out to Tina's family members with his sweet stories and generous words. He mentioned several of the family by name, including the two he identified as her favorite uncle and aunt, Harold and Grace. He encouraged the family members to reach out to each other in the days ahead and to cherish their many happy memories of Tina. He reminded the rest of us in the congregation of something I'd already read in the obit. If we wanted to honor Tina's memory, he said the family was requesting memorial donations to the local humane society. Pre-addressed envelopes were prepared and waiting at the exits.

Discreetly peeking around during the prayers, I was not surprised to spot a number of local antiques lovers. Some, I knew, were regulars at the shop and had probably gotten to know Tina there. Next to the Harrises sat a couple of people I recognized from the library, possibly fellow board members. Unsurprisingly, Gus was not among them.

Quite a few people I didn't know were sitting near the family section, including one woman who had passed a tissue to Tina's mother. They were likely friends of the family. Whatever everyone's reason for being there, I was grateful to see the show of support.

The service was nearing an end, and the only thing the minister left unsaid was the fact that Tina's killer was still on the loose. I didn't hold that against him, though, since a funeral wasn't necessarily the best place to discuss that sort of thing.

Soon, Reverend Smith prayed the benediction, and the family filed out. Tina's mother made her way down the aisle on her walker, carefully assisted by her only surviving daughter. The two seemed very comfortable with each other. Tony, who appeared out of sorts and out of place, put his hand on his mother's back, but the gesture looked contrived. I immediately felt guilty for even thinking that. After all, late or not, he'd shown up to pay his final respects to the sister he'd just lost in a horrible manner.

Detective Shelton, who was wearing a somber-looking black suit and gray tie, remained standing at the back of the chapel as the rest of us exited after the service. I wondered if he was there as a courtesy or if there was someone in the room he was checking out. Whatever the case, I sure hoped that would be the last Roseland funeral I attended for a while.

As we all left the chapel, I tapped Michele on the shoulder.

"Oh, hi, Emma. Sweet service, wasn't it?"

I nodded. "The minister did a great job, and I hope it comforted the family. Listen, I wanted to ask you about something you said at church yesterday. You mentioned that Tina had a few enemies, and I was wondering—"

"You know that I run my mouth too much," Michele said sheepishly. "I probably should have kept that to myself."

I smiled. She did love to talk, but she wasn't malicious.

Michele lowered her voice. "I was thinking about the fact that Gus Townsend and Tina got into it on the library board last year. Everybody in town was talking about it. Gus said it was important to her career that her work be included in that *Faces of Roseland* exhibit, and Tina almost prevented that from happening. And then there were those rumors about her and Hubert Harris, of course."

Huh? "What rumors?"

"He was spending an awful lot of time over there, helping Tina get her house ready to sell. Several of the neighbors were talking about it, and Harriet stormed over there one night when Hubert and Tina were outside, discussing the landscaping. According to one of my customers, who overheard the conversation, Harriet basically told Tina she needed to tend to the house herself and let Hubert get home."

I gave her a skeptical look. "Tina and Hubert? That's kind of hard to imagine."

Michele waved a hand. "I know, I know. Didn't say I believed all that, just that those were the rumors. Well, I need to get on back to the shop. Got a lot of new spring inventory to put out. And don't forget to bring me more jewelry when you get a chance."

After promising her that I would drop off some new jewelry soon, I said goodbye and caught up with Carleen, who had been speaking with the Harrises.

"Now that was interesting," Carleen said as soon as I got to her side.

"What was?"

"Harriet was asking whether I knew anything about who would get to sell the antiques Tina left behind, assuming her family doesn't want all of them."

"That's an awfully big assumption." I glanced at the Harrises, who were getting into a shimmering new white Lexus, not the faded ten-year-old Jeep Grand Cherokee that Harriet drove to garage sales. "And sheesh, what took them so long to ask?"

Carleen grinned. We decided to stop by the Cupcake Café for a soup-and-sandwich lunch. After we quickly ate and discussed the funeral, I mentioned that I still wanted Carleen to examine the possible Haskell brooch I'd found. She said that if I could spare five more minutes, she would be happy to take a look. So we walked to her shop, and I pulled out the brooch and asked for my friend's expert opinion.

"Oh my, this is gorgeous." Carleen's eyes widened. "My gut instinct tells me it's Haskell, but let me look at it in more detail." She pulled out her huge magnifying glass with the mother-of-pearl handle. "Hmm."

"Is that 'Hmm' as in good or 'Hmm' as in 'Too bad it's a fake'?" I was eager to know whether my brooch was the real deal or not.

"Give me a minute." Carleen studied the back of the piece then gently set it down on a black velvet display board and headed in the direction of her office. "I'll be right back."

I heard the creaking of wooden desk drawers being opened and closed, and I wondered what Carleen was up to. Less than a minute later, she returned with a file folder.

"This"—she proudly waved the folder in front of me—"is one of the jewelry files I started keeping years ago when quality costume jewelry began showing up on eBay. When I saw fine pieces that weren't pictured in any of my guidebooks, I printed out a copy of the eBay description and photos. Now, take a look at the printout on top."

She handed over the folder, and I eagerly opened it. The first printout was titled "Miriam Haskell Filigree and Floral Motif Pin or Brooch." The piece looked exactly like mine, and it had sold for $587 four years ago!

"What I remember most about that piece is the number of costume jewelry dealers I knew who were bidding on it," Carleen said. "Back then, eBay didn't have all the privacy settings they do these days, so it was easier to scope out your competition." She smiled as she reminisced about the early days of the eBay craze. Carleen confided that the printout merely confirmed what she'd already known—my piece was definitely Haskell.

"Look how fine that filigree is," she said with obvious admiration, handing over her antique magnifying glass. "See how the cutouts are nice and crisp? And notice how the gold itself has a lovely embossed look. No one but Miriam Haskell went to that much trouble. The prongs on these rhinestones are also typical of Miriam."

"Miriam?" I asked, teasing my friend. "Were the two of you on a first-name basis?"

"I'm not quite that old, Emma. But I certainly *wish* I had been on a first-name basis with her. You know who she was, don't you?"

I laughed. "All the women who lusted after her jewelry, I imagine."

"No, silly. Coco Chanel. She and Haskell took tea together in Paris. I've often thought how I'd love to have been a fly on the wall for *that* conversation."

"Me too." I studied the printout. I was elated with my magnificent vintage find. "You know, Chanel was known for her yards and yards of pearls, and Haskell liked pearls too. But Haskell's designs were much more froufrou than Chanel's, which always have that classic look."

"Maybe that's why they got along," Carleen pointed out. "Their styles didn't compete with each other." She handed over my brooch. "I wouldn't normally come out and ask such a nosy question of my friends who are occasionally customers, but I'd love to know what you end up getting for this piece, if you don't find that too intrusive."

"Not a bit," I said. "I'll be listing some pieces online as soon as I get the Gallery Stroll jewelry finished. Wouldn't it be great if this did as well on eBay as that brooch you saw all those years ago?"

After promising Carleen I would keep her posted on my selling experience with the Miriam Haskell brooch, I headed home. There, I fed Miriam Haskell's namesake and fixed a cup of brisk black tea before settling in at the kitchen table with my big red tackle box full of jewelry supplies. Now that I was deep into creating a new design, I needed to focus my scattered thoughts. I was good at eyeballing random beads and knowing exactly where they best fit into a jewelry design, but I wasn't so hot at examining random facts in a murder investigation and knowing where they fit. I'd carefully made all those lists over the weekend, yet even after attending Tina's funeral, I hadn't come up with a single new clue that would put us any closer to solving her murder.

Determined to finish more jewelry that afternoon, I reached for a silver chain with a vintage sterling silver heart on it and arranged a few beads and smaller resin heart charms on either side. I had rubber stamped the beige resin hearts with a design that mimicked vintage handwriting. By inking the script on the resin heart charms and adding them to the necklace, I had created new jewelry that looked like something discovered in an antique jewelry box.

Finally satisfied with the piece, I was ready to add the clasp and sign off on another one-of-a-kind Emma Madison Designs exclusive. With the Gallery Stroll coming up on Thursday, I was hoping that my jewelry would be one of the first pieces of art that women shopped for. With proceeds from the show—and profits from selling most of what was in that tin of junk jewelry from the garage sale—I was looking forward to boosting my savings account this month. I also planned to try some Facebook ads to help spread the word about my jewelry.

Before I could finish fantasizing about growing my jewelry business, fate intervened. I was attaching a lobster claw clasp and squeezing a sturdy jump ring into place when *ping*, my pink-handled jewelry pliers exploded. One half of the pair ricocheted off the kitchen cabinets, frightening Miriam Haskell, who had been picking at the remains of her breakfast.

I was at a standstill until I got some new pliers, so I grabbed my purse and car keys to make a quick run to Craft World. I mentally chastised myself for having put off replacing the old pliers. This time, I would purchase two of them and have a backup on hand.

When I was about a block away from Main Street, my eyes were immediately drawn to the ambulance parked in front of the Cupcake Café. Detective Shelton and another officer stood under the yellow-striped awning, and I wondered what on earth had happened. I quickly pulled into a parking spot in front of Carleen's shop and went inside. No customers were in the showroom, but Carleen was hovering near the front.

"Hi there. What's up next door?" I asked. "The police are out front, and it doesn't look like they're letting anyone past."

"There was a little brouhaha at Mavis's," Carleen said. "Apparently, Tina's family stopped by this afternoon shortly after you and I ate lunch there. I was getting the mail and saw a police car out front. One of Mavis's waitresses was leaving for the day, and she told me about it. She said Tina's brother got into a scuffle with the sister, Teri, and got arrested. Things turned ugly, and Tina's mother, Mrs. Le-Mann, was highly distressed by all the drama. I'm guessing someone who witnessed the fracas must have called an ambulance for Mrs. Le-Mann. Maybe you could go see if there's anything else we can learn about it."

I loved how she wondered whether "we" could learn anything else, but I wasn't about to miss out on that opportunity to nose around. "I'll go see if Mavis will spill the beans. Be back in a jiff."

Much to my chagrin, Detective Alan Shelton was now sitting at one of the black wrought-iron tables out front. He appeared to be idly drinking his bottled Coke and eating a large deli sandwich. He tipped his head as I walked by. It annoyed me that he might think I was there just to be nosy, particularly because I was there just to be nosy.

After entering the shop, I got in line behind a woman and a teenage girl trying to decide which cupcakes they wanted. It soon became clear that their visit was some leisurely mother-daughter outing, and they couldn't quite agree on their cupcake selections. The mother wanted only fudge truffle. The daughter insisted her father and brother would prefer bananas Foster. Shifting uneasily from one foot to the other, Mavis appeared to be uncharacteristically anxious, as though she wanted the customers to get on with their order.

The pair soon came to a decision. Two fudge truffle cupcakes and two bananas Foster cupcakes later, the two were good to go. Mavis pulled out a yellow striped box, filled it with the cupcakes, and tied it securely closed with baker's twine. The mother handed over a twenty and received her change. They left, and the only other customer in the shop appeared to be a college student, who was seated at one of the smaller tables near the front. With earbuds in, he was focused on his laptop and didn't seem to be paying us any attention.

"Looks like you saved all the fun for after I left here today," I told my frazzled friend.

"You're more than welcome to my share of the fun," Mavis said. "I just want to bake cupcakes and serve sandwiches, not have to referee a family fight."

I pointed at a tray of lemon curd cupcakes. "As long as I'm here, I'd like two of those to go, please. Now what I want to know is, what makes a man confront his sister right after he's left his other sister's funeral? And why did he get there so late?"

Mavis shrugged as she slid open the glass door of the pastry case and reached inside for my cupcakes. "All I can tell you is, I heard them having a heated discussion about their mother's silver." Mavis plopped a two-compartment cupcake box on the counter. "The sister said something to him about how if he'd kept his share of their family's silver, they wouldn't have had trouble paying for Tina's funeral. That's when he grabbed her by the arm, knocking one of those plastic vases off my table in the process."

"Was she hurt?" I asked.

"No. She just appeared to be highly aggravated. I got the impression she's one of those women who doesn't enjoy a lot of drama. When I asked if I needed to call the police, she said no and assured me she was fine. I was happy to let them sort it all out for themselves. But just their luck, Alan and another officer heard about the dustup as they were coming in for lunch, so they took Tony outside and had a little talk with him."

Alan, I noted with interest. I wasn't surprised that Mavis knew him.

"I heard Tony was arrested—"

"No, there was no arrest. But Alan did tell Tony to skedaddle and said he didn't want to hear anything else out of him."

"What about the ambulance for Tina's mother?"

Mavis looked confused. "There wasn't any ambulance for Tina's mother. Mrs. LeMann was embarrassed by all the hoopla, but she was fine. Oh, but wait. Two EMTs who are some of my regulars stopped by for lunch and parked here like they always do. Maybe somebody thought it was related to the LeMann family feud."

"So why is Detective Shelton sitting out front now?"

"Just as a precaution." Mavis came out from behind the counter and began wiping down the tables before the influx of afternoon customers. "He came back here to make sure there wasn't any more trouble. It's been quiet so far, and I'm sure glad of it."

I raised an eyebrow. "Now if Tina's brother has that much of a temper..."

"You don't think he might have killed her, do you?" Mavis asked.

"I don't know. That outburst doesn't mean he's a murderer, but it does tell us he's got an anger problem. And if you take a bad temper and factor in some bad blood over the family finances, that could sure lead to murder. Especially since they were arguing over some valuable family silver. And it's clear the three siblings didn't exactly get along."

A *whoosh* of air signaled the door was opening. Mavis and I both turned and saw Detective Shelton entering.

"Things seem to have settled down here, Mrs. Eastwood, so I'm going to head back to the station," he said. "Please don't hesitate to call me if you need anything."

Mavis smiled at him. "Will do, Alan. And thank you."

I paid for my cupcakes and left Mavis alone to get on with tidying up her shop.

After stopping by Carleen's to deliver the promised update, I drove to Craft World with several new questions on my mind. Could Tina's brother have killed her? And while he didn't have the courtesy to show up for his sister's funeral on time, he did show up in plenty of time to make a scene afterward. That was also curious.

But before I could devote any more time to playing Nancy Drew, I had to get some jewelry completed if I had a prayer of having a successful show at the Gallery Stroll on Thursday. I parked in front of the arts and crafts supply store and vowed that I was going in for pliers and nothing else. As I pulled into a space in the busy parking lot, I glanced longingly at the Making Memories Antique Mall. New items arrived there daily, but I couldn't shop there every day. I firmly told myself no, headed into the crafts store, and was soon breezing out the door with two new pairs of pliers in my bag. I made a mental note to inventory all of my supplies and see if any more of them needed replacing.

Soon, I was home and at my kitchen workstation again, giving that lobster claw clasp another shot. Within minutes, the sterling heart necklace was complete. I had a hunch that some woman at the Gallery Stroll was going to adore it.

"There." I held up the necklace, swirled it under the bright bulbs of the kitschy red-and-chrome light, and listened to the gentle tinkle of all those heart charms. Miriam Haskell breezed by on her way to her water bowl, so I sought feedback. "What do you think, Miriam? Pretty impressive, huh? Mark my words, this is a necklace that folks will be talking about at the Gallery Stroll."

I still have so much more jewelry that I want to finish before Thursday evening, and I have to stay current on packaging and shipping my online sales too. I was starting to feel anxious about how quickly the Gallery Stroll was coming up, and not just because I was afraid I wouldn't have enough jewelry to show. I didn't know what I was going to wear. I'd hoped to visit one of the downtown boutiques in search of a new outfit, but I was behind on my work and simply didn't have time to shop for new clothes. As I mentally flipped through my closet, my cell phone rang. It was Jen.

"Hey there. What's up?" If Jen called during the day, it was usually for something short and sweet. Our chatty calls waited until late evening when she was alone in her office, or even later when she was off the clock.

Jen got right to the point. "What was it you said about Alan Shelton's behavior at your friend's store the other day?"

"Just that he was so rude about me keeping out of the way when it was clear I was there to be with Carleen. Why?"

"One of the news reporters just had a little dustup with him. Said Alan was rather gruff and kept saying he didn't need any more reporters trying to solve his case for him. Does he know that you used to be a reporter?"

"I don't know why he would." I propped my phone against my neck as I used both hands to return jewelry supplies to the tackle box. "What was his problem this time?"

"Not sure yet. Something about an incident report he hasn't had time to write up since he's so busy working other cases."

I humphed. "I dearly hope he's looking into Tina's murder." I placed the tackle box back on the kitchen shelf. "He was at her funeral this morning, and unless he was a friend of hers and I didn't know it, I'm guessing he was there for some reason pertaining to the investigation."

"Surely he was," Jen said. "Listen, gotta go. Talk to you later."

After a busy afternoon and evening of jewelry making, I looked at the to-do list on my phone and thought about the rest of the week ahead. I wished I had taken time to ask Jen what I should wear to the Gallery Stroll. Jen was a clotheshorse, and she always had an opinion about what I should wear.

I walked into my bedroom. An antique oak wardrobe held the clothes that didn't fit into the room's lone small closet, its tiny space typical in older houses like mine. The wardrobe held my dressier clothes, so I looked through the shifts and skirts and hoped for a fashion miracle.

After rummaging around inside the wardrobe, I caught a glimpse of turquoise near the back. I'd completely forgotten about that vintage black, turquoise, and white Pucci shift I'd bought the year before. I wasn't serious about collecting vintage fashion—not as serious as I was about collecting costume jewelry, anyway—but I knew enough about the classic designers to know a Pucci when I saw one.

The shift had been a flea market find last summer. The seller had been touting her old English chintzware—cups, saucers, bowls, and plates galore. Each overpriced piece was marked with the name of the maker, the pattern, the age of the piece, the price, and the word "Firm." Yet the vintage Pucci was just twenty-five dollars, a fraction of its value. The woman had haughtily turned down anyone who'd asked for a discount on her old dishes, yet she'd sold me the Pucci for next to nothing.

Thinking about that cheap flea market vendor and her over-priced wares reminded me of my earlier conversation with someone else who was known as a cheapskate, Harriet Harris. She'd said Tina's belongings were all boxed up and waiting to go to her family. If Harriet was responsible for disposing of Tina's belongings, that meant Harriet would be first to know where those items ended up.

Maybe there was something among Tina's possessions that could provide a clue about who might have wanted to kill her.

As I hung the Pucci on a hook on the back of my bedroom door and got ready for bed, I plotted how I might get a peek at Tina's things. I didn't want Harriet to know I was curious about them, yet I had to find a way to stay in the loop about anything involving Tina and her family.

Because whatever Tina had left behind, there was a distinct possibility that it might have gotten her killed.

Chapter Eight

An unexpected Tuesday morning phone call hijacked my plans to spend most of the day at home, completing and packaging more jewelry. I was just reaching the edge of consciousness when my cell phone rang at 6:50 a.m. Rubbing my eyes, I looked at the screen and assumed it would be a wrong number, but Savannah was calling. "Hello?" I answered, groggy but already alert enough to be concerned.

"I know you might not be up yet, and I'm so, so sorry to call you this early, but I'm in a bind here. I've got to go out of town for a family emergency, and there's no one to work the gallery for me. I know because I was planning to fill in for someone today. Is there any possible way you can do it?" Her words came out in a rush, and she sounded stressed.

"Let me think." I fisted my mouth to suppress a yawn. "I know the morning's open, but I really need to catch up on some jewelry projects this afternoon. Do I need to be there the whole time, or can someone else take part of the day?"

"If you'll handle it until around one or so, Bob's agreed to take the afternoon shift. But I desperately need the morning covered."

Bob Mathis, a talented local woodworker and a fellow member of the Ross County Arts Council, was always reliable and would no doubt show up as promised. "Consider it done," I said. "I'll be there at ten, right on schedule."

"Great, and don't forget that whoever has the morning shift usually gets there early to turn on all the lamps, light the display cases, and do all that sort of stuff. Emma, you're a lifesaver!"

"Yeah, yeah, yeah." I laughed. "You know I don't like to do mornings too often, but for you, I will. And listen, I hope everything's okay with your family."

"It's my aunt who lives up in Blue Ridge," Savannah said. "She broke her hip last night. My mom's having a fit to get up there and help, and if I can drive her there this morning, it would really mean a lot to her."

"I've got it covered," I promised. "But be sure to keep your phone handy in case I have to text you with any questions."

As I sat in bed, trying to recover from the early-morning wake-up call, Miriam wandered in and began purring loudly. "I know, I know. If I'm up, that means you want your breakfast. Let me wake up first, will you?"

Padding to the bathroom, I yawned and mentally rescheduled my day. I brushed my teeth, washed my face, and looked in the mirror. I still had almost three hours before it was time to play shopkeeper. There was no reason I couldn't enjoy my usual pot of coffee, get some jewelry projects underway, then shower, dress, and arrive at the gallery well before the first customers arrived.

Still in my bathrobe, I went into the kitchen, turned the coffee maker on, and prepared to spread out my jewelry supplies. First, I texted Jen. *Working at the gallery 10-1. Come by if you can.*

She soon texted back: *Will do. Save me one of those blue scarves in the window.*

I wasn't sure which scarves she was talking about, but I figured I would find out soon enough. Whoever had displayed them in the gallery's street-facing window obviously knew what they were doing.

With my customary Pyrex mug of coffee on the table before me, I reached for my design notebook and flipped to the page with my jewelry to-do list. I'd finished some of the more elaborate new designs. Next, I simply needed to string a few leather cords with inspirational word charms that said "Create" and "Love" and "Inspire." Those were ridiculously easy to whip together, and I had been amazed the first time I sold one for fifteen dollars. I had less than a dollar in supplies and less than a minute of labor in each one, yet customers couldn't get enough of the simple necklaces. I quickly made another half dozen of them for the Gallery Stroll then reshelved my supplies.

An insistent meow interrupted my thoughts. "You're still hungry?" I poured cat food into Miriam's bowl and gave her fresh water before pouring a second cup of coffee. While I savored a new Colombian roast, I headed to my bedroom closet. The jeans and white knit tee I'd planned to wear wouldn't do for gallery duty. With a mug of coffee in one hand, I rifled through my armoire with the other, searching for my new coral blouse with the lace-insert sleeves. I would accessorize with one of my tasseled necklace-and-earring sets because customers often asked about whatever pieces I happened to be wearing. A live model was a great advertisement, and the price of the advertising couldn't be beat.

After a quick shower and blow-dry, I pulled on a pair of dressy gray slacks along with the blouse and jewelry. I blew a kiss to Miriam as I headed out the door for the drive downtown.

When I stepped outside, the blustery gray morning had me quickly running back inside for a sweater. I was twenty minutes ahead of schedule, precisely the amount of time I needed to stop by Mavis's for a cappuccino and a Danish.

When I arrived, the café was bustling with early-morning customers. The aromas of fresh-baked bread, cinnamon, and coffee filled the air as I headed to the service counter in the back.

"My goodness, aren't we out and about early this morning?" Mavis asked. She rarely saw me before noon.

"I got called on to work the morning shift at the art gallery," I said. "But I won't be fit for anything if I don't have a little more caffeine and some sugar first."

"Your usual?" She pointed at some pastries under a glass dome.

I nodded. Whenever I came to town in the morning and stopped by the café, I always ordered the same items—a caramel cappuccino and a cream cheese Danish. It might not have been the healthiest breakfast in town, but it was my reward for being wakened before my usual seven o'clock.

I told Mavis to come visit me on her break if she got a chance then waved as I headed to my car. I pulled up to the back door of the gallery at nine forty.

Heading into the building, I grasped my cappuccino and Danish in one hand and fished around in my purse for my shop key, which I kept on a separate key ring in an inside pocket of my purse-cum-tote bag. After I unlocked the door, I flipped on the overhead lights, walked across the creaky old floor to the middle of the shop, and set my belongings on the vintage wooden countertop.

The gallery was so peaceful at that time of day. I enjoyed watching it come to life in the morning. I loved to hear the patter of my shoes on the building's wide-plank floors and imagine who had first walked on them more than a hundred years ago. The morning light streamed through the old-fashioned plate glass windows, which added character and made the artwork and crafts behind them easily viewed by passersby.

A small bay window spotlighted the work of a different artist each month. This month, a gorgeous orange, green, and red African print quilt was displayed behind a handcrafted wooden chair draped with hand-dyed blue cotton infinity scarves. Now that I knew what Jen had been talking about, I chose the prettiest scarf and tucked it behind the counter.

Next, I turned on the lamps, including one that Bob Mathis had clearly made since it featured an intricate inlaid wooden base. I fingered the price tag and whistled softly—five hundred dollars. But for those who liked the unique and unusual piece, it was a reasonable price. Bob usually sold one or two lamps every month.

Passing by a table with several jewelry displays, including some of my own designs, I couldn't help noticing that most of my black-and-white sets were gone. I planned to create a few more one evening soon. I tapped a quick iPhone reminder about needing more black-and-white jewelry sets then headed behind the counter to stash my purse—and breakfast—out of the way.

The groan of the old door opening announced our first customer of the day. I popped up from behind the counter. "Good morning, and welcome to the..."

But I didn't feel very friendly when I saw who it was—Detective Shelton.

"To the gallery. Can I help you with anything?" I wondered whether he would remember me from the other day. I certainly remembered him.

He looked uncomfortable as well. "You're that friend of Carleen Wood who was at her shop on Friday."

"Yes. That was a horrible morning, and I was glad I happened to be there to see Carleen when she needed a friend. Tina was someone we all cared about, so I'm sure you can understand why we were so upset."

"Nothing personal," he said, "but we did have to investigate before we could let anyone disturb the crime scene. I hope you understand."

Even though I still felt he'd been overbearing that day, it sounded as though he were indirectly apologizing, and I would be gracious in accepting his apology.

"Certainly." I glanced around. "Are you looking for anything in particular?"

"I like to come by here first thing in the morning whenever I need a gift. Get a jump on the other customers." He smiled slightly.

I felt the tiniest bit of remorse about having judged him so harshly. "It's nice to know you shop here. Feel free to look around, and if I can help you with anything, just let me know."

He nodded and headed to a table of jewelry. After several minutes of picking up necklaces and placing them down again, he cleared his throat. "This set here on the display"—he pointed at the black velvet torso—"is it for sale too?"

I knew the set well—I had made it. "All the arts and crafts you see in this gallery are for sale. That's our policy."

"Great." He removed the pieces from the display and headed to the counter. "My sister and mother really like the jewelry I buy for them here. Something about how they're well-made pieces that don't look like all the other jewelry out there." He was obviously unaware I was the maker.

"That's certainly one of the advantages of shopping at a place like this." I tried to conceal a grin, wondering if I should I tell him I was the designer, but I decided not to. *Better to let him find out some other way.*

The detective didn't appear to be in the mood to chitchat, so I asked if he wanted his purchases gift wrapped.

"Yes, please," he said.

I reached beneath the counter for a small paper gift bag and some tissue.

"You know..." He hesitated.

I looked up from my gift wrapping, curious.

"We're working hard to find out who killed your friend." He looked sincere. "I probably don't have to tell you that we don't have a lot of homicides in this town, and we intend to keep it that way."

I was surprised to hear him refer to the case since he'd been so no-nonsense about it before. "I sure hope you find the killer soon," I said. "It's made a lot of us nervous to think a murderer is still on the loose around town. And of course we want to see justice for Tina since she meant so—"

His cell phone rang, and he excused himself, stepping near the front of the shop before answering the call. He kept his voice low, but I listened carefully and heard something that sounded like, "What do you mean he won't talk to us? He has to."

I tried to look busy, but I was curious to know what he was talking about.

"Listen," he said after he hung up from the call, "I need to get on to the station, so—"

"And your bag's all ready." I handed over the jewelry.

He tipped his head and made eye contact for just about a second too long. With his light-brown hair and handsome blue eyes, the detective actually wasn't that bad to look at, and I could feel my cheeks blushing.

"Thanks again," he said with a nod as he left.

The rest of my morning at the gallery flew by. In addition to the jewelry Detective Shelton bought, I'd sold two of Bob's wooden bowls, six packages of Savannah's watercolor note cards, and the last seven copies of *Goodness Gracious*, the local garden club's award-winning cookbook with one of Savannah's most popular floral paintings on the cover. Members of the Georgia Geraniums Garden Club north of Roseland were in town for the day and had snapped up all the remaining copies of the book. It featured recipes from local dignitaries—the mayor and council, the school superintendent, and several well-known local artists—as well as a few of the state's former first ladies, so it was a perennial best seller in all the downtown shops.

During the morning's only brief lull, Jen dropped by and picked up the scarf I had set aside for her. Bless her, she'd brought me another caramel cappuccino, so I was on a sugar high all morning. I was grateful for the energy boost, because the shop had a steady stream of customers. Most of them made purchases too, which kept me busy, and before I knew it, my shift was over.

Promptly at one o'clock, I handed the shop over to Bob and decided to make a quick stop by the Silver Squirrel. A woman with bright-orange-red hair was standing inside, and that could be only one person.

"Hey, Emma," Carleen said when I entered. "Come on in out of that wind. There's someone I'd like for you to meet. This is Tina's sister, Teri."

I walked over and shook her hand as she stood near one of the jewelry cases. "I can't tell you how sorry we are about your sister's passing," I said. "She meant so much to us, and I can only imagine how this must have affected your family."

Teri whipped a lace-edged hankie out of her purse. "Oh dear, and I thought I was through crying."

"I'm so sorry!" *Stuck your foot in your mouth again, Emma. Way to go.*

"No, no. It's me." Teri waved a hand. "I appreciate your kindness. Really, I do. It's just that I'm still weepy about everything."

I patted her on the back, hoping she wouldn't mind the gesture. "I'd be a hot mess if that were me. In fact, I'd probably take to bed and not leave the house for a year."

Teri managed a quiet laugh. "That's tempting, believe me, but I had to come by and thank Carleen for being such a good friend and employer to Tina through the years. And when I saw that she'd made a huge gift to the humane society in Tina's memory and sponsored the reward fund at the police department, well, I had to come say thank you in person."

"That wasn't necessary at all," Carleen said. "But I'm so glad you did. And since you're opening a new business in Roseland yourself, why don't we get together for tea in a few days? Emma, you could come too." Carleen glanced at me with raised eyebrows, as if to say, "You will, won't you?"

I immediately accepted her invitation. "I'd love to. And maybe we could discuss some ways for Teri to get involved in the community here in Roseland." I turned toward Teri. "If you're interested, that is."

Teri's smile was broader this time. "I'd like that."

"I'll give you a call soon to set it up, okay?" Carleen looked between the two of us.

We agreed to meet, and Teri soon left, saying she needed to get over to her antique mall and do a final walk-through of the space.

"That was a nice surprise," I said.

"It sure was." Carleen clasped her hands together and appeared content for the first time in days. "How thoughtful of her to stop by."

I thought so too, and inwardly, I realized I'd misjudged Teri after listening to some hearsay that might not have even been true.

Carleen cleared her throat. "Before you got here, Teri filled me in a little since she said she knew I'd probably heard about her brother's behavior at lunch yesterday."

"Sounds like she understands how the small-town gossip mill works," I said.

"Mm-hmm. It seems the sisters had recently butted heads with Tony about some missing family jewelry. Teri said she's still grieving over her sister and couldn't care less about the jewelry, but the bickering has only gotten worse since Tina's death. And that's probably not going to change since Teri just found out she's to inherit her sister's entire estate. Since Tina was single, she arranged to leave everything to Teri with the knowledge that Teri would then use the money to help make sure their mother was taken care of."

"So even if they were estranged in the past, it's obvious that they reconciled in time to make sure their mother was well provided for."

Carleen sighed. "Teri said she wished she and Tina could have become friends again much sooner."

My mind was whirling. "Did Teri happen to mention what jewelry was missing?"

"You know, I didn't think to ask," Carleen said. "Teri said she wondered whether perhaps Tina had gotten desperate for money and sold some pieces here. As I told her, I don't recall Tina ever selling me a piece of jewelry. I would have remembered that. She bought a few jewels here over the years—job hazard, I guess—but sell them? No."

After telling Carleen I needed to get home and finish up some more jewelry designs, I headed to my parking spot behind the gallery, retrieved my car, and drove home. On the way, I realized it was entirely possible that Tina had been sentimental about the family jewelry and had simply kept it.

And if she had, her killer had probably figured that out.

Chapter Nine

ate Tuesday afternoon, I packed up three of my newest jewelry designs to share at the biweekly meeting of the Ross County Arts Council. Networking with other creative souls was one of my favorite sources of inspiration. No matter which art or craft they preferred, artists brought a unique perspective to the table. I learned so much from my fellow artists and craftsmen, and through our arts council, I'd met friends like Trish Delgado, who made tile designs imprinted with old lace pieces, and of course Savannah Rogers, who painted those gorgeous watercolors of historic buildings, homes, and gardens around town. Many of us worked full-time from home or were retired, and the arts council was a great way to get us all out of the house and talking to one another.

Miriam Haskell sidled up to the kitchen table just as I was about to tuck the last of the jewelry into my canvas tote bag with the arts council logo on the side.

"Have I been neglecting you, Miriam?"

She raised her head, turned her stunning blue eyes on me, and gave a loud meow.

"Come here." I reached into the cabinet for some of her favorite kitty treats. "I'm going to leave you a few extra shrimp-flavored goodies today."

Her happy reply told me she appreciated the gesture, and I gave her a goodbye pat.

As I took my tote bag out to the car, I checked my watch and realized I would be early for the meeting. With a quick buzz by Mavis's, I could pick up some sweets as a surprise for everyone. We always had sodas and bottled water on hand, but snacks were a hit-or-miss treat, depending on the whims—and schedules—of those attending the meeting.

Twenty minutes before closing time, I walked into the Cupcake Café. Mavis looked up from wiping one of the tables near the display counter.

"Don't worry. I'm not here to hold you up. I just wondered if you had anything left that I could take to the arts council tonight."

"Now, Emma, you know I'm never without something sweet around here. I just baked some marbled cheesecake brownies to go on tomorrow's take-out plates. If you like, I can box up a dozen or so of those for your meeting."

"That sounds divine. Would you mind?"

Mavis headed to the back and washed her hands before reaching for the pan of brownies. "Haven't talked to Carleen too much since, you know, that awful tragedy happened. Do you know how she's holding up?"

"Doing pretty well, I'd say. The shop is keeping her busy these days, which is a good thing. But now that you mention it, that may just be a way for her to keep her mind off the, um, recent unpleasantness."

Mavis reached for a flattened yellow-and-white cardboard box and quickly fastened its notched sides into place. While she worked, I whipped out my cell phone and checked email. I had an order for five elaborate pearl-and-rhinestone necklaces for a group of bridesmaids. *Excellent.* Except that the customer—a favorite of mine and someone who'd frequently ordered from me before—was requesting a rush job and needed the necklaces in a week. *When am I ever going to find the time?*

"You know, Tina's brother was in here again this afternoon," Mavis said casually. "Had a woman with him this time. A much *younger* woman."

My head snapped up so quickly, I nearly hurt my neck. Mavis raised an eyebrow at me.

"You've got to be kidding," I said. "I would think he'd steer clear of here after that incident yesterday."

"That's what I thought too, but apparently he got hooked on my bananas Foster cupcakes after eating one yesterday and came back in for a whole box of them." Mavis appeared to concentrate for a moment as she paused and sealed the box of brownies with a yellow sticker before tying a bow with baker's twine. "He and that gal sat right here and whispered to each other for thirty minutes. Seemed happy as clams. Ate several of the cupcakes too. There was none of that drama like we saw in here yesterday."

"Any idea who the woman was?"

"No, and I hate to admit it, but I did try to find out," Mavis said with a sly—or maybe guilty—expression on her face.

I couldn't help grinning. Like me, Mavis was keen to know what was going on in her town. "Did you get the impression she was his girlfriend?"

"That would be my guess." Mavis handed over the box of treats. "If they come in here again, I'll try to find out more."

I hauled my oversized purse up onto my shoulder and carefully picked up the box by its string. "If they do stop by, would you let me know? I haven't made much progress in helping find Tina's killer, and I promised Carleen that I would. Anything, even a tidbit of something dropped by a family member, might be useful, especially if it's regarding Tina's brother... I mean, since we know so little about him."

"If he comes in again, I'll give you a ring, sweetie. Count on it."

I said goodbye to Mavis. As soon as she closed the door, she turned the Open sign in the store window to Closed and gave me a wave. Brownies in hand, I headed down the block and wondered about the mystery woman who had been with Tina's brother. It didn't make sense that he would be spending time in downtown

Roseland the day after his sister's funeral when he lived in Atlanta, a good ninety-minute drive away. His newfound interest in Roseland seemed rather sudden, and I was curious why he found our little town so compelling.

Right then, though, I was eager to get to my arts council meeting. The scent of chocolate had me salivating, and I was ready to tuck into one of Mavis's creations.

When I walked into the meeting room of the Roseland Public Library a few minutes later, Trish Delgado, our arts council president, was talking to Martha Barnes. An award-winning quilter and our group's oldest member, Martha was busy draping a black cloth over the display table.

Our library was one of the oldest in the state. From its beige brick facade to the mahogany-paneled rooms, the library was a town treasure. Its meeting room was highly sought-after by civic groups around town, and the arts council had dibs on it for every other Tuesday night. We stayed in the library board's good graces by regularly donating arts and crafts books as well as volunteering for their annual fundraising drive. It was a win-win situation for everyone.

"Hi, Martha. And here you go, Trish." I plopped down my purse and handed Trish the box of brownies. "What are you two working on these days?"

"I'm finishing up the binding on a Baltimore Album quilt made with batiks." Martha swept a gray curl off her face. "Hopefully, I'll have it to share at our next meeting."

"And from me, it's same old, same old," Trish said, opening the box and peering inside before setting it on the drinks table. "I don't feel like I've had an original idea in a year. To be honest with you, I'm getting tired of pressing doilies into wet clay all the time. But I'm going on an art retreat this weekend. Hopefully I'll come back inspired to try something new."

Martha, who'd already helped herself to a brownie, was busy wiping a corner of her mouth with a paper napkin.

"Where's the retreat?" I asked. I wanted to attend one in the next year or so and liked hearing about the retreats my fellow artists had enjoyed.

"Asheville," Trish said. "You know how North Carolina's such a hotbed of creativity these days." She plucked a small bottled water off the refreshment table, opened it, and took a quick sip.

"I've heard there's a bunch of New Age hippies up there too," Martha said. "Kind of makes you wonder just what exactly is in that mountain air."

Trish chuckled. "I don't pretend to know what's in the Asheville air, but I sure plan on finding out while I'm up there for the workshop. I can't wait."

A murmur of voices at the door caused all three of us to look up, and we saw Savannah and Gus arriving. Savannah held the large black portfolio she often used to transport her watercolors, and Gus appeared to be helping her make sure it didn't get bent. Gus rarely brought one of her assemblages to a meeting simply because they were too unwieldy to haul all over town. Her pieces included items such as bottle caps, feathers, gum wrappers, tin can lids, bicycle-chain links, beach glass, or even a used tea bag or two. We never knew what might make it into Gus's artwork, but it was always fun to find out.

Over the past few years, Gus had received press on the local, state, and even national level for some of her larger assemblages. One of them, *The Joys of Driving and Texting,* featured the outline of a female's body with a cracked cell phone in one hand and a crumpled steering wheel in the other. When Gus was going through what she called her uber-feminist phase, she created designs of corsets trimmed in barbed wire and gave the pieces titles like *A Woman's Work is Never Fun.*

Those who knew Gus only as "Augusta Townsend" through her press clippings assumed she was some angry leftist artist. They were often surprised to meet the friendly, curly-haired woman with the huge smile and the romantic Victorian clothes. Tonight, she wore a ruffled blouse and denim vest over a lace-trimmed denim skirt. I was always fascinated by Gus's clothing choices, which currently included the same bubblegum-pink ankle boots she'd worn a few nights ago. Peering over the top of the boots were the frilliest, girliest, most lace-adorned socks I'd ever seen.

"I read that piece in the newspaper about your Horizon Award," I told Gus as I offered her a bottle of water. "I love how they described you as a 'prominent feminist philosopher and artist.'"

"Wasn't that a hoot?" She chuckled. "The critics like to give these lofty themes to my work, and everyone else assumes I'm a nutcase because of the seriousness of my art. What they don't get is that I just want to see a reaction out of folks, good or bad. The worst thing in the world is indifference."

Savannah rolled her eyes good-naturedly. "They certainly can't be indifferent about *your* work." Savannah and her sister were a study in contrasts. All buttoned-up and businesslike in her day job, Savannah had until recently worked in corporate relations at a hospital south of Roseland and closer to Atlanta. Now that she was taking a sabbatical, her artwork was the place she could let her creativity shine through.

A few minutes before six, Shareta Gibson came in. Still in her midtwenties, Shareta was the member we loved most, as Trish liked to say, because she helped keep down our average age. Shareta's work was inspired by Africa and its rich history. Her latest pieces were infinity scarves she'd hand-dyed using items from nature just as her forebears had done.

"I sold one of your scarves this morning to the editor of the *Daily Tribune*," I said. "She saw them in the window and asked me to hold one for her."

"Cool, and hey, thanks." Shareta tapped me on the arm. "It's amazing how much attention that storefront display gets."

Some commotion at the doorway caused us both to turn our heads. Bob Mathis was trying to wrangle a large plastic laundry basket through the door without tipping it over. I hoped it was packed with some of his latest hand-turned wooden bowls. A retired bank president, Bob had taken up woodworking as his retirement hobby. He said he found woodworking much more enjoyable than banking.

According to the most recent arts council newsletter, Bob was working on a new technique that would combine more layers in his pieces. I knew that whatever he'd brought to show us would be spectacular.

As I was taking a seat, Michele Fairchild dashed into the room and apologized for being late. "Sorry, guys. I got busy talking with a customer and let the time slip away from me." Michele was one of the only non-artist members of the council, but she was a huge supporter of the arts. She also gave us excellent advice about marketing our work based on trends she saw in the retail world.

"So is this it tonight, folks?" Trish looked around the room. "I know there's just a handful of us, but Marsha called earlier and said she might not make it since one of her girls had a volleyball banquet to attend."

Bob grabbed a can of Coca-Cola and joined us at the table.

Trish shuffled a few papers and cleared her throat. "Before we begin, I want to point out that Emma brought us a box of Mavis's marbled cheesecake brownies. Caring for you all as I do, I'm going to accept the responsibility of trying one to make sure they're okay. So Bob, if you'd grab one of those for me—yes, right there on that napkin's good—I'd be much obliged." Since Trish was nearly six feet tall and slim enough to be on the catwalk, she could afford to eat all the brownies she wanted. "Emma, would you read the minutes from our last meeting?"

I pulled out my battered old burgundy leather portfolio, a leftover from my journalism days, then removed the copies of the minutes and distributed them around the table. Journalists—and in my case, former journalists—were often tapped to serve as either secretary or historian in any organization they joined. Everyone else was too nervous about writing for public consumption. I didn't mind serving as secretary for the arts council, though. The minutes took me only about thirty minutes to type up after each meeting. Plus, I figured my role as secretary inoculated me against having to accept one of the more unpleasant jobs like keeping track of membership dues or—perish the thought—hitting up all the local artists for donations for our annual silent auction.

I read the minutes, which were swiftly accepted and approved.

"If it's okay with everyone"—Trish's eyes left her notes and glanced at all of us—"I'll summarize what you've got on your handouts in the way of new business. As you can see, we're now up to nineteen paid members. I believe Savannah said a couple of members from the Greater Roseland Art Society are considering joining as well to help us cross-promote each other's work. Is that right?"

Savannah tilted her head. "That's the plan."

"Great, then that should put us over twenty soon enough."

Martha cleared her throat, and I fought to hold back a sigh. "Do we really want to get much larger?" she asked. "I think we've got the perfect mix of people right now."

I glanced at Michele and winked. Martha had been on the arts council since its creation thirty years ago—a fact she was not loath to share—and she was quite vocal about its membership. She claimed she wasn't opposed to growing our numbers but simply wanted "good growth." That usually meant the children of her longtime friends, whether or not the children were actually talented artists and craftsmen themselves.

Trish tucked a strand of hair behind her stylish glasses. "I believe we addressed that at last month's meetings, Martha. And you missed those two because you were visiting your son down in Florida, right?"

Martha nodded and pursed her lips.

"We agreed to cap membership at thirty, and since we're nowhere close to that right now, going over twenty isn't going to be a problem. If you have any questions, you'll see that Emma summarized the discussion in our minutes. Let me know if you have any questions after you've read over it. I always appreciate your input." Trish gave our eighty-three-year-old member a warm smile.

I didn't know how she did it, but Trish was great at defusing the tension in a room.

She pushed her glasses up on her nose and continued. "Now, you can see right here on page one that last month, we voted to cancel the next meeting since there's a conflict with the Taste of Roseland food festival. Many of us plan to have booths there that night. That is, if they decide to allow permits for arts and crafts in addition to food vendors. Heard anything more about that, Bob?"

The town's mayor, Jim Mathis, was Bob's younger brother. Bob was always eager to bring us any straight-from-the-horse's-mouth reports that pertained to the arts council. "Jim says he thinks they'll allow it because food vendors have been down the last two times."

Trish adjusted her glasses on her nose again. "The only other item I can see that we need to address is whether to participate in the regional art show going on in Gainesville next March. I know that seems a long way off right now, but we have to let them know by the end of the month, or they'll offer the spot to another group. I think it would be great to participate and get some publicity outside of Roseland. Maybe we could let a few folks exhibit their wares and distribute some brochures about our upcoming events. But I'd love to hear what everyone else thinks."

"I think we should do it," Gus piped in. "Savannah, wouldn't you like to have your watercolors there?"

"Sure, I would," she said.

"I know I'd love to get more exposure for my pieces, especially since I've got a huge installation going in their county library later that month," Gus said. "I don't see any negatives here, so why would we not do it?"

Trish spoke up. "No reason, I guess, just that we're accustomed to voting as a group on everything we do."

"Then let's vote." Gus held up a hand. "All in favor?"

"Wait a minute," Trish said. "We can't vote without a quorum, and we don't have a quorum tonight."

"It's not our fault we don't have a quorum. We're all here, for Pete's sake." Gus wasn't exactly a fan of *Robert's Rules of Order*. Neither were the rest of us, for that matter, but I could tell Gus's eagerness to vote made Trish uncomfortable.

"Tell you what," Trish said. "How about I poll everyone by phone tomorrow, just a yes-or-no vote, and we'll send out the results by email. That way, we'll all know what we're doing ASAP." She turned to Gus. "That work for you?"

Gus nodded.

Trish excelled at small-town diplomacy. Secretly, I hoped she would turn her two-year term as arts council president into a three-year term, an extension a few of us were quietly rooting for.

"Moving right along," Trish said, "Savannah, since we don't have a lot of official business tonight, why don't you tell us what you're working on and how you're marketing it these days. That's always my favorite part of our meetings, anyway. I get such great ideas from you guys."

"Certainly." Savannah stood and reached for her black portfolio. After laying it out on the table, she revealed a beautiful painting depicting some of downtown's most famous buildings—the court-house, the library, the historical society headquarters, and the garden club's ancient offices, among others.

"You know," Martha said, looking around as if to make sure she had everyone's attention, "my late mother was a founding member of that garden club, and her mother was one of the first officers of the historical society. So I must have a print of this. Would you mind dropping it by the house when you get a chance?"

"The prints haven't come in yet, but when they do, I'll be sure to let you know." Savannah smiled kindly at Martha.

"It really is gorgeous," Trish said.

We all agreed.

Trish continued to admire the painting. "And I love how you combined all these great buildings. Plus, I think everyone in town is going to want a print, so your marketing is practically built-in with a piece like this."

Savannah beamed. "I hope so because I want to use it as a fundraiser for Haven of Hope."

Haven of Hope was the area's shelter for abused women and chil-dren, and I'd donated some jewelry to their fundraisers in the past. Giving back to the community was not at all uncommon for the artists in our town. It was so like Savannah to want to use her work to benefit others.

"Are you selling the original or just prints?" I asked.

"They're going to have a live auction for the original at their an-nual banquet this fall, and they're already selling the note cards of this design. Their board members all got some of the cards to sell, and there's an ad for the cards in their monthly newsletter and on their website."

Gus spoke up. "I offered the shelter one of my corset pieces, one of those with the barbed wire. They said that when they hung it inside the shelter, it spooked some of the women. They were happy to auction it off, though, so I guess all's well that ends well." She shrugged.

I shared a conspiratorial grin with Savannah. I could see how Gus's work might be considered a little scary if someone didn't know her. I could also see how Gus's pieces conveyed strong messages about women and women's rights. Still, people liked what they liked. If I didn't believe that, I wouldn't have made a habit of including at least a dozen black-and-white necklaces in every art show and sale I attended. They really weren't that exciting to make. In fact, I thought they were a little too safe, a little too been-there-done-that. Sometimes, though, the buying public was more comfortable with a familiar design than a newer, more challenging one.

"Now, come on." Savannah gently elbowed her sister. "They were grateful for your donation."

"They didn't refuse to take the money, did they?" Bob asked.

Spoken like a banker.

Gus rolled her eyes and grinned. "No, of course not."

"There you go." Bob sat back with a self-satisfied smile.

"Shareta, what are you working on these days?" Savannah asked.

Shareta reached into her tote bag and produced a small woven basket. "This." She placed it on the table. "I've always wanted to learn some of the African weaving techniques, but I don't have room to store large baskets, so I've decided to make them in miniature."

Savannah reached for the basket. "How lovely," she said, passing the basket down the table.

"Will you be putting some of these in the gallery shop?" I asked. "These will fly right out of there, you know."

Shareta laughed. "That's actually the first one I've ever made, but once I speed up my production, I would love for the shop to carry them."

"Now Bob, I want to see those new bowls I've been hearing so much about," I said.

"I thought y'all would never ask." He walked around the conference table, picked up the plastic laundry basket sitting nearby, and set it on the table with a flourish. Gently, he removed the thick terry cloth towels separating his pieces and laid three bowls on the table.

"Wow! Look at that one." Trish reached for a bowl with a chevron design. It featured several different colors of exotic wood. "How exquisite."

Next was a glossy boat-shaped piece made of cherrywood. Bob said it was a practical piece that could be used for everything from salads to flower arrangements. "But the newest piece I've made is this one." He removed what appeared to be a simple large round bowl. As soon as he placed it on the table, we all gushed in admiration. The bowl featured inlays not of other woods but of turquoise. The bright colors appeared throughout the bowl's interior as well as the exterior.

"That's the most gorgeous wooden bowl I've ever seen," I said.

Dipping his head, Bob said a quiet thank-you.

"Gorgeous doesn't begin to cover it," Trish said. "And I know we agreed not to clean each other out at these meetings, but unless you've promised to sell that one to someone else, it's mine, Bob Mathis. I don't care if you display it at every arts and crafts show in and out of town for the next three years. Just promise me that bowl will come back to me eventually."

"Sold," Bob said, beaming. "But I do need it for a couple of art shows right now."

Obviously thrilled at her success in claiming the magnificent bowl, Trish turned to me next. "Emma, what's going on in the jewelry world? I always count on you to let me know what's in and out of style."

"Chokers and cuffs are in, chunky statement necklaces are in, and dinky little anything is O-U-T out," I said. "The bigger and chunkier, the better." I reached into my tote and pulled out a black velvet torso display. On it was one of my new vintage-inspired pieces, an eighteen-inch necklace with a large tree-shaped pendant. I'd suspended it from a double strand of silver chain that linked iridescent teal and green glass beads.

"That piece is amazing," Gus said. "Let me check it out." She reached for the display and carefully fingered the necklace. When she finally finished inspecting it, she passed it around the table.

"I've got the chain double looped right now," I said. "But you can also remove the pendant and wear it on the single thirty-six-inch chain. Women like having two options when it comes to chain length. Some customers prefer to slip a necklace over their head rather than fastening and unfastening it each time."

Gus whistled, clearly admiring my new piece.

Whatever else our arts council meetings accomplished, the get-togethers sure were great for my creative ego. And Gus wasn't known for being lavish with her praise.

"Really? You like it?" I asked.

"It's perfect, just perfect." She pointed at the necklace and gazed at each element. "I think I see what you were saying here too."

"Saying?" I asked.

"Yes. The large tree motif of the central pendant speaks of life and growth, and the teal and green beads represent the sky and earth. Am I right?"

"Actually, I wasn't trying to have this necklace say anything except, 'Hey, do you think I'm pretty?' and 'Buy me.'" I rubbed my fingers together in a show-me-the-money gesture.

Everyone laughed, including Gus.

"Honestly." Savannah shook her head. "Gus thinks that just because she sees everything in figurative language and symbols, everyone else does too."

"I still say there's symbolism in your work," Gus said. "In everyone's work, really. But please tell your necklace I said that I think she's very pretty."

"And she thanks you." I gave my most regal bow.

Trish laughed and began to flip through her notes, probably making sure she had covered everything.

"That green color is really pretty," Bob said. He never had much to say about my jewelry, so I was pleased by what was clearly honest praise.

"So you're a fan of green?"

"Oh yes, but then I've always liked emeralds or any green stones in women's jewelry. My mother loved emeralds. And you know, so did that gal who died up at the antiques shop last week."

My ears perked up immediately. "What do you mean?"

"Tina? Wasn't that her name?"

Suddenly, my senses were on full alert. "Yes, Tina Le Mann," I said. "But how do you know she liked emeralds?"

"Easy," Bob said. "I was in the pawnshop one day, looking for a replacement tool after one of mine broke. She came in trying to sell this big old emerald necklace she said had been her great-grandmother's, something passed down in her family. That old man that runs the place offered her several thousand dollars for it, as I recall, but she decided not to sell it. Said emerald was her mother's birthstone and her favorite gemstone and maybe she should just keep it after all. I'm not real sure why that made an impression on me, but it did."

"Was anyone else with her when she tried to sell it?" I asked.

Bob shook his head. "I don't think so. But then again, this was some months ago, so I can't be sure. Why?"

"The police still haven't figured out who might have wanted to kill Tina," I said. "If she had some expensive jewelry, that might be one reason someone would go after her. Although why they'd do so at the place where she worked puzzles me."

Everyone else was quiet, as though they were unsure of what to say next.

"She seemed like a nice person," Savannah said quietly, obviously trying to be helpful. "I didn't know her all that well, but she was always nice to me when I went in the shop to see Carleen."

"Tina was a sweetheart." I frowned. "That's why I'm even more convinced we've got to keep this case in the public's eye. We've simply got to find out who killed her."

Gus was pursing her lips and had a troubled look on her face. Again, I got the sense she was holding something back, but I had no idea what.

Meanwhile, I had bigger things to worry about, like a killer who remained on the loose in Roseland. I was getting antsy for a break in the case, and Bob had just given me what might be my best lead yet.

Chapter Ten

After the arts council meeting and Bob's news about Tina's family heirloom necklace, my mind went off in a million new directions, and I wasn't able to wind down until well after midnight. Naturally, since I was sleeping in the next day, Miriam woke me up when she decided I'd slept long enough and it was time for her breakfast. She pawed at the covers and even tapped my face. Eventually, I was forced to rise and get her something to eat.

"Oh, Miriam, I could have used that extra hour of sleep," I groaned as I pulled my terry cloth robe around me and padded into the kitchen. I'd left my iPhone in the bedroom, so when I heard a familiar ringtone as I opened a can of cat food, I decided whoever it was could wait until I got Miriam settled. She purred contentedly and started devouring her breakfast. Once my feline roommate seemed satisfied, I retrieved my iPhone and saw that Jen had left a voice mail. I tapped the screen to listen to her message.

"Hey, it's me. Listen, something's going on out at the antique mall you like, that one the Harrises own. I thought you might want to nose around. We sent the photog, but the police wouldn't tell him anything. All we've got is a photo of the store with a police car out front. See what you can find out and let me know, okay?"

Something was up at Making Memories? Harriet and Hubert sure seemed to be right in the middle of all the action. I wondered what was going on. There was nothing to do but get dressed and drive over there to check it out. I slipped on a pair of dressy jeans and a gauzy aqua top with bell sleeves then clasped a colorful beaded necklace around my neck. I was ready and on the road in fifteen minutes.

On the way, I clicked on my Bluetooth earpiece and called Savannah, the most well-connected Roselander I knew. Savannah had been
born and raised in the town, and she always knew more about its goings-on than anyone else.

She picked up almost immediately. "Emma, what's up?"

"I'm hoping you can tell me. I just heard a police car has pulled
up outside Making Memories, and I'm headed there now. Any idea
what's going on?"

"Oh, good grief. It must be the Harrises. They've just decided to
divorce, and I hear the negotiations aren't going very well. This could
get ugly."

"What are you talking about?"

"I don't know how much I can tell you, but their oldest daughter,
Hannah, is one of my friends from the Junior League. She told me
her parents have been having marital problems for years and are finally headed for what she says is destined to be a bitter divorce. My
guess is that something has already gotten out of hand."

"But they were together at Tina's funeral on Monday," I said.

"Hannah said something blew up between them last night, and
the Harrises won't tell their girls what it was." Savannah sighed. "She
did say that they've been arguing about who actually owns the antique mall, or which of them gets control of it, at least. It's a shame,
really. Those two have been married forty-something years. I wish
they could work it out."

"Me too." I wasn't wild about Harriet, and Hubert's reputation as
a womanizer hadn't exactly endeared him to me, but I hated to hear
they might divorce. I found it odd that all this Harris family drama
was occurring mere days after Tina's murder. The Harrises had only
recently listed Tina's house for sale, and from what Harriet had told
me, she and Hubert had gotten along well enough to conduct business together then. That couldn't have been more than a few weeks
ago.

"You still there?" Savannah asked.

I snapped out of my mental meandering. "Sorry. The wheels are turning as I try to figure out what's going on here. And I know this sounds selfish, but I've found a lot of my best junk jewelry at that mall over the past two years, so I'd hate for it to close because of all this." I felt a twinge of guilt at the realization that my own business interests were overshadowing what ought to be concern for a couple's failing marriage.

"I know what you mean," Savannah said. "Those of us who love old stuff hate to see a place close, especially one that's been doing as well as the Harrises' has. If I hear anything I can share with you, I'll let you know."

By the time our call ended, I was approaching the antique mall. Quite a few vehicles were there, but not a single police car was in sight as I pulled into a space and parked. *Did something really go on here this morning?*

The door's ubiquitous cowbell clanged as I entered, and Harriet looked up from a butterfly-clipped stack of papers she was studying intently. "Why, Emma, you're just who I needed to see," she said with an eager look my way. "Come over here a minute if you don't mind."

This ought to be good.

"What can I do for you?" I asked.

She pulled the top sheet out from the stack of papers. "Look at this necklace and tell me what you see." She handed over a print-out showing a striking necklace that appeared to be made of emeralds—large, clear, exceptionally green emeralds.

"That's a gorgeous necklace. Looks like some kind of rare, old estate piece," I said. "Why do you ask?"

"Because the police are asking if I have it." She shook her head as if the idea were utterly ridiculous.

"Why would they think that?"

"Remember when I told you about Tina LeMann having to sell her house? Those old boxes I helped her pack had some costume jewelry in them. I told that brother of hers I'd be glad to go through it all and see whether I could sell any of it for him here at the store. I never saw anything like this necklace, of course, but now he's insisting it had to have been in Tina's belongings. He's threatening to sue me for the return of a necklace I've never even set eyes on. He actually had the nerve to have the police come question me about it here this morning, right in front of my customers and everything."

So that's what the ruckus was all about. And why was Tony looking through those boxes if Teri inherited their sister's estate?

"You're sure you've never seen this necklace?" I asked.

"Quite sure. Wouldn't you recall if you'd seen something this ornate?"

She had a point. "Did they tell you anything about the necklace?"

"Alan said it was reported to be an old family heirloom, and that's all he could tell me."

"Alan?" I wrinkled my nose. "Would that be Detective Alan Shelton?"

"Yes, I taught him when he was in kindergarten. Why? Do you know him?"

"Not really," I said. "But I've run into him several times over the past few days and wondered how competent a detective he is, that's all. I haven't heard of the police making any progress in solving Tina's murder."

Harriet bristled. "Alan Shelton is one of the finest young men we've got in this town. If he's working on this case, I can assure you everything possible is being done to solve it. We just have to be patient, hon."

Her tone made me twitchy, but at least I knew where Harriet stood on the matter. "I suppose you're right. Listen, would you mind getting me a copy of that printout? I'd like to show it to Carleen in case the necklace shows up at the Silver Squirrel."

Harriet raised an eyebrow. "Don't you think it would be just as likely to wind up here?"

I had to think fast. "Oh, sure, of course it could. But a seller who isn't familiar with your place out here on the highway might assume a downtown shop would be the place to start." I crossed my fingers behind my back and hoped my fib wouldn't come back to haunt me.

"I see what you mean." Harriet removed the printout from her stack of clipped-together sheets of paper. She placed it facedown on the copier behind the front counter and pressed a button. The machine jiggled, whirred, and spit out a color copy that she promptly handed over.

I was about to head to my car with the printout, but then I realized I needed to come up with an excuse for having stopped by the antique mall in the first place. I looked around as if I were in a browsing mood and simply idling away some time.

"So, what is our resident jewelry designer looking for today?" Harriet seemed more relaxed than when I'd first come in.

"Clip-on earrings. I've come up with some designs where I string vintage beads and baubles on this glorious new silk ribbon I came across. But I'm fresh out of vintage earrings, which are always some of my prettiest vintage pieces."

"I'm sure there are plenty of them in here, but goodness knows if I could tell you where to look."

"I know my way around," I said, heading off with a wave. "No problem."

Besides, the browsing would give me some time to think. I needed to figure out why Tina had held on to such an expensive necklace. If she had to sell her house and use the money to pay for her mother's care, it seemed she would have wanted the money that necklace was probably worth. Especially if, as I suspected, it was fine jewelry rather than costume.

I headed down the farthest right-hand aisle of the store, as was my habit, and began pawing through baskets, tins, and boxes. Jewelry bargains were rarely found behind the jewelry counters of an antique mall. The best finds were often tucked into an old sewing basket or perhaps hiding in a rusted tin among the kitchenwares.

Shopping in antique malls and thrift stores was such a soothing, calming activity. Browsing artifacts of the past helped settle my mind, and imagining the former lives of all the pretty old things fed my creative spirit.

Making Memories usually had good quality merchandise, but Harriet's vendors tended to be in the same spots month after month. I'd shopped there for so long, I knew not only the contents of each booth but also who the vendors were and what their prices were likely to be.

I walked past a booth with primitive furnishings and antique bread bowls. Then I stopped by the booth with vintage linens and teacups. The white-and-cream shabby chic look never seemed to go out of style. Sometimes those booths had old jewelry or buttons I could use in my work. I looked through all the pretty vignettes but didn't spot a single jewelry piece that spoke to me.

Near the end of the aisle, at the entrance to a booth that had been empty for a few weeks, my eyes widened at the most wildly colored mahogany sofa I had ever seen. Upholstered with a hodgepodge of jewel-toned fabrics, from bright reds and oranges to iridescent plums and blues, the Victorian-style fainting couch looked as if it had been plucked straight from a Calcutta street market. I loved it.

The couch certainly wasn't traditional in any sense of the word. Victorian furniture usually featured thick, dark velvets and damasks, not the bright, happy colors adorning the couch before me. I reached for the dangling tag listing the price—sixteen hundred dollars. Cost-ly for a small-town antique mall but not bad for such an unusual piece.

Next to the couch was a black wrought-iron display rack with a colorful assortment of fabric purses completely filling its arms. Fringed, tasseled, and sporting bits of lace and vintage needlepoint, they were in the same intense red, orange, plum, and blue hues as the sofa.

A pretty silver compote held a small stack of business cards at the entrance to the booth. I took one and read the block print. "T. Le-Mann Interiors. Custom Upholstery Consultations Available."

So the colorful pieces were the work of Teri LeMann. I didn't know why she would be a vendor at Making Memories when she was opening a new antique mall of her own. And I was surprised Harriet hadn't mentioned that.

Tucking one of the cards into my purse, I made a mental note to ask Harriet about her new vendor before I left. But first, I had to take another look at that amazing piece of furniture. The couch was bound to draw a lot of attention, and Harriet was lucky to have it in her mall. One piece with pizzazz could often get people talking.

As I turned the corner to browse the next aisle, I was all but run over by another customer—Detective Alan Shelton.

"Excuse me, Miss Madison," the detective said, "but I have some work I need to do in here."

The officer's patronizing tone set me off. "Indeed? I suppose I was under the misguided notion this was an antique mall open to the public and where customers were welcome to shop. Have I somehow been misinformed?" Something made me go all Jane Austen whenever I got riled up.

The detective looked embarrassed. "No, no, you're right. Forgive me." He looked at his hand, which was clutching what appeared to be one of Teri LeMann's business cards. "It's just that I'm under a lot of pressure to get a break in this LeMann case, and... well, that's really all I can say for now. Please excuse me." With that, the detective sped to the front of the store and, I assumed, out the door because I soon heard the clattering of the bell.

What an infuriating man. My mind was reeling. *What was he doing here? Did he overhear me talking to Harriet earlier?* I certainly hoped not. He was giving me enough trouble as it was.

I needed to go home and get to work on my jewelry, but my shopper's sixth sense told me to check out a stack of metal tins at a kitchenwares booth. The seller had great prices, and she restocked so often that there was almost always something new to explore.

The first tin, an old baby-blue Currier and Ives oval one, contained sewing items. It had a few darning eggs inside, which Savannah collected. I would have to tell her to stop by. The next two tins were empty, but the one on the bottom was heavier and obviously had something inside. I popped the lid off and found some vintage button cards. I often worked buttons into my jewelry designs, and these were old and in mint condition. A small plastic bag was filled with orphaned earrings, including one marked Hattie Carnegie. Once I filed off the clip, that earring would be terrific on a new ribbon necklace. The whole lot was only eight dollars.

Eager to pay for my latest jewelry finds—and to question Harriet—I headed to the front counter. "I found just what I needed. And I must say that I love that fainting couch in the new booth back there." I waved toward the aisle where I'd spotted the couch. "When did that arrive?"

"That ugly thing with all the bright-orange and purple fabrics? Holly took that in yesterday. Said it's by Tina LeMann's sister, Teri. Not sure why she wants a booth here when I've been told she's going to compete with us and open her own antique mall in the old Piggy Wiggly, but hey, as long as she's current on her rent and gives us ten percent commission, I don't care."

"Maybe she sees it as free advertising to have her designs in your antique mall. And it's such a unique piece that I'll be surprised if it stays here long."

"You may be right." Harriet looked up as she peeled off the price sticker that was on the bottom of my tin and stuck it to a page in her spiral-bound notebook. "It always amazes me what customers like and don't like. You can never predict what's going to be the big seller here."

"I noticed Detective Shelton was in here too," I said, hoping Harriet might offer more information.

"He's actually a regular of mine," she said. "He collects first-edition crime novels. Comes in here every week or two, looking for a new one. I assume that's what brought him here today."

"I see." I handed Harriet the cash for my purchase. But I didn't see, not at all. Detective Shelton hadn't had a book in his hand when he'd nearly mowed me down earlier. And if he'd come into the antique mall simply to buy some old books, surely he would have just said so. I wondered whether he had slipped up when he claimed to be busy investigating Tina's murder. Something about his most recent shopping expedition wasn't adding up, and I planned to find out what that was.

But first, I needed to go home, get a cup or two of coffee in me, and spend the rest of the afternoon and evening getting my jewelry and displays pulled together for the Gallery Stroll the next night.

Chapter Eleven

Thursday morning and afternoon passed in a blur. After whipping out a few last-minute jewelry designs, organizing and packing for the Gallery Stroll, and showering and dressing for the evening, I barely made it downtown in time to set up at the Threads of Time Gallery owned by my friend Gail Ginn, an accomplished weaver. I had always associated weaving with the potholders that I learned to make at Girl Scout meetings, but Gail's weaving had little in common with my childhood crafts. She wove on large wooden looms that were taller than her, not child-sized plastic ones.

Gail used only hand-dyed fibers and threads in her work. The colors created the thick, rich designs that were her signature. Gail Ginn place mats, table runners, pillows, and throws were sold not only in Roseland but also in some of Atlanta's swankiest home furnishings boutiques. For many locals, it was acceptable shorthand to simply request "a Gail Ginn" for a birthday, anniversary, or Christmas gift. I had a couple of her pillows and planned to buy one of her throws in the fall if my jewelry sales were still going well.

Because of her reputation as an award-winning weaver, Gail's gallery was a tourist attraction all its own. Collectors loved to buy pieces directly from the artist, to say they'd been in her gallery and—if they were lucky—actually watched her perform her weaving magic. I was honored she thought enough of my jewelry to let me display it there at the Gallery Stroll each quarter.

And I was horrified that I was almost running late.

Gail was at a loom in the back of her gallery when I lumbered in the front door, huffing and lugging totes packed full of jewelry. As I plopped them down near the door and walked to the back to let her know I had arrived, she paused from whipping her shuttle in and out of rows of red, blue, and purple fibers long enough to wave one hand and call out a greeting. Whatever she was working on didn't look like much yet, but I knew that in Gail's gifted hands, it was likely another masterpiece in the making.

"Thought I'd get a head start on another pattern before customers arrive at five. I've reserved that round table up front for you, but feel free to move if you prefer another spot."

That table near the entrance was a piece of the gallery's prime real estate, so there was no way I would turn that down. "Sounds great."

"Need any help setting up?" Gail tucked an unruly brown curl behind one ear, hardly missing a beat with her shuttle.

"No. My displays are pretty lightweight, so I just need to get them up and start filling them with jewelry."

Gail glanced at me without slowing her work. "Groovy. I'll be back here if you need me."

I headed out to the car to unload my display boards. They were actually upcycled pieces I'd found by the side of the road. Abandoned shutters with all their dents and dings were perfect jewelry displays once I dolled them up with chalk paint. The louvers of the shutters were tailor-made for displaying the necklaces and bracelets I'd learned to artfully drape, wrap, and tuck into place.

The display board I loved most was an old distressed window frame whose shabby white paint job I'd left intact. With a little chicken wire installed where the panes of glass once were, it became the perfect place to showcase earrings, brooches, and rings.

A quick glance at my rhinestone bracelet watch told me I had twenty minutes before the first of the evening's shoppers arrived. It was a good thing I worked fast. In the beginning of my jewelry career, it would have taken me two hours to complete a setup. Now, I could do it in half an hour.

Several other artists arrived while I was setting up my space, but beyond a polite meet-and-greet, I didn't have time to pay them much attention. I would be neighborly later. For the moment, I needed to double-check the list on my iPhone to be sure I had everything needed to make the evening run smoothly. Business cards? Check. Flyers with info about custom orders? Check. Credit card reader for my iPhone? Check.

I was clicking items off the list one by one when Gail walked up and cast an approving eye. "Your style has gone rather upmarket, hasn't it?" She plucked a beaded bracelet from a display and held it up to the light, dangling it in the late-afternoon sun, causing the blue glass beads to sparkle.

"Upmarket? What do you mean?"

"I mean your work has gone from cute costume jewelry to a more elegant, streamlined look," Gail said. "Your pieces have always been notches above your competition, of course. But these days, I think they have a certain *je ne sais quoi* that is pure Emma Madison style. I think it would be impossible for another jewelry artist to copy your designs."

I beamed. To have an artist of Gail's caliber admire my work was humbling, and her support gave me even more confidence.

When Gail resumed clucking over all my displays, she gently flipped through the silver-soldered heart bracelets on a black velvet display rack while I set out a basket of pendants and earrings featuring old script. Words of inspiration never went out of style. Pieces with words like *Hope*, *Create*, *Inspire*, and *Live* had long been some of my best-selling items.

Live. How ironic that in a week where death had dominated the headlines, there sat a necklace with its simple "Live" message. I couldn't help thinking about Tina and how someone had viciously taken her life. With precious little being said about the murder around town, it was starting to look as if the killer had gotten off scot-free. Despite my promise to Carleen, I hadn't been able to provide very much help in solving the case.

As I worked on the jewelry displays, I knew what I needed to do. I would swallow my pride and visit Detective Shelton to ask how—not *if* but *how*—I could help with the investigation. I would ask him about the dustup with Tina's brother and the new antique mall being opened by Tina's sister, and I would let him know that some people in town were eager to hear of any progress being made in the case. My own leads certainly hadn't produced anything helpful. It was unthinkable to me that a killer might get away with murder right there in Roseland.

Glancing at my watch, I realized it wouldn't be long before those first customers walked through the doors. I tried to push the unpleasant thoughts of Tina's death to the back of my mind for the next three hours.

Focus, Emma.

Gail conducted a final walk-through of her gallery and made sure everyone was ready to roll. When she came back up front, she paused and admired one of my new script-motif pendants. The one she chose was hanging from a silk ribbon, and she asked me to save it for her. I told her I would be glad to set that one aside. I knew full well that I would quietly slip it to her later as a thank-you gift.

"I mean it, Emma. I've been at this long enough to know you're going to do a lot of business tonight."

I laughed. "No matter what happens with my sales this evening, you're sure great for my self-esteem." I gave her a quick side hug. "Now let's wait and see if the customers agree with you."

"They will, sweetie. But first, I want you to meet one of the other artists we're hosting tonight. His name is Justin, and I'm trying to introduce him to some of you younger artists in town. His use of color is extraordinary, and I can't wait for you to see his work." She gestured in the direction of a blond man about my age.

He was busy setting up wooden easels that displayed large oil paintings of mountain scenes. Even from a distance, I could see that his work was impressive.

"Are you game?" Gail asked.

"Sure." I always enjoyed meeting other artists. "Just give me a few minutes to tidy up my display here and get my baskets out of the way." I looked down and used my foot to slide a canvas tote under the skirt-draped table. "Besides, he looks pretty intense at the moment."

Justin had placed a painting on his last empty easel then appeared to be sorting through a stack of shrink-wrapped prints, probably copies of his most popular paintings.

"Well, then." Gail's eyes were still trained on his space. "I don't guess we should interrupt him right now. Just be sure you say hi to him before the evening's over."

I promised her I would make an effort to be friendly. And since Justin was new to the local arts scene, I could tell him a few things about all that was going on in Roseland. The local arts community had been very kind to me, and I liked to pay it forward.

Before the first customers arrived, I conducted a final fluffing of my display. I counted to be sure the seven dozen pieces I'd brought were showing to their best advantage. I stepped back to survey the entire table, then I leaned in to swap out a colorful, sparkly beaded necklace for a more traditional black-and-white model, which I draped on the black velvet torso that was the table's focal point.

"I like them both," a male voice behind me said. I turned around and found myself face-to-face with Justin.

"Thanks. I always obsess over which pieces best represent my work. I hope tonight's Gallery Stroll customers agree with you about that." I stuck out my hand. "I'm Emma Madison, by the way, and I gather you're Justin." I pointed at his name badge.

Justin gave me a smile and a warm handshake. "Justin Hayes, starving artist, one and the same, ma'am."

I liked his friendliness and felt instantly at ease. "Now that you've seen my display, I'd love to hear about your paintings. Gail is quite a fan, and that's saying something."

Justin led the way to his own corner of the gallery, near Gail's loom. I wondered whether she intentionally had him set up nearby so she could watch over the newcomer to town on his first night at a Gallery Stroll.

His larger paintings were displayed on easels, but some smaller ones were hanging on the gallery's exposed brick wall. All were landscapes of familiar scenic views, yet their moody quality was striking. Each painting seemed to capture the mountains at a specific moment in time.

"Your paintings are amazing." *And I would love to own an original someday.* "I've always wondered how artists manage to capture the look of that morning mist rising off the mountains. A touch of magic, maybe?"

Justin shrugged. "There's no secret to it. For me, the most important part is being able to see it in my mind first. I'm mainly a plein air painter, but if I can't be outdoors or don't happen to have my art supplies with me, I take a photograph that reminds me of what I was seeing in that moment. From there, it's just a matter of technically executing that vision with oils and canvas."

I fingered one of his shrink-wrapped prints. "You make it sound simple, but I know it's much more complicated than that." I continued to flip through a display of small prints and paused on one that captured a North Georgia mountain landscape at the peak of its autumn beauty. "Wow! This is stunning."

"You like fall too?" he asked.

"It's always been my favorite season. Especially around here."

Justin smiled but didn't say anything for a long moment. I wondered what he was thinking.

"Since it's almost five, I guess I'd better head over to my display and do one final check before the doors open," I said. "Good luck this evening."

"Good luck to you too, Emma."

I smiled and headed back to my display, glad Justin Hayes couldn't see my face. My grin would tell him far too much about what sort of first impression he'd just made.

I'D BEEN AT THE GALLERY Stroll for two hustling-and-bustling hours when I looked up in time to see Tony LeMann enter the gallery and head to the back with a young blonde—perhaps the one Mavis had spotted him with earlier in the week. He had a shopping bag on his arm, and it looked as though he were waiting in line to speak with Gail. The blonde eventually wandered over to my table and was browsing through some of my necklaces when Tony finally caught up to her and said, "Come on. Let's go."

"What? I like these." She pouted and twirled a strand of her long, nearly platinum hair.

"We're not spending a dime here if the owner can't even find time to speak with me. If you like jewelry, I'll find you some *real* jewelry," he said loud enough for everyone to hear. "Now let's get out of this so-called gallery before I say something I'll regret."

What a jerk! While I didn't expect everyone to love my jewelry, I'd never heard it dismissed so abruptly, especially at a friendly, community-wide event. I wondered what was stuck in his craw. My pieces had been flying off the racks all evening, and I was determined not to let the one bad apple ruin my good time. Lots of the downtown merchants, including Carleen and Michele, had stopped by to say hello. I'd noticed Carleen talking with Gail, and I wasn't surprised when I glanced up from making a sale and saw Carleen at the checkout counter with a new Gail Ginn scarf.

After more than three hours on my feet—greeting the Gallery Stroll regulars, chatting up all the newcomers, and talking about jewelry to more women and men than I could count—I was relieved when the last customer left. An exhausted Gail turned her shop's sign to Closed. I'd sold out of necklaces and bracelets and had only a few pairs of earrings to take home, so the evening was an unqualified sales success. But I was more than a little tired and hungry and ready to get off my feet.

I reached into my purse and searched for one of the Brach's Jelly Nougats I always kept in reserve. They were my all-time favorite candies and for an offbeat reason. I liked the taste of the soft taffy-like confections, but I absolutely loved the fact that those yummy cream-colored rectangles with their colorful candy centers looked like miniature jewelry boxes. I thought they were the prettiest candies ever made.

After unwrapping one of the sweets and popping it into my mouth, I slowly savored the taste as the piece softened. A tap on my shoulder startled me, and I accidentally tried to swallow the candy. I began to sputter and nearly choked on the mouthful of creamy nougat.

"I'm so sorry," Justin said. "I didn't mean to surprise you."

To my dismay, I began to cough and gasp. Justin watched me with a horrified look on his face. My eyes watered. A tickle seemed to have taken up permanent lodging in my throat, and I could feel my face reddening by the second.

"Are you going to be okay?"

"I'm fine." I wheezed, repeatedly trying to clear my throat. "Really." But my words set off another round of hacking. Mortified, I began to envision a headline that read "Jewelry Designer Chokes to Death in Tragic Incident at Gallery Stroll."

"I'll go get you a bottled water," Justin said. "Be right back."

Great, just great. I finally meet a nice guy, and then I choke to death in front of him. That ought to make a swell impression.

By the time Justin got back with the bottle of water, I had recovered from my choking episode and was well on my way to recovery—of my windpipe if not my pride.

"Thanks," I said before taking what I desperately hoped was a ladylike sip from the bottle. "I was so hungry, I was scarfing down a piece of candy."

"Funny you should mention hunger." Justin patted his stomach. "I was just thinking how I'd love to swing by Sombrero for some tacos. Any chance you'd care to join me?"

I looked at my watch. It was only a few minutes past eight, and I had to eat sometime that night. "Give me five minutes to schlep all these jewelry displays out to my car, and you're on."

He grinned. "I'll do better than that. How about I do some of the schlepping for you?"

After a hugely successful Gallery Stroll, I had assumed the night couldn't get any better.

Suddenly, I knew that it could.

Chapter Twelve

Around midnight, I finally crawled into bed and realized I hadn't brought my iPhone, which doubled as my alarm clock. I padded back into the kitchen and got the phone out of my purse. As I was setting the alarm on it, I discovered a screenful of text messages I'd obviously missed during the Gallery Stroll.

Jen's text made it clear I was in hot water: *Stopped by. U R gone. WHERE ARE YOU? Call me!*

I didn't know she'd planned to stop by, and I hadn't thought to look at my phone all evening. It had been turned off during the Gallery Stroll, and I'd been so busy that I hadn't had time to check for messages earlier. *Sheesh.* Jen knew I was normally a weeknight couch potato, so I could see why she might have wondered where I was. But I was a grown woman. She needed to chill.

I headed into the kitchen and prepared a cup of chamomile tea before texting Jen to say that I was still up if she wanted to chat. I took a sip of tea and soon heard the familiar ringtone. I tapped the screen and braced for a lecture.

"You had me worried sick! Why didn't you tell me you were going to be out late tonight? Where have you been?" Jen was pulling a late-nighter at the *Trib* and had taken a break earlier to stop by and chat. I thought she was going overboard on the worry, but I was eager to share my delicious news.

With my tea in hand, I walked back to my bedroom, fluffed a few pillows into place, and settled in for what I knew would be a nice long chat. "If you must know, *Mom*, I was in the company of a handsome new gentleman caller."

Jen whistled. "Girrrrrl," she teased, "you've been holding out on me."

"Not exactly. I didn't meet him until tonight. We were both in the Gallery Stroll and set up at Gail Ginn's, and afterward we went to Sombrero for a bite to eat. I have to tell you, I had the best time. I can't get over it. This happened so easily and so fast, it was like we'd been friends for years or something."

"Hey, being friends is a great way to start."

She was right on that point. After Todd had helped Jen buy her house, they'd kept in touch and were friends for months before they ever began dating.

"So tell me about him."

"I thought you'd never ask." I snuggled into the pillows and set my cup of tea on the bedside table. "He's an artist. Oils. Paints gorgeous landscapes, lots of mountain views. But they're unique, not the schmaltzy stuff like you see in some of the local souvenir shops that—"

"So what does he look like?" Jen asked.

I ignored her shallow question. "He's thirty-three. Has a degree from the Savannah College of Art and Design. Used to do illustrations for a magazine, interestingly enough, so he understands the shift going on in publishing these days."

"So is he a full-time artist, or does he have a day job?"

"He's like me, self-employed. Unlike me, he already owns more than one home. He inherited some money from a grandfather and used it to buy real estate when he entered art school. That not only financed his education but also gave him the freedom to paint since he wasn't depending on a day job to cover his mortgage."

"Smart man," Jen said. "So that's good. Proves he's not a slacker. And in today's dating scene, that's saying something."

I laughed and took a sip of tea. "Can't say I disagree with you there."

"Now are you going to tell me what he looks like, or do I have to beat it out of you?"

"Okay, okay. He's a good six inches taller than I am, sandy-blond hair, brown eyes, medium build. Likes to ride bikes. And yes, he's definitely good-looking."

"So is this Mr. Right?"

"Oh, good grief, Jen. Who knows? Let's just say I find him terribly *intriguing*."

"Intriguing, huh? That means you think he's hot. I can't wait to tell Todd. Listen, the scanner in here is going nuts, so there's probably some car wreck or house fire that I need to check on. Keep me posted on how it goes with da Vinci, okay?"

And as usual, Jen hung up without saying goodbye.

WHEN MY ALARM WENT off at the usual seven o'clock on Friday morning, the first thing I did was down enough coffee to get my wits about me and plan my day. Even though I'd had terrific sales the night before, I couldn't rest on my laurels. Friday was often a day I would hit garage sales, but that week, the local sales didn't sound too promising. The garage sale previews on the *Thrifty Shopper* Facebook page had shown beer steins, old electronics, Coca-Cola memorabilia, and baby clothes, none of which would help me make jewelry. Instead of hitting the sales, I decided to hit the thrift stores for a bead-buying expedition.

After I showered, dressed, and fed Miriam, I headed to my car and set out on a mission to visit as many local thrift stores as I could squeeze in before lunchtime. The shops were some of my best sources for jewelry elements and inspiration. Thrift store beads could be taken apart and restrung. Occasionally, the perfect beads happened to be trimming the neckline of an old threadbare sweater. I didn't mind taking apart an article of clothing in the service of a jeweled creation.

As I drove, I made a mental note to purchase a few brown beads in addition to blue ones if I saw some good deals.

My first stop, on the west side of town, was a shop with a half-off sale in progress, which was probably a strategy to get rid of some overflow. I scored a bag of assorted beads for a dollar and, while I didn't exactly need them, five paperback mysteries selling for a dime apiece.

The next thrift store on my list, one that benefited the local food pantry, was on the outskirts of downtown. They restocked every Friday, so perhaps they would have some new junk for sale.

As I pulled up, I spotted a familiar blue-green Prius parked near the front door. That looked like Gus's car. Roseland didn't have that many blue-green Priuses tooling around town.

Entering the shop, I scanned the small space and quickly spotted Gus, who was in a back corner of the store. Looking down, she quickly flipped through a stack of old pictures propped against a wall.

I quietly walked past a particleboard bookshelf displaying angel figurines, stopped a few feet from Gus, and cleared my throat. "Did you sell so many pieces last night that you've been forced to come here and restock?"

"What? Oh, Emma, it's you." Gus laughed. She stood and dusted off her hands on her wispy blue skirt. "Hey. Are you as relieved as I am to have that show behind us?"

"Yes and no," I said. "I always work too much and too late on the nights before a new show, but I made a lot of sales, so there's that. It sounded like you did pretty well over at the Foothills Gallery too, if the customer chatter I heard last night was any indication."

Her eyes brightened. "Can you believe I actually sold three of my assemblages last night? That's got to be a record for me."

Gus's work was pricey. I assumed three sales meant a very good night for her.

"I'm about to ransack the jewelry here." I gestured toward the glass display case up front. "But I've got to ask why you're so interested in all these hideous old pictures."

Gus was clutching a cheap print of garishly colored fall trees and a crude still life of a bowl of fruit. She cocked her head. "I like to say beauty can be found in anything, but yeah, these are pretty gross." She studied the fruit picture and shuddered in mock—or maybe not—disgust. "It's actually the frames I'm interested in. I want to cover a frame in some of my found objects. Since the frame will be bearing a heavy load of industrial-strength glue and tchotchkes, it's got to be a sturdy one. Some of these old frames will probably do the trick, and the price is certainly right."

She focused on the sign reading Frames—$1.

"So you're like me. You treat thrift stores as art supply stores."

"You got it. Listen, Emma..." Gus seemed hesitant, which was out of character for her.

"Yes?"

"How's your friend Carleen doing? Isn't that her name? The lady Tina worked for?"

My heart sank. I'd been trying not to think about that this morning, but the murder remained very much on everyone's minds. "Carleen's doing well, but we'd all be doing much better if the killer were caught."

Gus seemed sympathetic, and I realized she had just referred to Tina by name, as if she'd known her.

"Were you and Tina friends?"

Gus looked uncomfortable and set the two clunky pictures on the floor. "More like acquaintances. We both served on the library board. We didn't always see eye to eye, but I'm sure she meant well."

Thanks to Savannah, I knew what Gus and Tina had tangled over at the library, so I didn't press Gus on that point.

"You didn't happen to know any of her family, did you?" I wasn't about to pass up an opportunity to learn more about the LeMann family if I could.

Gus shook her head. "Never heard her mention them. But then, we spent most of our time at the library talking about raising funds to purchase more books." She examined the pictures on the floor and wiped some dust off the top of one of them. She seemed eager to change the subject. "You're still looking for old beads, right?"

"Always." I perked up. "Why?"

Gus's eyes sparkled. "I hear that a new antique mall is opening over on the bypass next week, so that'll be another place for us to check out."

I nodded. "One of the vendors at Making Memories told me about it the other day. Word has it their rent is going to be more affordable."

"Sounds like quite a few of the vendors are ready to leave Harriet's place. Kind of sad, really. She loses her husband, and now she loses part of her business."

"I assume you're referring to rumors that the Harrises are divorcing?"

Gus confirmed that. "If they weren't before, they sure are now. The latest rumor is that one of his little indiscretions got out of hand, and Harriet heard about it and hit the roof. Things got so bad, she made him leave this time."

It didn't surprise me that the old leech had finally gotten caught, but I was still sorry to hear that the rumors were true and that he and Harriet had indeed separated.

"Did you hear this from someone reliable?" I asked. "You know how the rumor mill in Roseland likes to work overtime."

Gus nodded. "Heard it straight from their daughter. Well, *overheard* it straight from their daughter. She was at the Cupcake Café this morning with a friend. I was there typing up last night's sales into a spreadsheet on my laptop and couldn't help overhearing them as I worked."

"This would be the younger daughter, the one named Holly?" I knew they had another daughter, Hannah, but I thought she lived out of town.

"Yes. She said something about her parents bickering and how she couldn't wait until their divorce was final. She wants a little peace in her life. The other girl at the café seemed to be lending a sympathetic ear. Holly didn't seem that upset about the news, now that I think about it."

"Wow. I hate to hear that for Harriet's sake, but I can't say I'm shocked." I felt guilty for prying, but the nosy former reporter in me liked to know what was going on in Roseland, especially when it regarded a man whose real estate listings included a home owned by a recently murdered woman.

So Harriet and Hubert are getting that divorce after all. Maybe that explains why Harriet was so hesitant about buying that bracelet she'd wanted at Carleen's store. If she had been thinking about a divorce, maybe she was curbing her spending for a while.

"Emma?" Gus's raised voice let me know I must have missed something.

"Yes?"

"Did I say something wrong? You seem... distracted."

"Oh, sorry," I said. "No, nothing's wrong. I was only thinking about why the Harrises finally decided to get a divorce, but that's really none of our business, is it?"

"As if that's ever stopped us from making it our business," Gus said with a wry grin.

"Listen, I guess I've wasted enough of your time this morning," I said. "If you're like me, you probably want to get home and recover from standing on your feet most of last night."

Gus picked up the two frames she'd set aside and propped them under her arm. "A massage is definitely on my schedule for the afternoon. Guess I'll see you at the next arts council meeting, then?"

"I wouldn't miss it."

Once Gus left, I studied the jewelry in the glass display case up front and spotted a few 1970s-era necklaces with some interesting textured beads. I never knew which volunteer from the food pantry was going to be manning the cash register, but today's volunteer was a chipper middle-aged woman who seemed eager to rack up a few sales.

"These are still a dollar each, right?" I asked.

"Honey, if you'll take ten of 'em off our hands, I can let you have 'em for fifty cents each."

Five bucks for ten beaded necklaces was cheaper than buying beads at the craft store.

"Deal." I started plundering. Once I looked past the tarnished pendants and the gaudy plastic rhinestones, I realized some of the beads were quite striking. Metal, glass, ceramic—yes, they would work nicely. In my mind's eye, I could see them mixed with vintage pearls and my handmade resin hearts.

Five well-spent dollars later, I left the thrift store and headed to the last one on my list. Along the way, I thought about Gus's odd reaction when I'd asked about her relationship with Tina. She'd said they didn't always see eye to eye. She hadn't seemed angry about it, but she obviously hadn't forgotten about her disagreement with Tina either.

I wished I knew why Gus seemed so uneasy around me lately. It was as if she thought I was investigating *her*.

Michele at the Feathered Nest used to serve on the library board, and she knew everything that went on in Roseland. Perhaps I needed to stop by sometime soon to see whether she could offer any insight on the ill will between Gus and Tina—the ill will that Gus had distinctly *not* wanted to discuss.

Chapter Thirteen

When I got home, I recorded the day's bead purchases in my old-fashioned ledger. Some of the chains the beads were on were irredeemably tarnished and clearly toast, so I trashed those and wiped off the beads with a soft cloth before sorting them into my red tackle box. One multicolored strand of beads—one of those great fifty-centers I'd purchased—cleaned up beautifully.

As I studied the colors, something started niggling at the back of my mind. It seemed as though it had to do with cleaning something, but I couldn't remember what. *Clean out my purse, maybe?*

I always needed to clean out my purse—or as I sometimes thought of it, my portable office. After gathering the purse from its perch atop a red vinyl-padded kitchen chair, I stood by the counter and removed a half-empty water bottle, my makeup bag, my over-filled key chain, several weeks' worth of store receipts, bill payment stubs, my monthly planner, an invitation to a bridal shower, and a folded piece of paper that didn't ring a bell.

Straightening out the paper on the countertop, I realized it was the printout Harriet had given me on Wednesday. I'd meant to drop it off with Carleen, but that had gotten crowded out by all the other activities of the week. I glanced at the kitchen clock and saw that it was 3:19 p.m. I still had plenty of time before she closed for the day, but first I studied the necklace some more. It was a beauty, with one large teardrop-shaped stone flanked by six oval ones, three on each side. The stones were so well cut, they sparkled even in the photo-copied image.

Carleen needed to see that printout so she would recognize the necklace if it ever came across her counter. Since the piece clearly wasn't in Tina's belongings—according to Harriet, at least—maybe Tina had actually ended up selling it to someone after all. And if the buyer was local, maybe the person would decide to sell it again.

Within ten minutes, I was walking through the front door of the Silver Squirrel.

"Didn't expect to see you today," Carleen said. "You were so swamped selling jewelry last night, I imagined you'd be recovering at home all day."

I laughed. "I did have a great night of sales. And guess what? After we talked the other day, I went ahead and listed that Miriam Haskell brooch, and it's already up to four hundred fifty dollars in one of my online auctions. You know, jewelry is definitely on a lot of minds these days." I pulled the printout of the emerald necklace from my purse. "I need you to take a look at this."

Carleen peered at me over her reading glasses, a puzzled look on her face. "Okay..."

She unfolded the paper and gave a low whistle. "That necklace is out of this world. And this note says our police department is looking for it. Why?"

"Tony LeMann thinks the necklace was in Tina's possession at the time of her death, and he's accused Harriet Harris of taking it. She gave me this printout when I was at her store the other day. I'm hoping this necklace doesn't have anything to do with why Tina was killed, but naturally I can't help wondering."

"But since Teri's inheriting everything, I wonder why he cares," Carleen said. "Even if the necklace were found, wouldn't it belong to Teri?"

"You'd think so." I tapped my chin. "Maybe he's planning to sue and thinks the necklace is something he has a right to."

Carleen folded the sheet of paper in half and was handing it to me when I told her to hang on to it. "I've already taken a picture of it on my iPhone," I said. "I'd rather you keep the printout since you're the one who might see it show up for sale here."

"Good point. Did Harriet say where they got the photo?"

I shrugged. "I can't believe I didn't think to ask about that. If the Roseland PD has the photo, they got it somewhere, and that arrogant Tony LeMann would be my guess." I wrinkled my nose.

Carleen grinned. "Not wild about Tony, are you?"

"Would you believe he had the nerve to walk by my display last night and tell his lady friend to quit looking at my jewelry, that he'd get her some 'real' jewelry. And—wait a minute. Real jewelry. What if Tony was referring to this necklace, and he's just pulling the wool over our eyes by letting everyone think Tina lost it?"

"But he's an attorney, right?" Carleen asked.

"Which could mean he's skilled at defending bad behavior." I sighed. "I hate to say it, but I think perhaps I need to pay a visit to Detective Shelton and let him know what I heard last night. I imagine he'll find this most interesting."

EVEN THOUGH IT WAS close to quitting time on a Friday, Evelyn Wilson, the Roseland Police Department's receptionist for the last thirty years, was extra friendly when I stopped by her office. I told her I needed to speak with Alan Shelton about a matter relating to the Tina LeMann murder investigation. She punched in his number on her desk phone, told him I was there to see him, and gave me directions to his office.

"I remember when you used to be in these offices daily," she said. "But I'm not surprised it took a certain handsome detective to get you back over here."

"You can't be serious." I found her suggestion rather ridiculous, but Evelyn didn't need to know that. "Detective Shelton has been more than a little put out with me since this whole Tina LeMann case began, and it's only out of loyalty to my late friend that I'm even here today."

"I'll let you two work that out." Evelyn winked at me as I passed by her desk. I rolled my eyes in an exaggerated fashion so she would know exactly how I felt about her gesture.

It certainly wasn't the first time someone had tried to play match-maker for me since I'd arrived in town years ago. Once word had gotten out that a new single woman had moved to Roseland, every-one—or so it seemed—had wanted to play Cupid. The merchants wanted me to meet their sons, my coworkers wanted me to meet their brothers, and once, the mayor had tried to hook me up with his painfully shy, geeky nephew, who was helping his uncle install some new computer software.

Evelyn obviously didn't know that I had absolutely zero interest in Detective Shelton. The first real shred of humanity I'd seen in him was when he'd come into the gallery shop earlier in the week. At least the man had good taste in jewelry. So far, that was the only nice thing I could say about him.

But if I could add a few details to his investigation, I was eager to help. First, I stopped by the restroom. I started to apply lip gloss but decided I didn't want the detective—or Evelyn, for that matter—to think that I had been primping for him. I definitely didn't want any-one to get the wrong impression of why I was there. My visit was purely business.

I walked down the familiar hallway with the worn, scuffed-up gray tiles. I'd been there many times when I first became a newspaper reporter, mainly to get copies of police reports but occasionally to in-terview someone for a feature story. I slowed my pace as I got near the detective's door.

Leaning against a tan metal file cabinet just inside his door, Detective Shelton was looking over a piece of paper and glanced up, clearly awaiting my arrival. "Miss Madison, please come in." He seemed in a good mood.

"Glad to." I entered and took a seat in the guest chair he offered before he sat at his desk. "I'm hoping I can give you a piece of information that might help us make some progress in finding Tina's killer."

"Help *us* make some progress?" He raised an eyebrow and crossed his arms.

I was determined not to let him ruffle my feathers. "Yes, *us*. You know—the police, friends, interested citizens. The community has to come together at a time like this. There's a danger to the entire town when a killer is on the loose, right?"

The detective seemed a bit baffled by my reasoning, but he simply nodded and drummed his fingers on his desk.

"Harriet Harris knows I'm passionate about old jewelry, and a few days ago, she shared a printout with me of the necklace Tony LeMann apparently told you was missing from his sister's things."

The detective coughed into his fist. "I'm afraid I'm not at liberty to discuss the details at this time. Is there something you wanted to tell me about the necklace?"

I paused. "Yes. You see, I was at the Gallery Stroll last night when Tony LeMann arrived at the Threads of Time Gallery with a woman I presume was his girlfriend. She was checking out some of my jewelry designs when Tony came over and told her they needed to leave and that he would get her some 'real' jewelry."

Detective Shelton stared at me blankly and shrugged. "And?"

"And you don't find that significant?"

"Why would I?"

"A man who claims to be missing some heirloom jewelry promises his girlfriend he's going to get her some 'real' jewelry? Real? As in emeralds, maybe?"

"That's quite a big maybe," he said. "But then... you probably know a lot about gemstones since you make jewelry yourself, right?" Unsmiling, he held my gaze.

Much to my chagrin, I knew I was blushing. *How does he know that?* "Yes, I do. But I'm much more familiar with semiprecious stones and costume jewelry than fine jewelry. I make jewelry primarily from new beads and stones and incorporate vintage jewelry parts as well. I've rarely worked with precious gems because I'm trying to grow my client list right now. I'd rather make and sell a lot of smaller, more affordable things. At least, at this point in my design career I would."

Good grief. Why am I babbling?

"Uh-huh." He looked back at the stack of papers on his desk, probably notes on the investigation.

I could tell I had lost his interest. "May I ask you a question?" I hoped his curiosity would get the better of him.

"You can ask, but I can't promise I'll be able to answer."

I chose my words carefully. "I know from Harriet Harris that Tony LeMann thinks his late sister might have had possession of this emerald necklace prior to her death. It seems to me that if she had such a valuable necklace, she could have sold it and wouldn't have had to sell her home. But if for some reason she died owning the necklace, she *must* have had a good reason for wanting to hold on to it, right? And a brother she'd lost touch with wouldn't be likely to have a photo of it, now would he?" I was hoping the detective would slip up and confirm that Tony had supplied the photo of the necklace.

"As I said, I'm not at liberty to discuss the details of this case, especially with someone who has decided to play amateur sleuth."

"Excuse me?" His comment struck me as incredibly rude.

"I see what you're getting at, Miss Madison."

I raised my chin and stared him straight in the eye to let him know that I wasn't easily intimidated. "And?"

"And I'm afraid I really can't tell you any more than that. But I would like to suggest that you let us handle this investigation. I'm sure I don't have to tell you that murderers are pretty nasty people. Whoever killed Tina would very likely have no problem killing a meddling friend."

I should have known our conversation was going too well. "Meddling? My abject apologies, then. I mistakenly thought *I* was doing *you* a favor by offering some new information today. I must have gotten confused somewhere in our discourse since I failed to understand that clearly, you have this case wrapped up and have precisely all of the information you need." I stood up to leave. "I won't waste your time by *meddling* in your case any further, Detective."

I retrieved my purse from the floor by the guest chair, incensed that he was so ungrateful for my attempt at being a good citizen. He seemed bent on knowingly overlooking some obvious murder investigation details that needed to be checked out.

"Miss Madison, please. I just meant to say you might want to show a little restraint in letting so many people know you're interested in this case. Word gets around fast in a small town like Roseland."

I stared at him, daring him to break eye contact first. "I can't imagine what you mean."

This time, the detective stared right back with what appeared to be belligerence. "Okay, then, let me spell it out for you. Mavis Eastwood of the Cupcake Café, who was recently interviewed by this department, says the only people she's spoken to about the case are her husband and her friend Emma Madison. Before the body was even cold, Carleen Wood, owner of the antiques store where the deceased was found, was talking about the case at length with one Emma Madison, a former newspaper reporter who is eager to see this case solved. Harriet Harris, owner of another antiques store, tells me one of her regular customers, a woman who designs jewelry that is sold at the local arts council gallery, is the only person who's asked her anything about Tina LeMann since the woman's death. Am I making myself clear?"

Yeah. It's clear that I have a bunch of blabbermouths for friends.

The detective cleared his throat. "Trust me, I'm not trying to antagonize you, Miss Madison. I just want to impress upon you that this isn't some scandal involving the town council. We're talking about murder here, and I'd rather you didn't get hurt attempting to solve this case."

How patronizing. In an instant, I realized that would be the very last time I offered to help Alan Shelton with anything related to the investigation. "Will that be all?"

He nodded. "Yes."

I turned and exited slowly in what I hoped was a most majestic manner. Even though I could feel my face flaming, I was proud that I was leaving the meeting with my dignity intact.

Less than a minute later, I was passing Evelyn's desk again. She called me over and motioned for me to turn around. "Come here a minute, hon."

"What is it?"

"You must have just run by the ladies' room. Right?"

"No, but I did when I first came in. Why?"

She tugged at the end of the trailing piece of toilet tissue streaming out of the waistband of my slacks then crumpled it up and threw it in her trash can.

"Thanks, Evelyn." I gave her a quick side hug.

So much for my dignity.

Chapter Fourteen

After lining up all of my supplies for easy access, I sat at my kitchen table with cotton swabs and a plastic container of jewelry cleaner. I gently dabbed at the vintage earrings I'd bought during the past week. Then I reached for my iPhone and swiped through the contact list until I found Savannah's number. I tapped it, and she picked up quickly.

"Hi there," I said, the phone propped between my ear and shoulder. "I never had a moment to stop and call while I was out running around the other morning, but I wanted to let you know I went by Harriet's, and the police weren't there because of any divorce proceedings. Seems that a valuable old emerald necklace is missing from Tina LeMann's estate, and Tina's brother has accused the Harrises—or Harriet, at least—of taking it."

"Why would he do that?" Savannah asked.

"I guess he thought that since Harriet and Hubert still had access to boxes containing some of Tina's old costume jewelry immediately after her death, that necklace might have been there as well."

"But if Teri is opening her own antique mall, why wouldn't she want to sell the items herself? Wouldn't the family have to split everything? And Tina's mother would be one of her heirs too, wouldn't she?"

"I've heard that Tina left everything to her sister so that Teri could use the proceeds to help provide for Mrs. LeMann," I admitted. "But you know, the more we learn about Tina and her siblings, the less this whole situation makes sense to me."

"Oh well, thanks for letting me know what you found out. I'd been wondering. And I also thought of something I probably should have mentioned to you already."

Now you've got my attention. "What's that?"

"This may be old news. In fact, I'm sure you probably already know about it, but Hannah Harris told me last night that her dad is opening an upscale consignment store downtown. She said it's going to feature only high-end clothing, jewelry, and accessories. 'More estate sale than garage sale,' as Hannah put it. The new-business announcement was printed in the newspaper last week, so I thought you might have seen it."

I was ashamed to confess that I was behind on reading the newspaper—I seemed to be behind on everything these days—but that particular bit of business news intrigued me.

Savannah continued. "The grand opening is next Friday, and there's a soft opening on Wednesday that a few people already know about. I'm invited, so you're welcome to go with me."

"You know that's right up my alley, so thanks for the invite." Looking at quality clothes and accessories was a great way to get inspiration for new jewelry designs. "I'll bet Hubert has some fine pieces tucked away, both the clothes and the jewelry, if he's opening his own store. That family doesn't go into business to lose money."

Savannah said she would give me a ring early next week so we could decide where to meet before the store's opening, then we hung up.

Jewelry had been on my mind all week—the jewelry I created, the jewelry the police thought was missing, and now the jewelry that Hubert Harris was going to sell in his new store. I couldn't help wondering whether his plan to open a new business was further proof that Hubert and Harriet were actually going through with their divorce. If their marriage ended, the new clothing and jewelry business might be his way of competing with her antique mall—if it truly ended up being *her* antique mall.

My gut told me there was some connection that I was missing. Tina had worked in a shop that sold estate jewelry. She'd listed her home with a couple who sold costume jewelry. But a family necklace was missing from her belongings, and none of her jewelry-savvy friends had ever heard about it.

I knew just the person to help me sort it all out. And fortunately for me, I would soon be having dinner with her and her husband.

Chapter Fifteen

J en and Todd were always fun dinner hosts. I'd gotten to know both of them during my first years in Roseland, before they were married, and the three of us had always loved to get together, usually to eat and gab.

"Anything new going on with the LeMann investigation?" Jen asked as I stood in her kitchen. Her famous cashew chicken stir-fry sizzled on the stove.

I paused to inhale the heady aroma of garlic and onions. "I was actually hoping to talk to you about that. I met with Detective Alan Shelton this afternoon, and that man is infuriating. He's clearly not making any progress on his own. I think he's mainly interested in telling me to keep my paws off his precious little murder investigation."

Todd, who'd been catching the day's sports highlights on the evening news, popped into the kitchen and refilled his Diet Coke. "You think he's got the hots for her?" he asked Jen.

"Maybe." She gave me a wicked grin.

"You guys can't possibly be serious," I said. "Besides, isn't he married? I thought I saw him wearing a wedding ring."

"Aha! You looked," Jen teased.

"Of course I looked. I'm single, and most single women notice a man's ring finger. I do that even when I'm at arts council meetings, and those men are in their sixties and seventies, for Pete's sake."

"Alan's not married," Todd said as he headed to the den. "We play on the same softball team during the summer. He wears his dad's old college ring. I'm betting that's what you saw."

So the detective wasn't married. That might be interesting to all the other single ladies, but it wasn't to me. He was good-looking, sure, but his looks weren't enough to make up for his condescending attitude.

Jen craned her neck toward the den, clearly making sure Todd was out of earshot for a second. "So if you won't admit you find Alan hot, at least tell me what's going on with the murder investigation."

I gave her an exaggerated sigh. "Now, I don't know if this is significant or not, but somehow I keep hearing about Harriet and Hubert's marital troubles. I don't see any direct connection to Tina, but they do seem to be some of the last people besides Carleen who saw her alive."

Todd came back into the kitchen, tossed the dish towel over his shoulder, and stirred the rice. "Hey, you two, can we get out of investigation mode and eat? I'm starving."

He was right. I'd been thinking and talking about nothing but the murder investigation for days. And I was supposed to be enjoying an evening with old friends.

As I dished up some of their mouthwatering cashew chicken, I resolved to mind my manners and focus on my friends... at least until Todd returned to watching his ball game.

"So how did your day go after you called me this morning?" I asked as the three of us ate.

Jen rolled her eyes. "The reporters haven't turned in their stories yet and aren't calling me back, the new boss is an idiot, and the IT guy is driving me nuts, so... it's pretty much business as usual." She crossed her eyes in the way that always made me laugh. "Todd and I are headed out of town Monday and Tuesday. He's got a real estate conference in Atlanta and thought it would be fun if we could hang out together before and after, maybe check out some of the hot new restaurants there. So I'm trying to get all the non-deadline stories edited before I leave. Naturally, no one is cooperating, so I'll probably have to spend most of the weekend at the office. But you remember how we roll there, so this isn't news. But first things first. Have you heard any more from the artist guy you went to dinner with the other night?"

"Yep." I smiled. "He called last night, and we're meeting for lunch tomorrow at the new sandwich place downtown."

"Fingers crossed," Jen said. "And you know I'll want to hear all the details. Now, what's going on with your murder investigation?"

"It's not *my* murder investigation." I waved away her comment. "I'm just doing a little snooping on behalf of a friend. But c'mon. We can talk while we do the dishes."

"Snooping, investigating, whatever. What have you learned?" Jen opened the dishwasher. "You rinse, and I'll stack."

"Deal. And not much, I'm sorry to say. But in case you asked, I did compose a list."

"Why am I not surprised?"

I reached into my jeans pocket and pulled out the list I'd made precisely so that I wouldn't forget any important details when Jen asked for them. "First, I learned that Tina had this hotshot lawyer brother, Tony, who might have had it in for her, but I haven't learned anything that would in any way tie him to her death. I think he's just a first-class jerk."

Jen pulled a face. "What do you mean you don't have anything on him? You've already told me he keeps showing up around town and making a scene wherever he goes."

"True, and they didn't get along, and I hear he does have a temper, but from what I can tell, he's no killer. And there's a younger sister too—Teri. She was at the funeral, sitting right beside her mother, and Carleen introduced me to her just the other day."

"Where did you guys meet up?"

"The Silver Squirrel, oddly enough. She seemed pretty cool, like someone I'd enjoy getting to know better because she's kind of artsy, but she's still reeling from her sister's death. I doubt she'll be a whole lot of help with the investigation into Tina's murder. I don't know much about her, but I did learn she has a booth at Harriet Harris's antique mall. Discovered it right before I had my latest run-in with Detective Shelton the other morning near her booth."

"You don't think he was checking it out for some reason, do you?" Jen asked.

"Why would he?"

Jen closed the dishwasher door. "I don't know, but you mentioned *her* booth and *him* being there. Just struck me as a coincidence, that's all. What'd you say the sister's name is again?"

"Teri LeMann."

We were finished with the dishes, and Jen motioned for me to have a seat at her kitchen table. "So why would this gal happen to be selling her stuff in the same town where her sister just got knocked off? Doesn't that seem a little creepy? If my sister had just been killed, I wouldn't show up all happy-go-lucky in the town where she died."

I nodded. "I'll admit it's strange, but I really liked Teri when I met her. It's obvious she's devastated by her sister's death. And frankly, since the two of them had reconciled not long ago, it's clear that Teri decided to locate here to be near family. That and Roseland's reputation as an arts-friendly town mean this is probably a good place for her to sell her designs. Otherwise, I have no idea why she decided to locate here."

"Who else is on your suspect list?"

"Would you believe Hubert Harris?" I asked.

Jen's eyes widened. "Not much surprises me anymore, but that would. Why Hubert?"

"He and Harriet both had immediate access to Tina's belongings once she was killed, the two of them are getting a divorce, and he's opening his own high-end consignment shop." I raised my eyebrows.

"In fact, I'm told that the announcement ran in your newspaper just the other day, thank you very much for telling me."

Jen brushed that off. "You know I can't possibly read every word that's in the newspaper. And Hubert's motive would be what? To kill her and get her jewelry?"

I nodded. "Then there's always the good old classic 'unknown assailant' possibility."

"And the motive would be?"

"A random robbery attempt, maybe? Or someone intended a sexual assault, but Tina fought back?"

"Who else was aware of that heirloom family necklace?" Jen asked.

"According to the police, only her siblings. Oh, and someone at the pawnshop downtown. One of my arts council buddies recalls Tina trying to sell the necklace there some months ago. I probably ought to let Teri know about that."

"Spell the sister's first name again?"

"T-E-R-I."

Jen reached for her phone and tapped a note. "I'm going to do a little digging around when I get back to the office tomorrow. Might as well find something useful to do with my time while I'm sitting there waiting on the reporters to file their stories."

"Let me know if you come across anything."

She gave me a thumbs-up. "Now, are you ready for dessert?"

"You made it?"

"No. You know the only thing I can cook is Chinese. It's a turtle cheesecake from the Cupcake Café."

I licked my lips. "My mouth's watering already." Mavis's cheesecakes were the stuff of legend.

"Todd, time for dessert," Jen called.

And for once that week, I could honestly say that my evening was ending on a sweet note.

Chapter Sixteen

With another busy week ahead, I had already decided to head to the park first thing Saturday morning for an extended walk. The morning air was crisp and cool, so I donned a lightweight fleece jacket and walked the few blocks to the park.

Getting out and enjoying the sunshine was always good for the body and soul. The new Ellis Avenue Park had been open only a few months, and already it was a hit with the locals—pet owners walking their dogs, parents strolling toddlers, and ordinary walkers like me.

The centerpiece of the park was a small brick fountain where visitors loved to toss coins and make a wish. City officials had decided the coins would be collected all year long then used to purchase gifts for the needy at Christmas. I loved living in a town so full of givers.

Deciding it couldn't hurt to toss a spare coin into the fountain and make a wish, I reached into my pocket and fished out a quarter. Without thinking twice, I wished that the police—or someone—would get a lead in finding Tina's killer. The murder was more than a week old, and that had sucked up most of my creative energy over the past week. It weighed on my mind, and it was clearly affecting my work.

When I'd tallied my online jewelry sales for the week, I found that I had far fewer packages than usual going out in the mail. That was probably because I had listed only a few of those great pieces from last Friday's stumbled-upon garage sale. While I did end up selling the Juliana bracelet for five hundred and ten dollars, which was a terrific price, I'd found it impossible to fully focus on my work with a killer on the loose and a friend who'd just been buried. It wasn't right.

I'd never been that close to someone who'd been murdered, and it felt very different from losing someone to sickness or a car accident. The tragedy of a murder—the injustice of it—was eating at me. As I walked through the park at a fast clip, I clenched my fists and pumped my arms. If the murderer had accosted me right then, I would have knocked his lights out.

That was probably why I didn't immediately notice when Holly Harris walked by pushing a stroller with her twin toddler boys, who appeared to be contentedly sleeping. She was talking loudly on her cell phone. "Dad doesn't care about the antique mall. He says to do whatever you want with it. Yes, I know what this means, and no, I'm not worried. Listen, I'm at the park with the boys right now, so we'll see you tonight, okay?"

I couldn't help glancing in her direction, but I was self-conscious about what I'd overheard and quickly turned away. To my surprise, Holly pushed her stroller over to where I sat on a bench by the fountain, where I'd stopped to retie a shoelace.

"You're Emma, right?"

I did my best to present my most innocent face. "Yes, I am. And you're Holly, the Harrises' daughter. How are you?" I didn't know her well, but we'd certainly crossed paths enough over the years that I didn't want to act as though she were a stranger.

"I don't know how much you overheard of my call with my mom, but I'd really appreciate it if you didn't say anything about that. I know you work at the newspaper and—"

"Actually, I haven't worked there in more than two years. And please don't worry. I wasn't paying attention to your phone call, so there's nothing to be concerned about." I had my hands in my jacket pocket, and I was glad she couldn't see that my fingers were crossed. I *had* been paying attention, but I was telling the truth when I said she had nothing to worry about.

"My parents are divorcing, and they're driving me crazy," Holly said, flinging a hand in the air. "But I don't want everyone in town to know. They've threatened to divorce before and worked things out, so hopefully that'll happen again. I need to remember to stop blabbing about it everywhere I go."

I recalled Gus saying that Holly was talking about her parents' bickering when she was at the Cupcake Café the day before, but I quickly decided not to mention that. "I can see why you'd be so upset. But surely this is all just talk. Hubert and Harriet have been together so long, I feel sure they'll work things out."

Holly offered a slight smile. "I hope you're right. I love both my folks, and I hate being in the middle of all their fighting. You know, last week was so awful. That lady who worked at the Silver Squirrel got killed, and then my parents got into a huge fight about what to do with the things she'd left in the house."

"Really?" *Perhaps I'm interested in the Harris family squabbles after all.* "Tina was a friend of mine. Not close, but I knew her from my years of shopping at the Silver Squirrel."

Holly bit her lip, as though she were unsure whether to tell me more. "Then I'm sure you knew she was having cash flow issues and decided to sell her house. Dad had just gotten a decent offer on it, but before they could do anything about it, she was dead. He wanted to put her belongings in storage to make showing the house easier the next time, regardless of whether he or another Realtor ended up showing it. He said Tina's mother obviously wasn't going to be moving back there, and whoever inherited Tina's estate would likely end up with her things. My mom said that was cold and that it was disrespectful to move her belongings so soon."

That was surprising. Harriet had never struck me as someone who was concerned about social niceties. "So this is why your parents are arguing?"

"Partly. Mom said if Dad hadn't gotten involved with Tina, maybe she would still be here. The listing of her house sure has been a bone of contention."

"Let's hope it all gets resolved soon," I said.

Holly's phone rang, and she answered it and waved goodbye to me before quickly pushing the stroller with her sleeping little boys. I was relieved when she left. I was starting to feel uncomfortable hearing about the Harrises' marital problems, even if it did seem that they were somehow related to Tina's death.

But how? That was the question.

AFTER A QUICK SHOWER and an abnormal amount of fretting over what to wear, I got ready to meet Justin. I'd agreed to join him for a light lunch before he headed up to Asheville for the weekend. He'd been asked to participate in a new gallery opening there on Saturday evening and didn't feel he could pass up the opportunity. I was happy for him and had a feeling he could expect an excellent show.

Justin had asked whether I would be up for trying out the new sandwich and sub place with him before he left, and I'd said sure. I was always game to visit a new restaurant, and friends had been posting photos of their mouthwatering sandwiches on Facebook.

I decided to wear my newest jeans along with a turquoise top I'd recently bought online. The top had the same bright turquoise shade as a rhinestone necklace that had been in my mega-find jewelry tin. I had so many turquoise and aqua pieces in my wardrobe these days, I knew the turquoise rhinestone necklace would get a lot of wear. And the great thing about wearing vintage jewelry was that when I got tired of a piece, I could either sell it online or work it into one of my upcycled creations.

As I looked in the mirror, I toyed once again with the idea of lightening my hair. It was currently a honey-blond shade, but I'd been thinking of going blonder. On the other hand, I knew I would probably have to spend time maintaining that lighter shade of blond. These days, time was at a premium.

At the last minute, I decided to pull my hair back into a sleek ponytail at the nape of my neck. I liked the way the style emphasized my blue eyes, probably one of my best features, and having my hair off my face also emphasized my new necklace and the large gold hoop earrings I chose to wear with it. Justin probably wouldn't notice my jewelry, but if I ran into any women friends—or potential customers—they might.

Once I slipped on my watch and said goodbye to Miriam, I headed to town and found a great parking spot just a few spaces down from Fellini's Sandwiches and Subs.

I walked in, and Justin glanced up from his iPhone, clicked off of whatever he'd been looking at, and slipped the phone into his pocket.

"Great to see you again, Emma." He stood and gave me a quick hug that felt comfortable and warm. I liked that he made me feel so at ease.

"You too," I said. "Ready to go wow the art lovers in Asheville?"

He grinned. "Ready as I'll ever be. And listen, you can sit here while I go order for us. Do you know what you want?"

"The turkey sub would be great. And bottled water to drink." After my morning of exercise at the park, I was feeling virtuous and didn't want to blow it. I was also trying to cool it after that humongous slice of cheesecake I'd eaten at Jen's the previous night.

"You got it." Justin smiled and headed to the counter.

I glanced at the back of the shop. The middle-aged man and woman tending the counter seemed super busy. They were making all the sandwiches themselves, and between ringing up customers and packing up takeout orders, they were hopping.

A whoosh of air entered the small space as the door opened, and like a bad penny that kept turning up, Tony LeMann walked in, this time with an attractive brunette by his side. *A different woman from the Gallery Stroll the other night?* I was fascinated. He might have been a jerk, but the guy sure got around.

Justin returned with our subs and drinks. He'd seen Tony too and said, "Don't look now, but your favorite customer from the other night just walked in."

I smiled. "Yes, and with another lady friend." While I managed to keep an eye on Tony and his latest companion, I was more interested in focusing on my lunch date.

Clearly, Justin was excited about getting his work into one of the more prestigious galleries in Asheville. He explained how he networked with other artists and how that benefited his career. In the fall, he planned to start offering a few painting classes in Roseland and see whether he enjoyed teaching.

I'd been thinking that when I had more experience under my belt, I might like to teach some jewelry techniques—but on a small scale. I wasn't sure Justin was interested in doing anything on a small scale, and I loved his passion and ambition.

All too soon, it was time for him to pull out and head to North Carolina.

"Do you mind if I call you when I get back tomorrow?" he asked.

"I'd mind if you didn't." I smiled.

I wished him good luck, and after another hug and a quick goodbye, he was on his way. Justin Hayes was quickly growing on me.

Chapter Seventeen

After I got home from lunch with Justin, I checked my phone and found I had a voice mail from Michele Fairchild at the Feathered Nest. She wanted to know whether I could bring some more bracelets by her shop. She had only three left, and she wanted to stock up again.

Michele had been one of the first local shopkeepers to carry my jewelry designs. While I sold pieces online almost every day through my website, there was something so satisfying about having my work in a local store where anyone who was interested could see and touch the jewelry. I was happy to learn my bracelets were selling well.

I checked my notebook listing the current inventory. Only a few of my stretchy bead bracelets weren't already promised to other customers and shops. Fortunately, Michele never minded which jewelry I sold in her shop as long as I kept her well supplied, and she liked it when I brought her something new and flashy.

Leather cuff bracelets were still getting a lot of buzz, and I had created a few new ones by combining vintage brooches, minus the pin backs, with wide leather bands. One of my favorite new creations was a large cream-colored band with a gorgeous rhinestone brooch that featured clear stones and a few seed pearls. Checking the items off my list one by one, I selected a dozen new bracelets, most of them cuff styles, and added them to my market basket.

Since I would be gone awhile, I made sure Miriam had plenty of food and water, then I drove to town and parked a few spaces down from the Feathered Nest. Two teenage girls were just leaving with some of the store's mint-green shopping bags, and a woman with two young children had just walked in before I entered.

Once inside the store, I inhaled deeply and smiled. Michele was a master at creating the ideal environment for shopping and browsing. Water gurgled softly from a small tabletop fountain set up near her old-fashioned brass cash register. Easygoing instrumentals played quietly in the background, and the soft scents from Michele's vast candle collection—the largest in the foothills area, according to her—gave a pleasant mix of berry and light floral fragrances. No wonder Michele's shop was usually busy.

"Hi there, Emma," she said. "I hope you've got some new jewelry for me."

The woman with two children looked up and smiled. Her eyes darted to me and my basket of goodies. Maybe she was a jewelry lover.

I held up my bag. "These are some new styles. Cuffs with vintage elements. I'd love to know what customers say about them, if anything. You know I aim to please."

Michele bustled over to the area of the shop with tables displaying small purses and wallets, hand-knit scarves, and locally made jewelry.

"I thought you had three bracelets left?" I picked up a small linen-covered bracelet display rack with a lone bracelet hanging on it.

"That was the count when I called you this morning," Michele said. "A woman came by at lunchtime and bought two as gifts for her sisters. Thank goodness I already had you bringing more."

I reached into the basket and pulled out a drawstring fabric bag. After unfastening it, I removed the new bracelets and added them to the display. It took a minute or so to arrange and tweak them, and soon I was happy with my balance of designs and colors—I couldn't simply plop a piece of jewelry on a display.

Michele peered over my shoulder. "Those colors are gorgeous. And those rhinestone parts are from old brooches?"

I nodded. "Every one of them. In fact"—I reached into the basket, produced a four-by-six-inch tent-style foldover card, and proceeded to read—"these one-of-a-kind designs feature vintage jewelry personally selected to best complement each piece. Contemporary leather cuffs with a nostalgic flair. A nod to the past with a hat tip to the present."

"You always have had a way with words." Michele took the card from me before rearranging a few things on the display table. She quickly snagged a candle from atop a stack of gift books and propped the card there instead. Michele was such a whiz with her displays. I always trusted her to show off my jewelry designs in creative ways I hadn't even imagined.

"That looks great. I'm going to snap a photo with my phone." If a display looked especially nice, I liked to have a record of it so that I could recreate it in another shop or arts and crafts show.

"Now come try one of the new cookie samples I got this week," she said. "I need to decide which flavors to order."

As I stepped over to the counter with my friend, I noticed the mom making her way to the display of bracelets. There was nothing to attract a shopper's attention like announcing that something new and different had arrived.

As the owner of one of the most successful gift shops in town, Michele often received samples of products from manufacturers who hoped to persuade her to carry a new line. She'd said that food items were always a best seller for her because they made great hostess gifts. They were good impulse purchases for out-of-town shoppers who wanted something to munch on during the ride home.

She handed me a yellow floral paper napkin with two small cookies. One appeared to have tiny butterscotch chips, and the other had flecks of red throughout. I guessed it was a berry flavor.

"Just take a bite of each," she said.

I did. The butterscotch-looking one was good and had a salty flavor I hadn't been expecting. "Mmm. Sea-salt caramel?"

"Nailed it," she said. "Now try the other one."

I placed the other half of the first cookie back on the napkin and picked up the second one. First, I sniffed. "Berry?"

Michele grinned. "Just take a bite."

I bit into the cookie, expecting a raspberry flavor. "It's strawberry," I said, surprised.

"Correct again." She clapped. "Berry cookies aren't anything new, but strawberry is a cookie flavor that's not that common in gift packages."

The cookies were delicious. "Which flavor are you going to order?" I asked around a mouthful of cookie.

"Now that you've confirmed my choices, both. I just wanted to be sure they're as good as I thought."

I balled up my napkin and handed it to Michele, who gave it a quick toss behind the counter.

Michele sidled up to the mother. "Do you mind if I offer your children a cookie?"

The pretty blonde smiled. "Not at all. Olivia, Ethan, what do you tell the nice lady?"

Michele held out the cute cardboard container, and the children eagerly reached inside.

"Thank you," they chorused.

"And we can't forget Mom," Michele said, tipping the box again.

"Thanks," the woman said. She then turned to me. "And I have a question for you since you're the jewelry lady, right?"

"Yes, I am."

"I want this bracelet." She held up a sage-green leather cuff with a pink rhinestone brooch attachment. "And I was also wondering whether you ever accept special orders."

"Happily." I reached into my purse and fished around until I found one of the business cards I never left home without. "You can find my online shop here." I pointed at a few lines on the back of the card. "And it also has my email address."

"I've got an old brooch that belonged to my grandmother, but the back came off years ago. I would love to have it made into a bracelet like this."

"No problem. I love special orders. Do you live here in Roseland?"

She nodded.

"Great. After you've checked out my website and decided what style you want, just let me know when and where you'd like to meet, and we'll get going on it."

"Super." She checked out with the green cuff bracelet and told me she'd be in touch soon. I said I would look forward to hearing from her, and I would, but as she and her cute munchkins left the shop, I secretly hoped she would hold off for a day or two. I'd gotten behind on special orders thanks to the busyness of getting ready for the Gallery Stroll. Then there were all the hours I'd spent trying to figure out who had killed Tina Le Mann.

As if reading my mind, Michele piped up, "So, any leads on that murder investigation? I haven't heard of any, have you?"

I shook my head. "The detective on the case assures me they're on it, but it sure looks like we'd have heard something by now, doesn't it?"

"I know what you mean." Michele tapped a finger on the counter. "And did I tell you I had my security company come inspect my alarm system? This murder has all of us shopkeepers on edge. I mean, I know they're saying it wasn't a robbery, but what if the killer really was trying to get Tina to open the safe or something? Can they be sure it wasn't a botched robbery attempt?"

"Guess we won't know until the killer is caught." Saddened again to think of the way Tina's life had ended, I added, "It still doesn't seem real to me that Tina's gone. She was such a fixture here on Main Street that I guess I never thought about her not being here one day. I don't know a soul who ever had an unkind thing to say about her."

Michele raised an eyebrow.

"What? Oh, you're thinking about that library board incident between her and Gus?"

"It was a pretty hairy ordeal at the time." Michele lowered her voice, which I found amusing since she and I were the only ones in the shop. "She and Gus first got into it at a monthly board meeting back during the winter. The board had met to vote on pieces for the *Faces of Roseland* exhibit, the one where children would paint some of their favorite local faces during crafts time, and the art on the walls was supposed to be portraits by local professional artists."

"Gus included, I presume?"

Michele cocked her head. "That's where things got bumpy. Gus had just gotten that prestigious grant from the state arts council and wanted to celebrate by having the library be the first to exhibit her award-winning piece, which happened to be the outline of a body that had died with a cell phone in hand."

I was confused. "But that wasn't a portrait. It was an outline."

"Exactly," Michele said. "Most of the board was willing to go along with it because, you know, it was Gus. But Tina insisted the piece didn't meet the criteria like the other *Faces of Roseland* selections. She almost managed to persuade the rest of the board to insist Gus substitute another piece or be excluded from the new exhibit. Gus, meanwhile, had already told the state arts council that her work was scheduled to be featured in the library, so the council was sharing that in their publicity about the new arts grants, which included a list of places where the winning works were exhibited. Gus said

Tina was trying to sabotage her career, and she vowed she would put a stop to Tina's meddling if it was the last thing she did."

The shop's door opened, and Michele turned her attention to the two women who had just entered. So seemingly mild-mannered Tina had taken on Gus. That sure sounded out of character for Tina. I wondered whether Gus had done something else to upset her. Maybe Tina simply didn't like Gus's artwork. Not everyone did. I'd heard the comments from those who thought Gus was a bit too out-there for Roseland and that her art was too edgy, too feminist, too... Gus.

On the other hand, I could see Tina's point about not including Gus's work in an exhibit that was, by definition, supposed to feature *faces* of Roseland. Award-winning artist or not, Gus needed to follow the same rules as everyone else.

The lively chatter from the new customers caught my attention, and I realized I'd been woolgathering again, standing there next to the checkout counter as if I had all day to pause and ponder. And I didn't. I had jewelry designs to complete and get in the mail. Besides, Miriam would be pouting if I left her alone for much longer.

I gathered up my empty jewelry bags and basket, told Michele I would see her at church in the morning, and headed to my car. The news about Tina and Gus had given me something new to consider, and I wondered whether I'd misjudged both women.

Soon, I was home and settled in for a quiet evening of catch-up work on my jewelry making and selling. Two days were left in the auction for the Miriam Haskell brooch, and already the bids had topped five hundred dollars. Whatever the final selling price, I knew I would be pleased with my profit margin. I was already thrilled at the return on my investment. If I could just find some grandmother's jewelry tin every week, I would be living on Easy Street.

I turned on the radio to catch a little of the Atlanta news and al-most turned it off when it led with the traffic report.

"We've just learned there's an accident on I-85 southbound near Spaghetti Junction, so you may want to find an alternate route if you're trying to make your way into the city on this sunny Saturday. And in other news north of the city, the owner of a Roseland real estate company has just been arrested for the murder of his former client, an employee at a downtown Roseland antique store. Hubert Harris was taken into custody around one p.m. and is now at the city jail, where he's awaiting a bond hearing. And in more breaking traffic news, we just heard there's another accident over on—"

I clicked off the radio, my heart pounding. I didn't care about Atlanta traffic, but I cared very much about Hubert Harris being arrested for Tina's murder! *Why didn't someone alert me? Why didn't Jen or Carleen call?*

Eager to see what others knew about the arrest, I grabbed my purse and reached for my cell phone. It wasn't in there. Then I remembered I'd last used my phone to take a photo of the bracelet display at Michele's shop. I must have left it there. *Rats.*

And I couldn't call Michele and ask her to look for it because I no longer had a landline.

After grabbing my jacket and car keys, I headed to the car and was soon back at the Feathered Nest. When I walked in, Michele was watching the door with a smile on her face. "Looking for this?" She waved my phone in its bejeweled rose-gold case.

"Thank goodness." I walked over and retrieved the phone.

"I knew you'd be back for it." Michele leaned over the counter and widened her eyes. "And I guess you've heard of Hubert's arrest?"

"Yes, I just heard it on the radio. I wanted to make a few calls to find out what's going on, and that's when I discovered I was missing my cell phone."

Before we could speculate about what might be going on, more customers came in, so I thanked Michele for the return of my phone and raced home. As I walked in the door, I hastily scanned my texts and voice mails. So much for blaming my friends for not calling with the news about Hubert. I had three texts from Jen, one from Savannah, and a voice mail from Carleen. I tapped the button to dial Jen.

"Why do you even have a cell phone? And where have you been? You're calling me about this case every blessed minute of the day, and now you can't return a text?"

"Hey, listen, I just got it. I accidentally left my phone at a shop where I was dropping off some jewelry and—oh shoot, it doesn't matter why I was out. Just tell me what happened. Why'd they arrest Hubert?"

Jen sounded breathless. "All the police will say is that they have some new evidence that led to his arrest. We called and asked that brother of hers for a statement on behalf of the LeMann family, and he was only too happy to give us an earful. He told a reporter the police found something in Hubert's possession, and it pointed to him as the killer. Do you think Hubert had that heirloom necklace you've been talking about?"

"I have no idea." I sighed. "I can't believe this. Hubert wasn't my favorite person, but I sure never thought he was a killer. Half the elementary kids in Roseland had him as their principal at one time or another. Good grief, the town must be buzzing."

"It's been nonstop in the newsroom," Jen said. "Everybody and their brother has called up wanting info, but of course no one wants to be quoted. You wouldn't believe how many of the teachers Hubert once worked with are calling us. They're saying things like, 'Well, you know, Hubert and I really never worked that closely together.' One of the men was his assistant principal for twelve years but claims he didn't know Hubert well. Give me a break. They've gone completely mad trying to distance themselves from the man. But I do have a question for you."

"Yes?"

"Why does the hotshot-Atlanta-attorney brother keep showing up in Roseland? You said Tina wasn't very close to her siblings. Yet the sister she reconciled with is keeping a low profile, but Brother of the Year pops his head up every time her name is mentioned. What's up with that?"

"A lot of us are wondering that same thing," I said. "And hey, I've got a few other calls to make, so I need to let you go."

"Call me if you hear anything juicy," Jen said.

I assured her that I would before I hung up and called Carleen.

She answered immediately and said she'd been glad to hear of an arrest in the case, but like me, she wasn't convinced Hubert Harris was the killer.

"Why do you say that?" I asked.

"I think Hubert and Tina got along too well after all that real estate business between them, plus he didn't have a good reason to kill her—at least not that we know of. And no, I don't think he would have killed her to get that necklace either. One of the few times he ever came into the shop, he said he was getting a head start on looking for a unique Christmas gift for Harriet. Tina helped him that day, and I knew he'd sold her the house. Before he left, he even winked at her and told her it was a pleasure doing business with her again."

I shuddered at the thought of Hubert winking at anyone. "Do you remember anything else about that day?"

"Tina seemed embarrassed by it—him openly flirting with her like that—but I told her that I knew he was a big womanizer, so I didn't think too much of it. Lots of people become friendly with the person who sells them a house. That was their only interaction that I can recall."

"How long ago was this?"

"Let me think. Six months ago? Last summer, maybe? Not a full year, I'm sure of that."

That interaction between Tina and Hubert struck me as a little odd. "But that doesn't mean something couldn't have happened later to make Hubert to kill her. We really have no idea what their business dealings were like, do we?"

Carleen sighed. "I guess not."

"Have the police said anything to you about arresting Hubert?"

"Of course not."

"That's what I figured. I hope Detective Shelton hasn't botched the investigation by jumping the gun and arresting the wrong guy." I simply couldn't accept that Hubert Harris was a killer.

"There's got to be someone around who knows why Hubert really got arrested," Carleen said. "While I'd hate to think it was him, I must confess that I'd love to believe the killer had been caught and this whole sorry mess was over."

I nodded. "Me too. But you don't think that's the case, do you?"

"No," she admitted.

"Neither do I."

"So will you call me if you learn anything new?"

Sheesh. Carleen is as nosy as I am. "You bet. And you do the same, okay?"

Next, I called Savannah, but the call went to voice mail. I wondered whether she might be consoling Hannah, the Harris daughter who was her longtime friend.

After I played with Miriam and checked my email for new online orders, it was nearly seven o'clock. My turkey sub had worn off long ago, so I made a salad with some leftover chunks of chicken, feta cheese, and Kalamata olives.

Only a few minutes into my meal, my phone rang. I reached for it and saw Savannah's name on the screen. "Hello."

"Emma, why didn't you call me sooner?" Savannah sounded distraught.

"Because I was out and about most of the day and didn't even learn about Hubert's arrest until I heard it on the radio when I got home. I was hoping you'd have some details you could give me."

"I could, I guess, but first I wanted you to know that Harriet Harris is sitting in my living room and is in the middle of a crying jag. She's asking to see you."

"Me?"

"Yes. She says she needs to tell you a few things to see how it might play in the newspaper. She said she trusts you because of some feature you wrote about her elementary school years ago."

Harriet has news and wants to spill it? "I'll be there in ten minutes. Eight if I manage to avoid traffic."

And I did.

Savannah and her husband, Paul, lived in a beautiful Victorian cottage on a street of quaint and highly sought-after historic homes, just a few blocks east of the town square. Many of the owners had lived in those old family homes for decades. Savannah and Paul had bought their house as newlyweds, back when old homes were a dime a dozen, and turned it into a real showplace. Their historically accurate renovation had won local as well as state historic preservation awards.

Parking along the street, I saw Harriet's black Jeep Grand Cherokee, a familiar sight at garage sales. I walked up to the house, knocked on the front door, and took a deep breath.

Keep calm and carry on. Still, I was dying to know what Harriet might want to reveal. Had Hubert really killed Tina? Maybe Harriet had known about it and the guilt got to be too much for her. *But what on earth does she want with me?*

Savannah opened the door and gave me a feeble smile. "I'm so relieved you're here. Harriet seems to think you may be able to help her."

"I can't imagine how, but I'm certainly willing to talk to her," I said.

We walked into the living room, where a red-eyed Harriet sat in a comfortable old floral-print wingback chair. She dabbed at her eyes with a tissue.

"Thank you for coming, Emma. It's so good to feel I've got a friend on my side in the middle of this mess."

A friend? While I didn't view Harriet as an enemy, I'd never really thought of her as my friend. But I put on my best game face and went along with that idea. "I heard about Hubert's arrest for Tina's murder, but I don't believe he did it. He didn't, did he?"

Harriet looked ashen. "Of course he didn't."

"Then why would the police think he did?" I asked.

She sniffed into her tissue. "Maybe... they sort of... *misunderstood*... some things I shared with them."

"Such as?" I prompted.

Harriet started crying again. To my surprise, I genuinely felt sorry for her.

"You've probably heard that Hubert and I were having problems and were going to divorce."

I bit my lip and slowly nodded.

"I'd been trying to get him to agree to a settlement before I got an attorney, but Hubert's been very unreasonable. He refused to let me keep the antique mall and said we need to sell it and split the proceeds. But that mall was my idea"—she jabbed a thumb at herself—"and I'm the one who built that business. I'm the one who works there almost every day. I can't believe he won't give me the antique mall without a fight."

Harriet was working herself into a dither, and I knew I needed to cut her off before she got any more wound up. "So you went to the police? Is that where this is headed?"

"Oh, right. After Tina's death, they naturally questioned Hubert and me since we were her real estate agents. I sort of mentioned to them that Hubert had been the one insisting she pack up the house so we could stage it and sell it sooner. I might have left them with the impression that he could have been the one who found that emerald necklace everyone keeps talking about."

"The necklace you showed me a picture of at the store the other day?"

She twisted her tissue. "Yes."

Harriet looked as if she were about to embark on another crying spree, so I decided to distract her. "Look, Harriet, I know people sometimes say things they don't mean in the midst of, um, family problems, but what exactly did you say about Hubert and that necklace?"

"I told them that if that necklace was still in the house when Tina was preparing to move, it would have been just like Hubert to knock her off to get his greedy hands on it."

Savannah, who'd been sitting quietly and listening to our exchange, gasped. "You don't really mean that, do you, Harriet?"

"No." Harriet cut her eyes at Savannah. "Hubert wouldn't hurt a flea. He might be a selfish son of a—"

I broke in. "Okay, okay. We get the picture. But now you've got to tell the police you embellished the story and that Hubert didn't kill anyone."

"And there's something else I told them."

I closed my eyes and motioned for her to continue.

"When I went through Tina's things, I found a letter she'd written to Hubert but apparently never gave him. It said in no uncertain terms that she was tired of him hitting on her and that she was going to file a complaint with the local board of Realtors if he didn't stop coming by. I might have suggested that this was another good motive for murder and—"

"Harriet! You didn't," Savannah said. "You've got to tell the police you exaggerated about that too."

"I can't do that. What if I get sent to jail? What will my customers think?"

Searching for the best way to say what Harriet needed to hear, I cleared my throat. "You know, they're going to think a lot worse of you if they find out you let your husband go to jail for a crime he didn't commit. I think you need to call Detective Shelton right now. If you like, I'll stay here with you until the police arrive."

"You will?"

"Sure. I'll be glad to." I nearly choked on my words. Suddenly I was Harriet's BFF? *What a strange position to be in.*

Harriet took a shaky breath. "Okay, I'll call Alan, but you've got to stay here with me."

Savannah eyed us quietly and rose from her chair. "I'll go make us all some coffee. Can I bring you two a snack? A slice of pound cake, maybe?"

I shook my head, and so did Harriet. The last thing I wanted to do was eat. My stomach was in knots. I was unnerved enough thinking that a real murderer was still out there without having to worry about the fake one Harriet had falsely accused. I wanted to get the overly long day behind me, go home, and crawl into bed.

Home, it seemed, was the only safe and sane place to be these days.

Chapter Eighteen

"Miriam, don't you think there ought to be a church for feline members like you to attend?"

My sweet kitty purred and rubbed up against my legs as I sat at the kitchen table, munching a piece of toast and downing the most high-octane coffee I had in the cabinet. After sleeping past nine, I was starving, and I needed something to keep my stomach from growling before I headed to the eleven o'clock service at church. No way could I have made it to early church after I'd been summoned to Savannah's house for what had amounted to a late-night counseling session with Harriet Harris.

I shook my head and tried to clear the cobwebs. What a bizarre evening it had been. Detective Shelton had arrived at Savannah's house minutes after Harriet's call. As I could have predicted, he hadn't been one bit pleased to hear how she had embellished her tale to make Hubert sound like a cold-blooded killer. While her comments weren't the entire basis of Hubert's arrest, they had certainly added fuel to the fire for the officers who were already hoping to pin the murder on someone.

The detective had warned Harriet about the possibility that she might face legal trouble if she didn't cooperate fully from that point on. She had quickly agreed, and I was pretty sure she'd been scared straight by her encounter with the law—even though that particular officer of the law was her former pupil.

Harriet had cried, sniveled, and made it abundantly clear that she had no plans whatsoever to apologize to Hubert, much less visit him in jail, which I thought was sad. Surely once Detective Shelton shared the news about Harriet's vengeful rumormongering, Hubert would be released.

I would give it more thought after I got home from church. The only other thing I had on my calendar for the day was afternoon tea with Carleen and Teri.

When I got to church, I decided there was a mind reader behind the pulpit. *What is it with pastors these days? How do they always know to preach on a verse that's exactly what I need to hear?* We had a visiting pastor that day, and he spoke on the verse in Matthew that read, "I was sick, and you visited me. I was in prison, and you came to me." *Can't a girl take a day off once in a while? Please.*

But even as I drove home, I knew what I had to do. I changed out of my dress and heels and slipped on some black slacks and a simple blue blouse. I wondered if Hubert would even talk to me, not as a former reporter and certainly not "on the record" but rather as someone trying to be a friend. I had nothing to lose by paying him a visit, but I possibly had something to gain.

THE CITY JAIL WAS A nondescript gray block building that hadn't been on my radar in years. I'd been there a few times when I first became a newspaper reporter. I didn't imagine I would know the faces there anymore, but there was nothing to prevent me from trying to get in to see Hubert. He might not want visitors, but if I were ever stuck in jail, I would certainly be eager to see anyone who came my way. *Nothing ventured, nothing gained.*

A tall, thin black woman sat behind the desk. "Can I help you?"

"I'd like to see Hubert Harris if he's allowed to have visitors. Is that possible?"

"Is he expecting you?"

"No," I said. "But I wanted to let him know I'm available if he'd like to talk."

"Are you family?"

"No."

The woman raised an eyebrow and looked me over.

I wanted to say, "Don't go there," because her face told me she thought I was too young to be Hubert's girlfriend, but on the other hand, she'd probably seen it all in her line of work.

"I'm an old friend," I said, hoping that explanation was sufficient. *Friend. There's that word again.*

The woman looked me up and down and apparently decided I didn't pose an immediate threat. She flipped through the pages of a clipboard on her desk. "Let me see here. No, he hasn't had a visitor today. I'll go see what he says since it's up to him. What's your name?"

"Emma Madison."

"I'll be back in a few minutes." She stepped into another room, where I assumed she was using the jail's ancient intercom system to communicate between prisoners and visitors. She came out with her same no-nonsense attitude in place. "Mr. Harris said he'll see you, and you'll have thirty minutes. Sign in here. And I'll need to see your driver's license."

"Great." I tried to sound more confident than I felt.

When I stood and hefted my huge purse up onto my shoulder, the woman scowled. "You know you can't carry that back there with you, right? Only a driver's license and a single car key. I'm assuming you've got a car outside where you can lock that up."

I assured her that I did. I quickly ran outside, stashed my purse in the trunk, and zipped back to the desk.

"Please pass through the metal detector," the woman said.

I did, and a buzzer sounded immediately. *Wonderful.* I had chosen that day to wear a chunky cuff bracelet, a necklace filled with metal charms, and an underwire bra. The officer wanded me and waved me through.

I'd forgotten about being screened, but of course they had to do that. Criminals and their friends weren't the most honest of visitors. I was sure the jail staff didn't want a knife or gun slipping through undetected.

A twentysomething officer with a soul patch ushered me down a dimly lit beige hallway and into a small room. I had been expecting a cubicle and a wall of glass, even though I suddenly remembered that the last time I'd been there to write a feature story about one of the officers, I had conducted the interview in one of those same rooms. In my years away from the crime beat, I had clearly glamorized it. I had been imagining *Law and Order* when Roseland's jail setup was more *Mayberry R.F.D.*

Now I had to think about what I was going to say to Hubert. *"Hi! How's it going?"* No, that would be a little flippant. *"Hubert, I'm so sorry."* I might or might not be sorry, depending on whether he was a murderer, but I was convinced more than ever that he was not.

Before I had time to fret any further, the heavy metal door swung wide, and Hubert entered wearing his jail-issued orange jumpsuit. Orange wasn't Hubert's color.

"Emma," he said. "I don't know what you're doing here, but I'm hoping you can help get me out. It seems that my soon-to-be-ex-wife led them to believe I'm a killer. I swear I did not kill that girl!" Either he was the best actor since Tom Hanks or he was telling the truth.

"I know you didn't," I said, and I finally meant it. "I just wondered if you have any idea who did."

He shook his head vehemently. "Not a clue. And I've been sitting here, racking my brain, believe me. Tina was the perfect client, and I never had a cross word with her. I went over with Harriet a few times to talk to her about staging the house, setting out a few annuals for curb appeal, that kind of thing. But I barely spoke to the girl during those visits. Harriet always did the talking."

Now that, I could believe. Harriet tended to run the show no matter where she was. I had no problem picturing her bossing Tina around about how to help them sell her house.

"Did you ever see any visitors when you were there?"

"Almost never." Hubert wrung his hands from his seat behind the table. "One day last week, I dropped off some flyers for her to give to anyone who might stop by after seeing the For Sale sign out front. You know, I did hear what sounded like a bit of an argument between her and some man. Tina told me that was her brother, and they'd had problems for years. Seemed kind of embarrassed about it, but shoot, every family's got problems." He looked rather downcast. "Just ask Harriet. She'll tell you all about ours."

So Tina had recently had an argument with the brother she rarely saw. "Did you happen to hear what the argument was about?"

"Best I could tell, he mentioned a lost piece of jewelry, and they were arguing over whether their mother could afford to stay in that nice new assisted-living place across town. As I recall, Tina insisted nowhere else was nice enough, but the brother was saying it cost too much money. He wanted them to find another place."

I glanced at the large round clock on the wall. "Listen, my time's almost up, but if you think of something—anything—that could be related to this case, would you give me a call when you get out? I'm sure you'll be released on bail soon. And if there's anything I can help you with, I'll be happy to look into it."

"Thank you," Hubert said. I thought he was going to cry. "It's hard having your reputation ruined because of a nasty wife, so I sure do appreciate you taking the time to help clear my name. You hear?"

Is that what he thinks I'm doing? Helping clear his name? I was only there because of my friend's murder. "We just need to get to the truth about what happened to Tina. That's what we all want, isn't it?"

He smiled appreciatively and shook my hand. I was about to ask him one more question when the guard came to the door.

"Ma'am, your time's up," he said. "You'll have to leave now." Unlike Detective Shelton, this officer seemed friendly, as though he didn't consider me a nuisance.

"Thank you so much, Officer. We were just finishing up."

I glanced at Hubert. He stared longingly at the door, probably wondering when he would next get to enjoy the view from the other side. I stood and told him goodbye, and the guard escorted me to the area where I'd first entered.

Back at the car, I got my purse out of the trunk and tried to decide what I should do with the rest of my afternoon. Hesitantly, I checked my phone for messages. These days, I could never predict when the thing was going to blow up. The only message I had, though, was a text from Carleen saying that I could feel free to park in her driveway when I joined her and Teri for tea.

We weren't having tea until four o'clock. That would give me plenty of time to have a snack, spend some time with Miriam, and maybe even enjoy a brief nap. It sounded like the perfect way to spend a Sunday afternoon.

TERI LEMANN AND I PULLED up to Carleen's Federal-style brick house at the same time, and Teri seemed pleased to see me arrive.

"I was so glad when Carleen said you would be joining us," she said.

"Since I don't get invited to tea very often, I didn't dare want to miss out, especially when Carleen's the hostess."

We strolled together up the brick pathway and past her well-manicured lawn. Carleen had obviously been watching and welcomed us inside. It hadn't taken me long at all to get ready since I simply put back on the navy dress and heels I'd worn to church, accenting my cardigan with a beige Bakelite teapot pin. Both Carleen and Teri wore dresses as well, so I was glad that my church clothes were appropriate attire.

We went inside and took our seats around the small dining table that I knew had been passed down in Carleen's family. She confessed that she'd had an ulterior motive for asking me to join her and Teri for tea. "Teri read on the arts council website that you're on the board. After meeting you the other day, she asked whether I thought you could give her the scoop on what it takes to connect with the local arts community. I told her she could ask you herself over tea."

I laughed. "Brilliant strategy. And as you know, I love to talk about the arts in Roseland."

Carleen nodded. "Yes, I know that quite well. But before you launch into that, let me tell you both what's on our tea table today."

Carleen had prepared a repast that looked as if it were intended for more than just three. On the bottom tier of the three-tiered server were salmon pinwheels, cucumber sandwich rounds, and small triangle sandwiches with egg-olive salad. The second tier held plain and cranberry scones with clotted cream and jam. On the crowded top tier were sweets, including lemon squares, chocolate sea-salt truffles, and pistachio and caramel macarons. Two elegant floral china teapots sat simmering on silver warmers. One pot contained Earl Grey while the other was filled with a peach-flavored green tea. Our dessert plates had sterling silver pastry forks next to them, forks I'd learned to recognize thanks to my frequent visits to the Silver Squirrel. The elegant silver serving pieces sat alongside some delicate china I imagined was Haviland, which Carleen had been collecting for decades.

"So now," Carleen said, "feel free to give Teri your best inside info on the arts council."

"With pleasure." I turned my attention from the yummy-looking food back to Teri. "And I have to start by saying that I'm just one member, so I can't guarantee the other board members will vote for your pieces to go in the shop, but based on what I've seen, you would have a great shot at getting on the list of exhibiting artists the next time a spot opens up. Your work is so distinctive, like that sofa I saw at Making Memories earlier this week. That was a stunner and much more high-end than what I usually see in antique malls and second-hand stores."

"Thanks." Teri smiled appreciatively as I went for a refill on my Earl Grey. "I know it's not everyone's cup of, well, tea"—we all laughed—"but I do think there's a spot for my work in some of to-day's homes with more eclectic furnishings."

"Sure there is," I said. "And with all the galleries in this town, everybody's going to want to scoop your furniture right up. I just know it."

Teri's eyes softened, and she bit her lip. "You can't imagine how much that means to me. I'm so pleased Carleen was willing to arrange for us to talk this afternoon."

"It wasn't exactly a hard sell." I grinned. "Carleen knows I never turn down a meal, and of course the fact that you're Tina's sister... well, we were both so fond of her, and it's such a pleasure to finally meet you, even if it was under some terribly sad circumstances."

Teri started to tear up. "I can hardly believe she's gone."

Carleen reached over and patted her hand. "It's okay. We're still reeling from all this ourselves."

"Carleen's right," I said. "I was in and out of the Silver Squirrel all the time, and while your sister was a great employee for Carleen, she was also someone I'd come to know as a friend. Tina gave so much to this community, and I can only imagine how much you must miss her. And I just want you to know, Carleen and I won't rest until we find the person who took her life." I began to choke up and had to blink back a few tears.

"Thank you, both of you, so much," Teri said. "And please forgive me for getting so emotional. I think working on my furniture and other art projects is what's going to keep me sane."

I took another sip of tea. "So how did you get started with your furniture designs?" I thought it was a good idea to steer the conversation in a different direction.

"Funny you should ask." Teri dabbed the last of her tears with a tissue she'd retrieved from what appeared to be an authentic Prada purse. Maybe that furniture business of hers was already doing well. "One day, I was reading a decorating magazine and saw where they had draped an old quilt across the back of a Victorian sofa. I remember thinking that the quilt's fabric looked nicer than the sofa's burgundy velvet upholstery. I had an old throwaway sofa frame in the garage, so on a whim, I upholstered it with a vintage quilt, and the rest is history. That first piece sold almost the moment it went in a gallery, and now I can't seem to make them fast enough for all the women who want them. In a way, that one magazine image really launched my furniture design business."

I smiled. "I get lots of ideas from jewelry and craft magazines, so I know what you mean. Those 'aha' moments can give you a whole new perspective on your work."

Teri perked up and seemed particularly eager to talk about her furniture. "It really was like a lightbulb clicking on in my head, and I knew right then that I wanted to use all these unusual fabrics to upholster furniture."

She was so animated, I realized we needed to let Teri talk about upholstery as much as possible. "So what sort of fabrics do you use?"

"Old quilts, vintage tablecloths. I even used an antique rug once because it was worn so thin that it draped well. The design on it still looked great, so I used it to cover a seat on a chair."

Carleen, reaching for another cucumber sandwich, asked Teri how she had learned to upholster.

"I took a class that was offered in Atlanta one summer," she said. "Once I learned the basics of folding and tucking fabric and a few finishing techniques, I was good to go."

"Those technique classes are great." I rubbed my hands together, excited by the memory. "I learned to solder jewelry by taking a class in Atlanta, and now I'm framing all kinds of stones and charms with silver solder."

"That reminds me"—Carleen pointed at me—"you know that old stone you found behind the shop the other day? I polished it up, and I do think it's an old emerald. No one's claimed it, so stop by and get it sometime. Maybe it'll find new life as another piece of jewelry."

"Super. I'll come get it when I'm out and about tomorrow." Unable to resist, I reached for one more pistachio macaron.

"I've heard your work is amazing," Teri said, "so I had to check it out for myself. I went in the Foothills Gallery and bought one of your beaded necklaces just the other day." Teri already seemed in much better spirits after talking about her artwork as well as my own.

I thanked her and asked more about her work. "What was the reaction when you started approaching shops about your furniture with these unusual fabrics? I know in the jewelry world, at least, customers like to copy the latest looks, but they don't always want to be the first to wear them."

Teri chuckled. "I know what you mean. The traditionalists wouldn't be caught dead with the kind of furniture I create. Initially, I decided to go where there was already a more relaxed lifestyle, the beach. The Gulf Coast has so many cute little boutiques and galleries. Some of them were only too happy to have a large, colorful piece of furniture to help brighten up their shop. To their amazement—and my own, really—they couldn't keep the pieces in stock. They practically flew out the door."

"Is that so?" Carleen looked impressed. "I thought everyone at the beach wanted watery blues and greens and white slipcovered sofas."

"Not everyone." Teri grinned and added, "Fortunately for me."

"Did you ever consider moving to the beach since your work did so well there?" I asked. If her work sold well on the coast, I didn't understand why she would want to reinvent the wheel in much-less-touristy Roseland.

"My family was all back here." Sadness clouded Teri's face. "I wanted to be near Tina and my brother, Tony. Of course, now that Tony's the only sibling I have left, and since I'll be the one primarily taking care of our mother... well, I felt I had little choice about where to live."

Before I knew it, two hours had passed, and while I wanted to get home, I didn't want us to end our otherwise lovely teatime on that sad note. I told Teri that if she would get me a few photos of her work, I would be glad to pass them around at the next arts council board meeting.

"I've had some glossy brochures printed up to leave with local business owners, but I dashed out of the house so quickly today that I forgot to bring them. Would it be all right if I just dropped them off at Carleen's for you early this week?"

"That would be great," I said. "In fact, our next board meeting is coming up soon, and I'll make sure I have them then. Why don't you give me your email address, and I can get in touch with you if the board has any questions."

"Sure." Teri reached for the Prada and pulled out a card. "It's right here on my business card."

"Terrific." I fingered the card. "And if you happen to be able to drop those brochures off with Carleen sometime tomorrow, I'll be working at the gallery shop in the morning and can pop over and get them when I'm done."

Teri said she would be out meeting with some new clients in the morning and would stop by Carleen's with the brochures. Then she said it was time for her to be heading home as well, so we both said our goodbyes and thanked Carleen for the delicious teatime.

Whatever had gone on between the LeMann siblings, Teri Le-Mann seemed like a genuinely kind and super-talented woman. She'd lost her only sister under terrible circumstances, she had a first-class jerk for a brother, and if I could do anything to help her feel welcome in Roseland's arts and crafts community, I certainly would.

When I got home, I spent a little time going over my calendar for the week ahead and writing down my jewelry-making goals. With Easter, Mother's Day, and graduation season around the corner, I knew that women's gift shops would likely do a booming business. I wanted to be sure my designs were in as many places as possible in addition to having many of them online.

I'd finished my planning and was about to turn on Netflix when my phone rang. It was Justin reporting on the fabulous time he'd had in Asheville. To my surprise, after a little hemming and hawing around, Justin admitted that the real reason he was calling was to see whether I would be interested in joining him Monday night at The Loft, one of Roseland's newest fine-dining restaurants. I told him I would be happy to join him, and when I got off the call, I immediately started thinking about what to wear.

I wondered if I was seeing too much of Justin too soon, but I quickly dismissed the thought. He was a great guy, a talented fellow artist, and for the moment, I was quite comfortable seeing him as often as we could arrange it.

Chapter Nineteen

Monday was my regularly assigned day to work a morning shift at the arts council shop, and before it opened at ten, I stopped by Mavis's for a caramel cappuccino and Danish to go. Monday was often a slower day for us, but unlike some neighboring small towns, Roseland had chosen not to close up shop on Mondays and risk running off any shoppers—especially tourists—who decided to come our way.

The breakfast hour regulars were finishing up at Mavis's when I arrived. As she rang up my purchases, I said, "I'm unveiling some new jewelry designs in the shop today. And Savannah's bringing by some new watercolors of downtown landmarks, so stop by if you get a second."

Mavis handed me my change and smiled. "If we have a halfway quiet morning, I'll be over. I think the girls here can handle it long enough for me to pop over there for a few minutes. I want to check out your jewelry before it gets gone this time."

The previous month, Mavis had said she intended to stop by and purchase one of my ever-popular black-and-white sets. But by the time she'd stopped in, all of them were gone. I didn't like to be too pushy in promoting my jewelry, but I wanted Mavis to know she couldn't dillydally around and expect to get the best selection. I had offered to bring some pieces by the bakery, but she'd insisted she wanted to check them all out at the gallery shop.

I parked in the alley behind the shop, got out of the car, and reached in the back for my canvas market basket full of jewelry. After slinging my tote-slash-purse over a shoulder, I clutched the to-go sack from Mavis's in my left hand and slung the market basket over my right arm. Fumbling only slightly, I clicked my key to lock the car and headed to the back door of the gallery shop.

A piece of mail appeared to be wedged between the door and doorknob, but I couldn't grasp it while I was impersonating a pack mule. Instead, I thrust my key into the door's lock and barged into the shop with my belongings in tow. Once I plopped my purse, basket, and snacks onto the counter, I walked back to the door and retrieved a business-sized envelope, which curiously had my name written on it.

Maybe Trish Delgado from the arts council had left a list of things she wanted me to tend to. More likely, it was the downtown shopkeepers' association letting us know about an upcoming event they wanted our help with. But that still didn't explain why my name was on it. Before I could speculate further, I tore into the envelope and removed a single trifold sheet of paper. It appeared to have been printed on a computer, and my eyes scanned the words rapidly.

Emma, You may want to rethink your involvement in the Tina Le-Mann murder case. Appearances aren't always what they seem, and neither was she. You may be biting off more than you can chew, and I'd hate to see something happen to you. A Concerned Friend.

I stared at the letter in disgust. *Who wrote this?* My mind started racing. Why on earth should I back off on trying to find out who murdered my friend simply because some cowardly person had written me a letter?

On the other hand, I was beginning to learn things about Tina that I hadn't known before. Like her problems with her family. And that dustup when she was on the library board. Maybe the letter writer was right. Maybe I *was* biting off more than I could chew.

But I knew one thing for sure: I was not about to be cowed by someone who didn't have the courage to sign his name.

I flung the letter on the counter, reached for my caramel macchiato, and took a sip. *Ah.* The hot, sweet liquid was exactly what I needed. *Letter, schmetter.*

Then it occurred to me that the letter with my name on it had been left at the store on the very morning I was scheduled to work, before the very hour I was to arrive. Someone obviously had known I was going to be there. Maybe the letter was a not-so-subtle personal threat.

I peered around the shop. Two doors led to storage space, and a short hallway led to an office and tiny bathroom. I wasn't about to check them out while in the shop alone. A loud *creak* caused me to quickly turn toward the back door and glance out the window, but no one was there.

You're letting your mind run away with you, Emma.

I glanced at my watch. Nine forty-five. I went to the counter for my purse and pulled out my cell phone. I tapped a quick message to Jen and received a response instantly. *Be there in 5 minutes.*

Meanwhile, I decided to prop open the front door of the shop. If a killer was waiting somewhere inside and grabbed me before Jen arrived, at least someone on Main Street would be able to hear my final screams.

Annoyed more than shaken by the anonymous letter, I walked around the store and straightened the jewelry display, fluffed a stack of Shareta Gibson's latest hand-dyed scarves, and generally tried to compose myself while I waited on Jen. Then I got angry that someone would dare to threaten me.

I looked at my cell phone. Four minutes had passed since the text from Jen. I walked to the front door and leaned against the doorjamb. Thirty seconds later, my friend turned the corner, clearly having hustled to get there in five minutes from the newspaper office.

"Right on time, as I knew you would be," I said.

"Hey, what's wrong? You look like you're ill."

"Do I?" I didn't realize the letter was affecting me physically, but Jen knew me well.

"It's probably nothing." I motioned for her to follow me to the counter. "But the strangest thing just happened. This letter was waiting for me when I arrived." I handed her the letter and drummed my fingertips on the counter while she read it.

Jen placed it on the counter. "You've called the police, haven't you?"

"No. I got here literally only a few minutes ago. It's probably no big deal, but—"

"Emma, you need to call and at least get them to make a report about this. What if it's important?"

"What if it isn't and I'm wasting their time?"

Jen's face had that look I never liked to see—her chin was firm, and her eyes were fiery. "Are you going to call the police, or am I? I'm not leaving here until you do something about this."

She was right, of course. Although I hated involving the police, the letter—and the threat—might be important.

I called the Roseland Police Department, and Evelyn answered. We exchanged greetings, then I quickly got to the point. "I'm afraid I've got another incident to report. It may be nothing, but when I got to the gallery shop this morning, a strange letter was waiting for me, and it said I needed to back off the Tina LeMann murder investigation."

Jen looked on as Evelyn fired question after question at me through my cell phone.

"You sure you aren't hurt?"

"No, not a bit. I'm fine, really."

"Are you there by yourself?" Evelyn sounded concerned.

"No, a friend is here at the shop with me now."

"And this letter definitely had your name it?"

"Yes, but just my first name."

"Did you see anyone when you came in? Was anyone else in that alley entering a business?"

"No, no one was around at all that I could see."

"And you're going to be there for a while, right?"

"Mm-hmm, for the rest of the morning."

"Hang tight, and make sure that friend stays with you. I'm sending someone from the department over now to check on you."

"Okay. Thanks." As Evelyn ended the call, I set my cell phone on the counter and looked at Jen.

She crossed her arms. "Well? What'd they say?"

"Evelyn said she's sending an officer over and to make sure someone stays with me until the police arrive. I didn't think about that—the letter writer might come back if he or she knows I'm here alone right now. Sorry. I didn't mean to tie up your morning."

Jen looked at her watch. "It's been seven minutes, and I think I can spare that. Besides, I couldn't live with myself if something happened to you." Lightening the mood, she added, "Because then who would listen to me gripe about the newspaper business?"

I grinned. A few minutes later, a flash of navy blue appeared at the front door. And it wasn't a customer. It was someone from the police department. I could have predicted who it would be.

"So, I hear we've had a bit of excitement up here today. Morning, Jen," Detective Shelton said, nodding.

She smiled. "Good morning, Detective."

I grimaced. "It's the kind of excitement I could do without. As I told Evelyn, it's probably nothing, but this letter was waiting for me at the shop this morning. It seems designed to stop me from looking into the murder investigation."

"May I see the letter?"

I started to hand it to him, but he held up a hand. "Let me glove up first." He pulled out a pair of latex gloves and snapped them on before quickly reading the letter. "And again, where did you find this?"

I explained that the letter had been propped on the knob of the back door when I'd arrived.

"Who has handled this letter? Just you?"

I dipped my chin at my friend. "And Jen."

"I'm going to need to take this and see if we can get any prints off it, just in case."

"That's fine, but first..."

"Yes?"

"Do you mind if I snap a picture of it with my cell phone?"

"Why?"

Jen saved the day on that one. "Maybe something in the words will jog her memory?"

"Yeah, that's it!" I said, perhaps a bit too eagerly.

The detective raised an eyebrow. "Okay." He unfolded the letter and held it flat for the photo. "Go ahead."

I clicked a shot. Two, for good measure.

"Thanks," I said as he placed the letter in an evidence bag.

He looked me in the eye and paused only for a moment before he spoke. "You're welcome." Glancing around the shop, he appeared to take in the doors and the hall. "No one else is in here this morning? Just you?"

"I sure hope it's just me." I casually walked over to one of the closet doors and opened it. "This is a supply closet"—mercifully, no killer was folded into the tight space below the shelves of cash register tape and gift bags—"and this is the bathroom." I opened the door and flipped the switch. The room was empty.

The detective nodded. "Good, but I'd like to keep someone posted here for a bit to be sure nothing unusual is going on."

"And meanwhile"—he turned to Jen—"are you going to be here for a while? I don't think it's a good idea for her to be here by herself, all things considered."

Jen shook her head. "I've got to get back to the office. But I could probably take a few breaks and stop back by."

"Really, I'll be fine," I told her. "Look, Detective, I'll call you if anything else odd happens today, okay?"

Jen looked torn about whether to leave.

"Why don't I hang around here for an hour or so and see how it goes?" Shelton asked.

"That's a great idea," I said, though of course I didn't mean it. "Jen, see, I'll be fine. You go on with your day. Okay?"

"Will you call me if you need anything?"

"Sure will," I said. "And don't worry. Everything's going to be fine."

Jen looked around the shop—at what, I didn't know—and gave me a quick but tight hug. Then she left in a whirl.

"Why are you so sure this letter writer didn't mean you any harm?" Detective Shelton asked.

I gripped the edge of the counter and leaned forward. "For one thing, if someone genuinely wanted to shake me up—and they obviously knew what time I usually get to the shop—there was ample opportunity for them to harm me right as I arrived this morning. If the letter writer had intended to do something to me, that would have been the perfect chance. I was alone, there were no witnesses, and it was a quiet Monday morning. For anyone who wanted to harm me, it doesn't get much better than that."

"Maybe. Maybe not. Did you stop to think that the person who wrote this could have been the killer?"

I gulped. Actually, I *had* considered that. But hearing him suggest it made it seem more real, except for one thing. "A killer wouldn't have given me a warning. He would've gone on and killed me, wouldn't he?"

"You seem to have thought of everything, haven't you?" Detective Shelton's tone indicated that he didn't exactly mean it as a compliment.

"I'm just saying that my gut instinct tells me this wasn't Tina's killer."

Officer Shelton stared at me.

"What?" I asked. "What's the problem?"

"The problem right now is you." His face was beginning to turn red. "You've made yourself front and center of this case the whole time I've been working it. Now, when I should be out following up on other leads, I'm sitting here protecting you because some bad guy who might or might not be the killer seems to know that you're all caught up in this thing."

"Then by all means, feel free to leave." I stabbed a finger at the front door. "I already told you that I think it's overkill for you to stay here. I know my neighbors on either side of this store. One call, and they'd both be over here in an instant."

The officer shook his head.

"What?" I asked again. "Why are you doing that?"

"Emma, you're still assuming that some criminal, someone who might have a knife or a gun, is going to show up and give you time to contact your friends. Excuse me for saying so, but that's a bit naive."

The front door opened. It was Mavis. I imagined she was coming in search of that new jewelry. "Well, hi there, Alan. Fancy seein' you here. Now, Emma, I'm looking forward to getting first dibs on those new jewelry sets. Where are they?"

Three of the tables had some of my jewelry on them, and Mavis was soon bouncing from table to table, shopping for sets with the Emma Madison Designs logo.

"I'm afraid I haven't had time to get any of the new ones out yet," I said. "Detective Shelton here stopped by for a... um... a *chat*, and I'm afraid we've been so busy, it put me a bit *behind* here this morning." I gave him the stink-eye to let him know he was interfering with my work. On top of that, I didn't feel one bit safer with him in the room.

Mavis snapped her head his way. "Alan Shelton? Are you interfering with this young lady's business? If you want those free doughnuts to keep coming, I suggest you let this young woman get her work done."

Detective Shelton sighed and headed toward the door. "You've got my number," he said to me. "And I would appreciate a call if anything *else* happens this morning." He ran a hand through his hair and shrugged before leaving.

"What was that all about?" Mavis asked. "And what did he mean by 'if anything *else* happens this morning'? Have I missed something?"

"Nah, not really," I said, eager to put the unpleasantness behind me. "The detective had a few more questions about something that might be related to the Tina LeMann murder. But you're here to talk jewelry, not investigations, right?" I reached for my market tote and carried it to the largest of the three jewelry tables.

Mavis was already up to her elbows in jewelry sets and seemed more than willing to drop the topic of police visits and murder investigations. "Ooh, that green set is gorgeous! You made this too?"

"You like it?" I asked, pleased by her enthusiasm. "That's a new color combination for me, mixing the dark greens with the turquoise and aqua stones."

"I love it." She fingered the necklace. "I'm going to be giving a workshop for cake decorators next month, and I want to look a little more professional than I do in my day-to-day uniform." Her uniform was actually a large yellow smock with the Cupcake Café logo em-

broidered on a front pocket. "This will be perfect. And oh my goodness, here are those black-and-white sets. I don't know if I like the
pearl ones or the glass ones best." She held the beads up and let the
glass catch the reflection from the sunlight streaming through the
front windows.

No matter how many sales I made, I would never get tired of
watching women appreciate the simple beauty of a piece of jewelry.

Mavis twirled the necklace and earrings in the air. "Would you
look at that?"

Thanks to the light hitting at precisely the right angle, a rainbow
of colors swirled across the stark white walls of the shop and led our
eyes straight to the front of the room. Outside our front door, Detective Alan Shelton sat on a bench, quietly continuing his visual patrol
of Main Street—right there in front of the shop.

Glancing at her watch, Mavis said she needed to get to the bakery. I quickly rang up her purchases, and soon she was out the door
with a big bag of jewelry.

While I kept an eye on the detective to make sure he wasn't scar-
ing off our shoppers, I answered a text from Carleen, who wanted to
know if I cared to join her for lunch at Mama's Place, a great little
hole-in-the-wall soul food restaurant tucked into a hidden alleyway
downtown.

Emma: *Can't be there till 1. Will that work?*

Carleen: *See you there then.*

A few minutes later, the door to the gallery shop creaked open,
and two women entered, deep in conversation and never drawing a
breath. "I heard he threatened to cut her out of the antique mall on
the highway, and she got mad and told the police he did it. Can you
believe that?" the blond woman asked.

Her brunette friend was quick to offer her opinion. "I wouldn't
put anything past those two. They were some of the stingiest people
in town when I lived here back in the nineties. Looks like they would

have either killed each other or worked out their problems by now, doesn't it?"

It always amazed me when customers acted as if the shop owner—or clerk, in this case— were deaf. For all they knew, I could've been a friend or family member of the very people they were talking about.

And assuming they were talking about the Harrises, I was indeed a friend of theirs—or at least it seemed that way. I was Harriet's friend because I helped her explain to the police why she'd "accidentally" led them to think Hubert might have killed Tina. And I was Hubert's friend because I believed he wasn't a killer and that I wanted to help find the real one.

When the women finally paused for air, I piped in while I had the chance. "Good morning, ladies. I won't bother you while you're shopping, but if I can help you with anything, please let me know."

The blonde dismissed me with a wave of her hand. "Uh-huh, okay. Thank you, dear."

The women kept up their gossiping as they strode over to a jewelry table and picked up piece after piece, not really looking at the jewelry but continuing to talk a mile a minute.

"All I know is, if Richard ever cheated on me like Hubert has always cheated on her, I would kick him out of the house and never let him back in. I'd take that man for all he's got."

Ain't love grand?

"What *I* heard was that she accused him of murder just to get back at him. Her daughter, Holly, was at the gym yesterday—and I don't know why, because it never seems to do her a bit of good—and she was on the phone with her mother, accusing her of letting him go to jail purely out of spite. Holly was practically *screaming* into the phone, and all of us on the exercise bikes and treadmills were *rolling* our eyes at each other. *Such* bad manners. Of course, Harriet was always kind of rude that way too, if you ask me. I used to hate how she would be *gossiping* with someone at the front counter whenever I went into that antique mall."

Pot, meet kettle. I nearly snorted the bottle of water I'd been sipping behind the counter.

I could have predicted that the two women would leave without buying anything and that they would leave without offering me the courtesy of a goodbye. I hadn't volunteered at the retail shop very long before I learned to recognize the types.

The brunette seemed fascinated with the blonde's account of Hubert and Harriet's problems. I thought it was sad, and not just because a couple's marriage was on the skids. It was sad that Harriet's daughter would discuss their private matters in public for the world to hear.

On the other hand, I knew I was being a complete hypocrite. Although it wasn't nice for such matters to be aired in public, I had no objections to using what I'd just overheard. I realized there was another angle I'd failed to pursue with Hubert. If he'd really been having all those affairs, Harriet might not be the only woman in town who had wanted to see him behind bars.

As soon as I had the opportunity, I intended to ask Hubert some uncomfortable questions about his well-known womanizing.

THE SIZZLING SOUNDS of chicken frying were music to my ears when I opened the weathered blue door at Mama's Place.

Opened fifteen years ago by one of the best African-American cooks Roseland had ever seen, Mama's Place was something of a legend to those few souls fortunate enough to know about it. I had been introduced to Mama herself many years ago when I first moved to town. The reporters at the newspaper ate there regularly, especially those of us who were young, away from home, and missing our mothers' home cooking.

Mama—LaNelle Jenkins—had been cooking for her large family all her life. It had long been her dream to open her own restaurant. When a tiny back-alley space between a carpet factory and a barber shop had become available, Mama did what the naysayers had said couldn't be done—she'd set up a commercial kitchen, brought in a few of her young-adult children to help, and started dishing up plates of her famous Southern cooking.

Mama didn't advertise, she didn't run specials, and she didn't put up with any foolishness in her restaurant. Her menu consisted of whatever she had a mind to cook that day, and anyone who didn't like it was free to dine elsewhere. A paint-by-number portrait of Jesus and a plaque stating the Golden Rule hung above the checkout counter and served as the restaurant's primary decor.

Monday was fried chicken day, and I was practically drooling just thinking about it. Carleen and I knew we would have to claim a table no later than one o'clock unless we wanted to get take-out plates. My friend was already sitting at a table covered in red-checked oilcloth and nursing a red plastic tumbler full of sweet tea when I walked in.

"This food smells divine," she said. "It's been months since I've had time to come over here for lunch, and oh, have I missed it."

A waitress asked for my drink order, and like Carleen, I wanted sweet tea. Soon, I was guzzling Mama's delightful nectar, which she sweetened with her special simple syrup. I hadn't realized how parched I was.

Carleen wasn't the only one who loved to eat at Mama's. The regulars included blue-collar workers, lawyers from the downtown offices, the local police force, store clerks with just an hour to get in and out, and small business owners like Carleen. I looked a few tables over, spotted Trish Delgado and Shareta Gibson with their lunch plates, and waved. Mama considered us all part of her extended family.

"Hey, doll. What'll it be today?" Mama asked Carleen, sidling up to our table with her notepad in hand. Mama wrote our orders on one of those old-fashioned flip-style notepads, the ones with the mint-green lined pages and a carbon copy underneath. I had no idea where she still found them, but clearly, electronic cash registers and credit card readers attached to iPads were light years away from ever coming to Mama's.

"The fried chicken, of course," Carleen said. "I've been tied up with work far too long, and I have been seriously missing that fried chicken of yours."

"You got it, baby," Mama said. "What do you want for your vegetables? We got butter beans, green beans, mac 'n cheese, stewed okra, squash casserole, and fried green tomatoes."

"Mmm, I'll take the okra and the squash casserole." Mama scribbled it all down in a practiced shorthand that was no doubt unreadable to anyone but her and the family members who helped in the kitchen. "And I already know what you want, sweetheart," she said to me. "Tell me if this isn't right—fried chicken, fried green tomatoes, and mac 'n cheese."

I knew the old punch line about how only Southerners considered macaroni and cheese a vegetable, but I didn't care. Not when I was dining at Mama's. And not when she was known to slather her perfectly cooked macaroni noodles with extra butter and cheddar cheese.

"Am I that predictable?" I asked.

"Honey, that's not a bad thing." Without asking, Mama swiped my half-full tea glass. "Let me get you a refill." I heard her as she turned the corner and hollered out, "Marion, get a large sweet tea to table three!"

I turned to Carleen. "I thought your idea of hosting that tea yesterday afternoon was a great way to break the ice with Teri and help her get to know us. I noticed she didn't have much to say about her brother. Did she happen to mention anything about him after I left?"

Carleen paused while one of Mama's daughters slid a fresh glass of tea my way. "Not much. I know that Tina's mother is still in the assisted-living place—and apparently a little frail after burying a daughter this week—and Teri is going by every other day to check on her. Did you realize that's how often Tina went out there to see her mother? I can't imagine when she had time for herself in between all those visits."

I nodded. "It seems there's a lot we didn't know about Tina. Including some bad blood between her and her brother."

Carleen's eyebrows shot up. "You learned something about Tony?"

"Mm-hmm." I finished a sip of tea. "I didn't think that yesterday was the proper time and place to mention it, but after church yesterday, I went by the jail to see Hubert. He said that one of the last times he ever saw Tina, she was having an argument with her brother. The conversation was hard to overhear, or so Hubert says, but it had something to do with a missing piece of jewelry."

Carleen had a faraway look in her eyes. "I wish..."

"You wish what?"

"I wish I could remember what Tina told me about emeralds that time."

"You two discussed emeralds? Like those in the missing necklace?"

"That's the strange thing," Carleen said. "I have this vague memory of something she said one day that had to do with emeralds, but it wasn't actually a jewelry conversation per se. It's on the tip of my tongue... or maybe the tip of my brain. I've tried and tried, and I cannot for the life of me remember what it was. Oh, I hate getting old!"

Carleen was only in her midfifties, so I had to laugh at her remark. "Maybe you just need to try *not* to think about it so much.

You know, that old advice about how if you give your brain a rest, the missing piece of information will muscle its way to the front."

Carleen relaxed her shoulders, reminding me of one of the wilted tulips in front of my house. "I guess there's nothing else I can do except give that a try, because grasping to remember it sure hasn't helped. I have this feeling it was something important, though. Now if only I could remember what it was."

"Here you go, ladies." Mama delivered our fried chicken plates with a flourish. She eyed my refilled tea glass with a firm nod, quickly looking over at Carleen's, which was still three quarters full. "If y'all need anything else, you just give me a holler, hear?"

We thanked her, and after she left, I whispered, "Do you think there's any chance Mama would adopt me?"

"You wish." Carleen tore into her large piece of fried chicken with more gusto than I would have expected from a refined and ladylike antiques dealer.

As I tucked into a perfectly breaded fried green tomato, Carleen told me a little more about what she'd learned in her recent conversations with Teri LeMann. She and Teri had sure hit it off, which was fortunate for Teri since Carleen was such a solid, dependable friend—something Teri apparently could use these days. Teri said Tina had left behind some old family silver, and she wanted Carleen to take a look at it and help her determine the value. It sounded as though Teri was trying hard to make new friends in Roseland.

"Since they have the same last name, I assume the sister never married?" I asked.

Carleen speared a forkful of squash casserole. "Actually, she did. Teri was married until just last year, it turns out, but she went back to her maiden name after the divorce."

"Know anything about her ex?"

"Just that he was addicted to gambling. She said she finally got fed up and made him leave. She was a little shy about telling me any more about him, and of course I didn't want to pry."

"Oh, come on. Pry, pry," I said with a laugh. "We need info here."

Carleen smiled softly. "I know we do, but you know what I mean. I barely know Teri, so I'm depending on her to lead the conversation whenever we get together. She says she's trying to settle Tina's affairs, but I'm not convinced there's that much to settle. I believe she's just lonely and needs someone to talk to, especially now that her sister's gone."

"So I gather she's not into selling antiques herself, just wants her vendors to sell them at the new antique mall?"

After wiping a well-manicured finger onto her second paper napkin of the meal, Carleen finished another mouthful of chicken before replying. "It's not exactly that she doesn't like antiques. She appreciates them, but her passion is what I would call upscale crafting. Her high-end furniture pieces aren't the sort of thing you can put on eBay or Etsy, but she's had some success selling them through antique malls and small-town boutiques. From what you've told me, that sofa she has out at Harriet's right now is a real showstopper."

"It's gorgeous," I said. "It's the kind of furniture you might see at the occasional boutique every now and then but few other places. I guess there's not that big a market for colorful overstuffed furniture at a time when brown leather sofas and white canvas slipcovers lead the market."

Carleen balled up her well-used napkin and placed it to the side of her plate. "I don't think Teri's work would be my cup of cappuccino, but good for her for finding a niche and running with it."

We'd both cleaned our plates by then, and one of Mama's daughters discreetly popped over to the table and removed them. Waiting until a break in our conversation, she asked, "Any dessert today, ladies? We've got caramel cake, fried peach pies, and chocolate layer cake."

We both begged off, even though we knew Mama's desserts were to die for. I made a mental note to stop by sometime and pick up a dessert. Jen would definitely be all in on joining me for sweets.

Since customers were still waiting for one of the diner's coveted ten tables, Carleen and I gathered our purses and got ready to leave.

Mama was in her spot behind the register as I paid my tab. "How was it?" she asked.

"Terrible!" I said. "It was so bad, I think I'll come back tomorrow and give you another chance to get it right."

She roared, and Carleen and I pulled out our cash, the only form of payment accepted. We paid our bills and prepared to leave.

I was standing in front of the door when it swung open abruptly, hitting me in the arm. "Ouch!" I said, rubbing my shoulder.

The door opened again, more slowly this time, and Detective Alan Shelton walked in. I rolled my eyes.

"Oh, sorry, Emma," he said.

I looked him in the eye. "No problem," I said as I breezed by.

"Now what was that all about?" Carleen asked. "It looked like an innocent mistake to me, but you sure gave Detective Shelton the evil eye."

I shrugged. "Maybe. I'm getting more irritated by the day that he hasn't been very helpful in finding Tina's killer. Every time I start to do something that could move the case along, he's waiting to criticize and accuse me of meddling."

"Have you ever thought that maybe he's trying to keep you out of harm's way?" Carleen asked. "The police always know more about an investigation than they let on. What if he's afraid of you getting too involved in this case?"

I humphed. "Right now, it doesn't appear that anyone knows too much about this case." In fact, it seemed only one person had a keen grasp of Tina's murder and what was going on with the investigation surrounding it. And that, I was sorry to say, was her killer.

When Carleen and I parted ways along Main Street, I was intending to head home and get to work when I remembered two things. First, I'd meant to ask her about those brochures Teri was supposed to have dropped off for me. And second, I'd been planning to show Carleen a new creation I had stashed in my purse, a Scarlett O'Hara–inspired necklace I'd been working on for weeks. I'd finally strung the pendant and beads on a simple green velvet ribbon that perfectly set off the colors in the necklace. I'd christened the piece "Fiddle Dee Dee" in honor of its inspiration, the Southern belle who'd famously wore a gown made of green velvet curtains. I was eager to get Carleen's reaction, and a quick trip by her shop would take only a few more minutes out of my day.

"Knock, knock," I said as I entered the Silver Squirrel.

Carleen looked up and smiled. "I was supposed to give you these brochures." She tapped the small stack of them on the countertop before her.

"I just remembered to come get them," I said. "Plus, I wanted you to see a new necklace I finally completed." I whipped out a flat silver box and pushed it across the counter toward Carleen, who carefully opened the tissue inside.

"You made this?" She leaned forward and examined the heart-shaped soldered glass pendant that was the focal point of the necklace.

I nodded. "Finished it over the weekend."

"Gorgeous," she said. "I love how you used the green glass beads along with your pendant. If I had half your talent, I too would be making jewelry instead of occasionally selling it. So call me a jealous fan."

"Are you 'pea green with envy,' as Scarlett O'Hara once put it?"

Carleen's eyes widened, and she started to speak, but something must have caught in her throat. For a second, I thought she was going to choke. She slapped the glass countertop, dabbed at her watering eyes, and wagged her head vigorously. "That's it! You've nailed it, Emma!"

"Nailed what?" I didn't know what she was getting so worked up about.

"You know how I told you there was something I was trying to remember, something related to emeralds? One day, Tina and I were talking about families who bicker over the furniture and jewelry left behind after a loved one dies. Happens all the time, right?"

"Uh, right, I guess."

"Trust me, you hear about these squabbles frequently in my line of business. Tina told me about having a family heirloom that one of her siblings was determined to get. When I suggested someone was 'pea green with envy,' like Scarlett O'Hara wanted her enemies to be in *Gone with the Wind*, she said no, it went much deeper than that. She said their envy was more of the *emerald*-green variety, yet she didn't seem to want to say too much more about it." Carleen was more animated than I'd ever seen her, waving her hands around and talking a little too loudly. At my surprised expression, she lowered her voice a fraction and continued. "I always assumed Tina was re-ferring to the degree of family jealousy over the necklace. But now, I can't help wondering if she was literally referring to emeralds. Maybe I just failed to pick up on it at the time!"

"And Tony LeMann is obviously the one who was more interest-ed in *things* than in his own family," I said. "Would you feel comfort-able telling Teri about your conversation with Tina?"

"I think I probably need to." Carleen tapped her lips with her in-dex finger. "And Teri is stopping by tomorrow at closing time, any-way. When she dropped off those brochures about her furniture, she said she wants to bring me a gift, something that once belonged to

Tina. I have no idea what it is, and of course it's completely unnec-essary. She said she's so appreciative of my help that she wants me to have something of Tina's. I hate to accept it, but I hate to decline it as well. She still seems so grief-stricken over losing her sister, I want to do whatever I can to make her feel better."

How thoughtful. "Sometimes the best thing you can do is simply accept the gift and say thank you. Who knows? Maybe doing some-thing nice for someone else will be cathartic for her."

After promising Carleen she'd seen the last of me for the day, I headed home to work on jewelry for a few hours, leaving me plenty of time to complete some pieces and clean up my workspace before going to dinner with Justin.

That afternoon, my goal was to craft some new resin jewelry, which had first come on the scene in the seventies and was sudden-ly—and inexplicably—all the rage again. I'd been utterly fascinated as a young teen when I first discovered the trendy jewelry encasing almost any object whatsoever within neat little blocks of Lucite, the trademarked version of acrylic resin that was invented in the thirties. I'd worn a necklace encasing a miniature Mr. Goodbar, a source of much fascination among my junior high classmates.

Memories of that schoolgirl necklace got me thinking about all the jewelry trends through the years. From charm bracelets and Add-a-Bead necklaces to floating hearts and mood rings, jewelry was a strong memory for most women, who could easily chronicle their lives through the jewelry they'd once worn. I smiled as I thought of my old college roommate, Carson, who still had a Mickey Mouse watch that she'd kept since she was a girl.

Carson, in fact, was the one who had inspired me to try resin casting. I'd reminded her of that old Mr. Goodbar necklace during a phone call one night, and she'd told me I ought to try to recreate it for old time's sake, so I did. After searching online, I had found a mold for making resin circles, ovals, squares, and hearts. I was ready to start designing some new resin pieces for an arts market I would attend later in the spring.

After digging into my tin of vintage jewelry bits, I pulled out some pieces I thought might make good resin fillers. One small plastic Ziploc bag contained nothing but mismatched rhinestones. Those jewels had fallen out of other pieces but were too pretty to throw away—like the rhinestones I'd recovered from beneath that seller's table at Making Memories a week ago. Some emerald-green stones caught my eye, and I added them to the smallest of the circular molds and added the resin.

Emeralds. I can't get away from them these days.

Using another of the round molds, one about an inch and a half wide, I added a distressed bottle cap whose interior was stamped with the word "Dream." After filling the remaining molds with assorted rhinestones, beads, and bottle caps, I carefully poured in the resin. I had already learned the hard way that the stuff was almost impossible to get off a surface once it spilled there. Caution was the name of the game.

Soon, all the cavities of the molds were filled, and my resin pieces were curing. I capped the resin bottles, put all my supplies back in place, and spent a few minutes petting an unusually needy Miriam Haskell before I showered and got ready for dinner. Justin was going to pick me up, and I wanted to be sure I was dressed to the nines before he got there.

AFTER BEING ON THE go for so many days, I was happy to slow down and spend some time simply selecting an outfit and getting dressed for a nice dinner out. I chose a simple black wrap dress and accessorized with vintage pearly earrings—clip-ons that I'd converted to pierced—and a matching choker. The final touch was a stretchy pearl bracelet I'd made with a vintage cameo button at the center.

Tossing on a lightweight ivory sweater, I figured I could easily shed it if the room was too warm or keep it on if the air-conditioning was on full blast. We Southerners were notorious for optimistically cranking up the air at the first signs of spring.

Justin picked me up promptly at six forty in a big black Explorer for our seven o'clock reservation. Dressed in a dark-gray suit and tie, he looked even more handsome than usual. He'd brought me a small bouquet of yellow tulips, and I wondered how he knew they were my favorite flowers. I quickly stepped inside and put them in water before he ushered me to the car and opened the door.

"Nice ride," I said. "You've certainly got a lot more room than in my little car." I pointed at my red Fusion in the driveway.

"And you probably get a lot better gas mileage." Justin looked over and smiled, then he got behind the wheel, and we headed to the restaurant. "You know, I drove a smaller car for a few years, especially when gas prices got so outrageous, but now I need the space for all these paintings and prints and easels. I used to spend hours trying to cram everything into a subcompact. Finally, I gave up and got something more practical for transporting the artwork. It saves time in the long run, and that's what counts."

I laughed. "You sound as time-crunched as I am these days."

Soon we were turning in to the brick-paved parking lot in front of The Loft. Few parking spaces were left.

"Looks like we got here just in time," I said.

"You're not kidding." Justin walked around to my side of the car and opened the door. *Such a gentleman. I like that.*

The Loft was one of the hottest new restaurants in town, so I had been only too happy when Justin got a reservation and asked me to join him there for dinner.

Since Roseland's defunct mill buildings were no longer used for the textile trade, town officials had been eager to find other uses for them. Fortunately, our town's largest old mill building was in good shape and had some great architectural features. After an apartment complex had taken over most of the building with loft apartments, there had been enough room left to create The Loft, an upscale restaurant on the building's third floor.

When we entered, Justin told them our reservation was under the name "Hayes." Our server, a pleasant college-age blonde, wore The Loft's uniform of black pants, a crisp white shirt, and a black apron with the discreet gold-and-black Loft logo.

Soon, we were seated and browsing heavy black leather folders containing the evening's menu. Since I'd eaten a hearty lunch at Mama's Place, I was surprised when my stomach gave a low rumble. Everything on the menu sounded good. The description of the veal piccata with freshly made linguini made my mouth water, but so did the chicken marsala. Seafood had long been my favorite, though, so I ordered a house salad and the broiled salmon with fresh asparagus.

Justin ordered the veal. If I'd known him better, I would have asked to try a bite, but that seemed like a second or third date kind of request. No use rushing anything.

Our drink orders came quickly—unsweet tea for Justin, water with lemon for me. A loaf of crusty bread and a tray of herb-infused olive oils arrived at the same time, and we were soon slicing off pieces and sampling the oils.

"You said the other night that you're on the board of the arts council," Justin said. "So how did you get involved with them?"

A lot of people in town still knew me from my reporter days, so it was refreshing to find someone who knew me simply as Emma, a jewelry designer and not the small-town news reporter who had written features for a few years.

Before answering, I finished the bite of fresh bread I had just dipped in olive oil. "I got to know a lot of the arts council members back when I worked for the newspaper. They were a great bunch of people. Hardworking, talented, some super volunteers. So I always said that if I ever came up with an arts and crafts passion of my own, I'd get involved." I paused to sip a drink of my ice water.

"Then how did you make the leap from newspaper reporter to full-time jewelry designer? I'm sure that didn't happen overnight."

I nodded. "When newspapers began shrinking and even going out of business a few years ago, I could see that I needed to think seriously about my career, to have a backup plan. I thought about going back to school and getting more training, in digital journalism this time, but that wasn't where my heart was. I started spending every spare moment working on my jewelry designs, and these days, my jewelry commissions keep me busy."

Justin smiled. "I love your story, Emma."

I could feel myself blushing. "But it's not terribly exciting."

"Are you kidding me? Think of how many people dream of going into business for themselves and never have the guts to do it, but you did. So yeah, that does sound exciting to me." Justin finished his salad and sliced off more bread.

"As far as the arts council, that was a logical place to go to learn more about the business side of the arts and crafts world. I had no idea so much would be involved in marketing and selling my work. Imagine my surprise when I heard my fellow artists analyzing the market and talking about color trends and popular images in design. That was really eye-opening. I had always assumed that making jewelry would take up the vast majority of my time, and as I'm sure you've learned, those days of simply making art and sitting back and relaxing are forever gone."

"If that was ever really the case to begin with," Justin said.

"Touché. So that's the saga of how I got involved with the arts council and why I'm involved today. Is that a little TMI for you?" I laughed and realized I was slightly nervous. Even though it wasn't exactly a blind date, the evening still had that blind date vibe. And Justin's chocolate-brown eyes were awfully handsome.

"No, it's not too much information at all. And frankly, I think it's always smart to analyze your market." Justin got a twinkle in his eye. "Even painters do that, you know."

I raised an eyebrow. "But your work is mostly landscapes and portraits. How could you possibly change those based on a market analysis?"

"You know the story behind the painting of Madame X?" he asked.

"Some." I nodded. "I know John Singer Sargent originally painted her with the strap hanging down, which was considered scandalous at the time. And if I remember correctly, he went back and painted that part of the portrait again, right?"

"Correct." Justin saluted me with his glass of tea.

"Obviously a smart move," I said. "But I'm betting you've never had to redo a portrait like that, have you?"

Justin shook his head. "No, but I've certainly read the art magazines and websites and visited enough galleries to know what sells. I do plenty of work that's only for me, and paintings that I certainly hope someone will like, but I'm not ashamed to tell you that I watch the kinds of things that are selling well when I'm coming up with ideas for new pieces."

"What's something you've painted recently that you might not have originally planned to create?"

Justin looked thoughtful. "The houses here in Roseland, for one thing."

"But paintings of houses aren't anything new."

"No, but the fascination with them here sure is. Individuals often want a painting of their own home. In a town like this one, though, there's such an emphasis on history that I often come across people who want paintings of several historic homes, not just the one they happen to live in."

"That's not true in other places?"

Justin sliced off another piece of bread. "Not at all."

I was glad I didn't have to worry about eating daintily around him.

"And another thing I've started painting is more landscapes. Those seem to sell well in all places and at all times. What about you? Have you created any new jewelry in response to something the public wants?"

"Have you heard the phrase 'Throw a bird on it'? That's been the motto in the jewelry world for the last few years. Wire nests with pearl 'eggs' and those dangly owl necklaces that look like the 1970s pieces our mothers wore. Yeah, bird stuff has been a real hit for jewelry designers. Does that say something about us, that we've suddenly rediscovered birds?"

"You want my cheap pop-culture analysis?" Justin asked.

I nodded, intrigued to hear what he had to say. At that moment, though, his analysis would have to wait because our meals arrived.

My salmon was the perfect shade of pink, and Justin's veal piccata had lemon slices in a rich, buttery-looking sauce. The tantalizing scents threatened to make me light-headed.

I smiled at him. "Maybe I can hear your analysis after we've gotten a few bites of this great food in us."

Justin looked relieved. He must have been as hungry as I was.

It was always strange to share the silence with someone I didn't know well. I wondered what he was thinking. I also wondered whether I should have declined the rich cream sauce with my asparagus. I had to admit it was delicious.

Justin cleared his throat. "This veal is excellent. How's your salmon?"

"Melt-in-your-mouth good. I like to think I'm a bit of a seafood connoisseur, and I must say this is cooked perfectly."

"Glad to hear it." He took a drink of his tea. "Ready for my pop culture analysis about birds now?"

"Sure." I coolly touched my chin and gave him my best *Thinker* pose. Really, though, I was trying to surreptitiously make sure I didn't have any cream sauce dribbling down my chin.

"Okay. So we live in this highly technical, less industrial but increasingly man-made world, right? Well, I think the renewed interest in all things nature is the 'natural,' if you will, reaction to that, a corrective measure. When you see people committed to organic gardening, or setting out birdfeeders, or searching out new farm-to-table restaurants, it's all a reaction against the technical and the man-made."

"And so we give them birds?" I asked, barely able to contain the amused smile I felt tugging at the corners of my mouth.

"Exactly," Justin said. "And so we give them birds."

A commotion near the front of the restaurant caught our attention. "Is this a restaurant or a private club?" a haughty voice asked so loudly that many of the diners turned around in their seats to look.

It was Tony LeMann, and after we'd heard a little more of the conversation, it became apparent that he was complaining because he and the blonde with him couldn't get a last-minute seating for dinner.

"Oh no," Justin said, a weary expression overtaking his face. "Him again. After his latest run-in with Gail Ginn, I hoped that was the last I'd see of him for a while."

"What happened with Gail?" I leaned in.

Justin rolled his eyes. "Wait till he's out of range, then I'll explain."

The manager was called to the front of the restaurant. Though I could hear only snippets of the conversation, it soon became clear that Tony had called earlier, asked about the usual crowd size on a Monday night, and assumed he could get a reservation. The beautiful and much younger woman at his side—not someone I'd seen with him before—looked off coolly, as if she were not embarrassed but simply bored that Tony was making a scene.

"I'm so sorry there was a misunderstanding," the manager said. "If you can wait just ten or fifteen minutes, I believe a table near the back will be opening up shortly." He pointed at a corner table, but Tony was already shaking his head.

As he glanced in the direction of our table, I quickly turned my head. Curious as I was, I didn't want to be seen watching the whole kerfuffle. I was relieved when I heard Tony say, "Just forget it. I can't imagine the food here would be that great, anyway." He turned to his lady friend. "We might as well head toward Atlanta, where the *good* restaurants are."

In one fluid movement, he spun around, companion in tow, and stormed from the restaurant. *Whew.* I was glad to see him leave. And based upon the now relaxed faces of the manager and waitstaff around him, so were the employees of The Loft.

Justin swallowed his last bite of veal piccata and cleared his throat. "How do you know him again?"

"We've never actually been introduced." I glanced toward the entrance to be sure Tony hadn't changed his mind and returned. "But I've seen him around town a few times lately, and I know who he is. He's the brother of my late friend Tina, the one who worked at the Silver Squirrel downtown."

Justin grimaced. "If you haven't been around him, then you might not know that Tony LeMann has never heard the word *no*. I was at Gail Ginn's the other day to start making plans for the next Gallery Stroll. Tony came in—with no appointment—and said he was headed out of town and wanted to, as he put it, 'give your little shop an opportunity' to carry his girlfriend's artwork."

I was eager to hear more. "Seriously? Does he not know who Gail is? Or how insulting it was to tell Roseland's famous weaver what her 'little shop' needs to sell?"

Justin shook his head. "Honestly, I don't think he had a clue. But Gail explained that she allowed only fine arts and crafts in her gallery, not the sort of decoupaged pieces his 'friend' makes. Tony wasn't too thrilled to hear that. Said he was sorry to hear that Gail wasn't interested in his friend's 'one-of-a-kind' offerings and even implied that her own weavings were second-rate."

I finished the last of my meal and placed my napkin on the table. "Then he obviously doesn't know Gail's reputation or the quality of her work."

Justin nodded. "And he doesn't know how to help his girlfriend if he thinks he can buy his way into any place in town that he wants. Like Gail's shop. Or this restaurant, for that matter."

"Buy his way? Did he actually offer to pay Gail?"

Justin grimaced. "That was the shocking thing. He whipped out his credit card and asked how much it would take to get his girlfriend on the schedule at Gail's next Gallery Stroll. When she told him there was no charge for exhibiting in her gallery, Tony scoffed and said, 'Everyone's got a price. And whatever yours is, believe me, I can afford it.'"

"You can't be serious?" I whispered to make sure no one could overhear us.

"Serious as a heart attack." Justin laced his fingers together on the table. "From what Gail told me, Tony LeMann does have the money he claims, and he loves to flaunt it around town. Her husband's an attorney too, you know, and he's had a few dealings with Tony in the past. In fact, Gail thinks Tony might've worn out his welcome in Atlanta and is thinking of coming to Roseland so he can be a bigger fish in a smaller pond."

Wow. If Tony had that kind of money and wasn't helping with his mother's assisted-living expenses, it wasn't because he *couldn't*. It was simply that he *wouldn't*.

We agreed that Tony was getting off on exactly the wrong foot in Roseland. By that time, our server had returned to see if we were interested in dessert. The crème brûlée and other offerings sounded quite decadent, but I couldn't eat another bite. Justin said he was full as well, so he paid our bill, and we were soon headed to my house.

Justin and I chatted all the way home, and I appreciated how easy he was to talk to. Still, I couldn't help feeling a little apprehensive as we approached the house. *Should I invite him in? Will he expect a kiss?* Furthermore, I needed to package some jewelry pieces for one of my customers so I could get them in the mail the next morning.

Justin pulled into my driveway and came around to my door.

"It's been a lovely evening, Justin, and I wish I had time to invite you in, but I've got a bit of jewelry work to take care of this evening."

He smiled. "No problem at all. I have a few hours of business to tend to myself, so maybe next time."

Next time. I liked the sound of that.

Then Justin grasped my right hand, brushed his lips across the back of it, and said good night. It was such a gentlemanly gesture, and it made me like him even more.

Once I climbed the porch steps and unlocked the front door, I turned around. Justin sat in my driveway, clearly waiting to see me safely inside before he waved goodbye.

Inside the house, I flipped on the living room light and was about to step inside the kitchen to get the teakettle going when I looked down in horror. My red tackle box and beads were strewn across the floor, which looked like the debris field following an F5 bead tornado. The glass pane in the side door to the kitchen was shattered, with shards of glass scattered across the beads.

My heart skipped a beat. "Miriam? Are you okay? Miriam?" I cried out.

Then, before I did anything else, I grabbed my cell phone out of my purse and called the Roseland PD.

As soon as the police assured me they were on their way, I continued calling out for Miriam. At last, a pitiful meow came from the living room, where she was hiding under the sofa. I coaxed her out, held her close, and waited on the porch for the officers to arrive.

However, the first car that pulled up wasn't a patrol car but Jen's blue Honda Civic. "I thought you were supposed to be on your way to Atlanta with Todd."

Jen ran up the porch steps and gave me a hug. "And I thought you had a big date tonight."

"I did, but I came home and found that someone had broken into my house while I was gone. So I walked in and—"

Just then, a patrol car pulled to the curb. Detective Shelton apparently wasn't on duty that evening, which suited me fine. Instead, as Jen looked on, I led the two officers inside and answered their questions about where I'd been, who I'd been with, and how I'd spent my evening. They took photos of the damage and dusted for prints. After I'd spent two exhausting hours talking to the officers, they finally said good night. I put on a pot of coffee and got ready to clean up the mess with help from Jen, who had kindly volunteered to stay and assist.

It had been such a fine evening until I returned home, and I gave Jen the rundown as we corralled thousands of wayward beads and baubles.

"So why didn't you go to Atlanta with Todd?"

She gave me an eye roll. "Because the *Daily Tribune* apparently doesn't expect its reporters to actually turn in stories on time. And you know me. I couldn't just leave the dirty work for someone else to take care of while I was off having fun."

Fortunately for me, Jen had been at work and listening to her police scanner when the officers got dispatched to my address. After about an hour of painstaking work, the two of us had managed to restore some semblance of order to the kitchen. I assured Jen that she could go home and I would be fine.

"What makes you so sure the perp won't come back again while you're here?" Jen crossed her arms and narrowed her eyes at me.

I pointed out the kitchen window. "That unmarked patrol car. He told me he's going to be parked in front overnight as a precaution."

Craning her neck, Jen took a look and seemed to begrudgingly accept that answer.

After thanking my friend for the help, I walked her to the front door, told her goodbye, and gave a slight wave to the officer behind the wheel of the silver car on the other side of the street.

Safe or not, though, I knew I wouldn't be getting much sleep that night.

Chapter Twenty

When I got up Tuesday morning after a restless night, I was still angry at whoever had violated my house. My morning was spent waiting on service calls from a glass company and a locksmith. And as a result of the vandalism, I now needed to go by Craft World to pick up some new jewelry cleaner and organizing supplies. I wished I knew who the vandal was so I could send them a bill. I drove to the store on a mission, with no time for leisurely bead shopping. I would get in and get out.

With my shopping basket full, I marched toward the front of the store. Gus Townsend stood close to the registers, obviously about to check out. That was odd. Gus had always claimed she never set foot in any chain stores that sold craft supplies. She would sniff and say, "I detest those stores." Gus had always said it was important to support only the smaller, independent craft supply shops. *To each his own.*

I didn't always have the luxury or the time to run to Atlanta in search of beads and wire. And I sure didn't that day. I walked up to Gus. "So, what are you doing at Craft World today?"

"C-Craft World?" she stammered. "Oh, um, just picking up some canvases. You won't tell anyone I was here, will you?"

I frowned. "Not if it's a secret, but what's the big deal?"

Gus bit her lip. "It's a big deal when you're trying to maintain a reputation as a fine artist."

My face must have shown that I was puzzled.

"Look, I know you've been busy with this Tina LeMann murder thing, and I was sorry to hear about what happened at your house last night—"

"How'd you know about that?" I asked, instantly on alert.

"Jen told Savannah about it at the coffee shop this morning, and Savannah told me."

"Good news travels fast, eh?"

"Yeah, I guess. But here's the thing, Emma. I really am sorry your friend Tina got killed, but she wasn't always as nice to everyone as she was to you. She hated my artwork and told a few people she thought it was an embarrassment to Roseland every time the town was mentioned in connection with my work. I know you've heard that we tangled when she fought me on the *Faces of Roseland* exhibit last year, but I had to speak up. I don't think she handled that very well, but that doesn't mean I'm glad she's dead. Do you understand that?"

In her swirling green skirt, lacy socks, and granny boots, Gus didn't exactly look like a natural-born killer.

"I guess I see your point now," I said. "And hopefully we'll find out who killed her soon so this will all be over."

After saying goodbye to Gus, I headed home to the thankless task of cleaning and sorting a few thousand beads, buttons, and charms. After a few hours, I realized my cell phone was ringing for the first time in a while, so I dug into my purse and retrieved it. No name appeared on the screen, but the number was a local one. I tapped the green telephone icon and said hello.

"Emma, hey, I've got some things I really need to talk to you about." The male voice on the other end sounded serious. It was Hubert Harris. *So he did get out.*

"Something that's related to the murder investigation?"

"I don't know. Maybe," Hubert said. "I'm not sure, but I want to tell someone, you know, in case anything happens to me."

That sounded ominous. *Does he think Harriet has a contract out on him?* "Okay, Hubert. Sure. Where and when do you want to meet?"

"It's pretty warm out. What would you think about meeting at the new park? I thought I'd go for a walk and get some fresh air, especially after being cooped up for a while. I've been doing a lot of thinking here lately."

I was certain he had. "Sure thing. I can be there in fifteen minutes. That work for you?"

"See you then."

I noticed I'd missed a few texts while I was deep into my afternoon of jewelry sorting, but I scanned all the messages and didn't see anything that sounded particularly urgent. Jen asked me to call her as soon as possible, but she always said that. Savannah had left a text reporting that Harriet was calling her twice a day to cry on her shoulder and asking what I thought she should do about it. None of that was as important as finding out what Hubert had to say. I would drive to the park, learn what was on his mind, and have plenty of time later to catch up with my friends.

When I got to the park in downtown Roseland, it was deserted. The skies had become overcast earlier in the afternoon, and that had sent all the moms and kids scampering. I spotted Hubert right away. He quickly stood from the bench where he'd been sitting, and he clenched his fists as I approached.

"There are some things I want to tell you," Hubert said, getting straight to the point. "But I'm hoping I can tell you in confidence. I know you used to be a reporter and all, but you don't do that anymore, right? This is off the record, okay?"

"Listen," I said, "even though it will all be in my brain, I give you my word that I won't act on it unless absolutely necessary. And if I have to do that, you'll be the first to know."

Hubert seemed a little bothered by that deal, but it was the best he was going to get. I had nothing to lose.

"If that's how it's got to be, then I guess that's how it's got to be." He glanced around nervously, as if making sure we were the only two people in the park. He cleared his throat and began. "I know you've lived in this town long enough that you've probably heard some rumors along the way." Hubert looked at me and nodded, indicating that he was waiting for me to acknowledge his comment.

"I've heard a few things." I was starting to feel a little uncomfortable about the turn of this conversation.

"And you've probably heard I have an eye for the ladies." Hubert briefly turned away, his face reddening slightly.

Suddenly, I felt embarrassed. Hubert Harris's personal life was really none of my concern. "I've heard something about that a few times, but your private life isn't my business." I was trying to be as gentle as I could.

"Truth is, I'm just an old guy who likes to flirt," he said. "And some of the gals these days like to flirt back. I know Harriet doesn't believe it, but I've never been unfaithful to her. Not once. Not one single, solitary time."

"Okay." *Where is this headed?*

"My point is, I've learned the hard way that not every woman I flirt with sees it as innocently as I do." Hubert stared at the grass and traced a bare spot with his loafer. "I had a few young teachers back in my day who thought I was going to divorce Harriet and marry them, but I never had the slightest intention of doing that." Hubert looked up then, possibly to gauge my reaction.

Again, I wondered why he was confessing to me. I didn't know what his past indiscretions could possibly have to do with Tina's murder.

"A few months ago," he said, "I started what I thought was an innocent little flirtation with your friend from the antique shop."

"You flirted with Tina?" That was something I hadn't expected to hear from the horse's mouth. Our conversation was getting more bizarre by the moment.

Hubert pulled out his handkerchief and wiped his brow. I started to ask him to wipe mine too.

"Yeah. I enjoyed talking to her when Harriet and I met with her about selling the house. Seemed friendly enough, and she was young and attractive, so..."

I was thoroughly confused. *Did he have a fling with Tina?* No, he'd just told me that he never cheated on Harriet. "So, what, then? You got involved with Tina?"

"No, no." He waved his hands to let me know I was off base. "Just telling you that I engaged in a little harmless flirting with her."

I chewed my lip and only half tried to conceal my irritation. Maybe Hubert's stay in the slammer hadn't resulted in any productive soul-searching after all. He was starting to waste my time. "So what are you saying?"

"Only that I'd been flirting with Tina, and that really seemed to set off another gal who was a bit of an oddball. I didn't realize it at first, but this woman seemed to be on a mission to get Harriet and me to break up. I tried to remove myself from that situation as quickly as I could."

"Uh-huh." I tapped my foot, uncertain where our strange discussion was going and sensing that I should encourage him to move things along.

"I met her one day over at a house I was listing for sale. I was putting a sign in the yard, and she said she was new to town and needed directions to an antique mall nearby, which happened to be mine and Harriet's. I offered to lead her over there. Be neighborly, that kind of thing."

I cocked my head, and Hubert had the decency to at least look a little ashamed.

"I figured out pretty quickly this gal was looking for a sugar daddy, and I told her I was a happily married man, and I was. At least, as happy as a man can be while married to a woman like Harriet."

That time, I couldn't help grinning.

Hubert cleared his throat and continued. "Anyway, this woman started coming by the antique mall when she knew it was my day to work there. She called the cell phone number that was on the business card I gave her. This gal obviously had some issues."

"And?" I asked. "Does this have anything to do with Tina LeMann's murder?" Maybe he needed to see a counselor or minister instead of confessing all his sins to me.

"Maybe," he said. "I met the woman when she convinced me to let her look inside the house Tina was about to vacate. I didn't find out until later that it was her sister, Teri."

My heart skipped a beat. *Teri, whom I'd come to know and like?* Sure, I'd found Teri a bit odd at first, but suddenly, I had a feeling that her *odd* was more like *dangerous*. I could hardly spit the questions out fast enough. "Why did Teri want in the house so badly?"

"Something about a family heirloom Tina claimed to have," Hubert said, causing a chill to run down my spine. "Now that Tina's gone, and I was the one listing her house, I get the feeling the real killer's still out there and trying to pin this thing on me."

Then I remembered something that made my blood run cold. *Carleen is meeting with Teri any minute now at the Silver Squirrel.* If the woman was as unhinged as Hubert was suggesting, Carleen might well be in danger.

I leapt to my feet. "Come with me, Hubert. I think I know where Teri is, and I may need your help!"

Chapter Twenty-One

I ran to my car, hopped in, and had it in Drive before Hubert even got his door open. He was still buckling up when I sped out of the park.

"Where are we going?" he asked, looking almost as terrified as I felt.

"The Silver Squirrel!" I marveled that Hubert hadn't figured out what was going on yet. "Have you got your phone with you?"

His head bobbed up and down.

"Then call 911 and tell them to get over to Carleen's!"

Hubert made the call, tripping over his words as he relayed the information to the dispatcher. My hands gripped the steering wheel, and I prayed we wouldn't be too late. My tires slung gravel as I wheeled out of the park's unpaved parking area.

Hubert looked confused. "Won't the shop be closed by now?"

"Yes, and that's what worries me. Your pal Teri has been playing the grieving sister, and she's meeting with Carleen right now."

"Carleen? What could she possibly want with her?"

"I'm pretty sure Carleen has an emerald that's been missing from that necklace, and I have a feeling Teri has the rest of it."

Hubert seemed bewildered. "Oh... now wait a minute, you don't think she would hurt her just to get that emerald, do you?"

"If she killed her sister like I think she did, of course she would!" I said, impatient that he could be so clueless. If he hadn't been flirting with both sisters in the first place... But that sort of thinking wasn't helpful. I needed to get to Carleen.

225

A red light caught me just before I pulled up in front of the shop, threatening to snap my already frayed nerves. I barely remembered to put the car in Park before I turned to Hubert and told him I was getting out. "You stay here while I try to get inside and see what's going on with Carleen and Teri."

Hubert looked stunned, but I didn't have time to explain anything more.

Running up the sidewalk in front of the shop, I saw the Closed sign, but a light was on in the back, where Carleen's office was located.

"Carleen!" I yelled, banging on the door. "Carleen, I need to talk to you. It's important."

Peering through the glass window, I could see a shadowy movement at the back of the shop, but no one came out of the office. I prayed I wasn't about to discover a second dead body there.

Realizing I might have a better view from the back of the Silver Squirrel, I ran to the alley behind the shop. *Did I make it here in time? What if Teri's hurt Carleen? Lord, please don't let there be another murder...*

I started banging on the back door as soon as I got there. "Carleen, open up!" I knocked and knocked until I thought my knuckles would bleed. Still no answer.

Then I thought of a way to get Teri's attention if she was actually in the shop. "Carleen, please let me in. I found the earrings that match that emerald I found behind your shop."

As if by magic, orange-haired Teri LeMann stepped out of Carleen's office, but there was no sign of my friend. *Did Teri kill her?*

Teri walked calmly to the door, opened it a crack, and gave me a Cheshire cat smile. "Hello there, Emma. Carleen's not feeling very well this evening. In fact, she's currently dealing with her upset stomach in the ladies' room. She said to tell you she's happy to hear you found the emerald earrings and for you to just leave them with me."

I tried to appear calm and rational. Giving Teri what I hoped was my warmest smile, I pretended that I believed her lies. "Oh, hi, Teri. I hear that a nasty virus has been spreading around town. Is that what's wrong with her? Anything I can do to help?" Slowly, I was wedging my foot farther into that slim opening.

"No, thanks. Carleen was just giving me a last-minute appraisal on some family silver before she goes home for the night. So what's this about some emerald earrings that you were mentioning?" Teri was the picture of confidence, as if she had no idea I was on to her. But she had a steely gleam in her eyes that I didn't like.

"Tell you what," I said, clearly surprising her when I shoved my entire right leg into the door and barged in. "I think I would really feel more comfortable giving these directly to Carleen."

Teri stumbled backward and didn't seem at all pleased that I had busted in on her "last-minute appraisal." Only then did I notice the small black revolver she had been holding behind her back.

Her smile evaporated, and she pointed her gun at my side. "I'm afraid you'll need to go join your friend now."

Don't act scared. "And what if I don't?"

"And what if I put a bullet in your head?" Teri placed the gun near my left ear to show me she meant business. With a hand jabbed sharply into my back, she marched me into Carleen's office.

"Emma!" Carleen cried when I entered the room.

"Are you okay?" I asked.

She looked shaken but appeared unharmed. "Yes, I'm fine, but—"

"But you're not going to be for long if you don't both shut up," Teri snarled. "And you"—she pointed the gun at me—"can hand over those earrings now."

I gulped. "Um... ah..."

Teri smirked. "Just as I thought. There aren't any matching earrings, are there?"

I bit my lip, unsure of what I should say, and tried to shift my purse without her noticing. If I could grab my cell phone quickly enough, then—

"And put that hideous purse of yours on the sofa. Now."

I did as she directed.

Carleen sat in her toile chair, nervously fiddling with what appeared to be the missing emerald necklace I'd come to know so well.

I knew I had to keep Teri talking if Carleen and I were going to get out of there alive. "So that's the infamous emerald necklace, huh?"

"For your information"—Teri waved her gun between the two of us—"Carleen already handed over the missing emerald, and she's putting it back in the necklace before I go. I thought the stone would be at your house last night based on what you said at tea on Sunday, but apparently not. Looks like you just keep a bunch of cheap trinkets around to work with."

So that was who had vandalized my home. Teri was lucky I didn't have a gun at that moment myself.

My heart was about to beat out of my chest, but I somehow managed to think calmly. "It's obvious that you killed your sister over this necklace, but what I don't understand is why you planned to kill her here rather than at her house." If I rambled on long enough, maybe Carleen and I would have a chance to catch Teri off guard and grab the gun before she used it on us.

"What makes you think I ever *planned* to kill her?" Teri was inches from my face, and I felt the cold metal of the gun on my arm. "I asked Tina if I could meet her at the shop that morning to discuss the fair division of our mother's property when the time comes—the things Tina hadn't yet cheated me out of, anyway. She said she was tired of arguing over the necklace, and she wanted her"—Teri waved her gun at Carleen—"to examine it before we had it appraised and sold, splitting the proceeds between all three siblings."

"So you didn't come here intending to kill Tina?"

"Of course not," Teri spat. "But when I got here, Tina told me she'd changed her mind about splitting the money from the necklace. She said she was going to suggest to Tony that we sell it and put the money in the bank to help pay for our mother's care."

"But you didn't like that idea, did you?" I asked. *It would sure be nice to see some blue uniforms coming through the doors here. Any moment now...*

"No, I didn't like that idea! When Tina pulled out the necklace that morning, I decided it was the last time she would ever hold that over me. I was going to take it and sell it on behalf of the family, giving each of us an equal share."

Carleen piped up. "And Tina tried to stop you."

"Yes." Teri had a far-off look in her eyes. "If only she hadn't done that, things might have ended differently. But Tina grabbed that stupid candelabra off the desk and threatened me with it, so I had to act in self-defense!" She looked enraged, as if the memory was wreaking havoc on her mind and sending her into a frenzy once again.

"So how did you lose the emerald?"

"That was Tina's fault too. After she pointed that ugly piece of silver in my face, I tried to grab it from her. Then she jerked the necklace away and started to attack me with the candelabra and chased me down the hall. I was forced to protect myself. When she tripped on the rug and fell there by the back door, all I wanted to do was get out of here. So I grabbed the box with the necklace, but she never bothered to mention that one of the stones had already fallen out. I guess I lost the emerald when I sped out of here Friday morning."

"So you killed your sister just so you could have this necklace?"

"My sister only held on to the necklace because she knew I had always wanted it. And my brother doesn't need the money. So really, I'm just making sure this piece of jewelry goes to the person my mother would want to have it."

Why are the police taking so long? Hubert called them ten minutes ago. Please, God, help me keep her distracted until help arrives.

"You must feel quite satisfied to finally have this necklace in your possession, right?"

Teri looked at me quizzically. "That's not really your concern, is it?" Her voice dripped sarcasm. "I tried to warn you as nicely as I could to stay out of all this, but you couldn't take the hint."

A light bulb went on in my head. "You're the one who left that letter for me at the Foothills Gallery!"

Teri's only reply was an evil grin.

"So why didn't you call the police if it was an act of self-defense?" I hoped I wasn't pushing my luck, but I was desperate to hold her off until the police arrived. Besides, if I was about to die, at least I would go out with all my questions answered.

"It was much better to have everyone think it was a botched robbery attempt. Plus, my brother and I had been seen at Teri's house—our mother's house, actually. Despite what you gullible people have been led to believe, Tina tricked her out of it."

"Why do you say that?" I cocked my head. "I heard she wanted to sell her house to help pay for your mother's assisted-living care. Surely the sale of that necklace would have helped too." That time, I was asking out of genuine curiosity more than any effort at stalling—although stalling was still an excellent idea.

"Our mother never should have left her house and gone into that so-called assisted-living place. That was just Tina's way of getting the house for herself. And you know what? I'm *glad* she had to sell the house. She never deserved it, anyway!" Teri had a maniacal look on her face, so full of rage that I wasn't sure what she might be capable of.

With my nerves already stretched thin, I glanced at Teri's hand, which was still gripping the gun. *As long as she doesn't pull the trigger...*

Standing next to Carleen behind her desk, I had a view of the half-open doorway where Teri stood. A slight shadow appeared to her left. I tried not to focus on it, deliberately keeping my eyes trained on her. I didn't want to alert her that anything was off.

"Did your mother favor Tina and your brother instead of you? If so, that must have made you really angry."

"Both of them were just greedy liars who stole my mother's affection and my inheritance," Teri said. "Tina got what was coming to her, and my brother will get his too before this is over with."

I shuddered. With any luck, that shadow I'd just seen meant someone was there to help us make it out of there alive.

"So that"—I pointed at the necklace on Carleen's desktop—"is the cause of all this trouble?"

Teri's eyes darted to the desk, where Carleen was checking the prongs holding the replaced emerald. Her hands were shaking slightly, and I could tell she was frightened.

"Hmm. Now that's interesting." I craned my neck as if trying to peer at the emerald. I purposely had a skeptical look on my face as I examined the necklace.

"What's interesting?" Teri asked.

"Oh, nothing, probably. It's just that something about your necklace looks a little different from the one that I saw in that print-out from the police."

Teri eyed me silently, as if she knew I was up to something. "Do you have it with you?"

I shook my head. "No, but I have a picture of it on my cell phone."

"Get it. Now." She waved the revolver in the direction of my purse on the sofa.

I took a deep breath. "It'll take me a minute to find it. This purse is so large, I just throw everything in there and go, you know."

Carleen studied me with a worried expression. She probably wondered why I was babbling about a disorganized purse at such a time.

I dug into the pockets, rummaged around in the zippered pouch, and fished an arm down inside while I chewed my lip and kept my gaze trained on Teri.

She followed my movements with a cold, hard look on her face. "Hurry up. Find that phone before you waste any more of my time. I'm getting tired of waiting."

Grasping the phone, I uttered a relieved "Got it" and quickly pulled it out. With a tap, the screen came to life. I flipped through my image gallery until I came to the photo of the necklace. Carefully, I reached out to Teri with my phone and watched her hands as she grabbed it. "If you enlarge the photo," I said, "you'll see what I mean."

I waited until the moment that her fingers began to enlarge the image. Then I clutched the bottom half of the lipstick-shaped canister of pepper spray I'd just retrieved from my purse, aimed it straight at her face, and pressed the button.

"Aaargh!"

My aim was perfect. Teri's hands flew to her eyes. She dropped both the phone and the gun, which I snatched from the floor and immediately trained on her. She was red-faced and sputtering a string of obscenities I seriously doubted had ever been heard inside the Silver Squirrel.

The office door banged open, and Detective Alan Shelton rushed in. He quickly shuffled me out of the way and pointed his gun at Teri, who was gasping for breath. Her face nearly matched her hair, and I couldn't tell whether the red on her face was because of anger or because of her body's reaction to the pepper spray. I was just glad she'd been stopped.

Several other officers arrived too, and a female officer slapped a pair of handcuffs on Teri. The officer began to read her the Miranda Warning.

"It was an... accident!" Teri cried. "You can't... do this!" Her breath was coming in short rasps.

"Oh, but I can do this," the arresting officer said. "Come on. Time to go. Party's over." She jerked Teri to the door of the office.

"You're hurting me. And my face still feels like it's on fire."

"Really? Well, I sure do hate that," the officer drawled, unfazed.

Teri's face sure looked as if it were on fire. She was obviously trying to glare at me but was having trouble keeping her eyes open, probably from the effects of the pepper spray.

I glared back, hopeful it would be the last time I had to see the orange-haired crazy woman. I wanted to collapse in relief, but first, I turned to Carleen. "Are you all right?"

She burst into tears and embraced me in a tight hug. "She was going to kill me, Emma! She told me I had to place this emerald back into the necklace before she left, but it was clear she wasn't going to leave me here to testify against her."

Detective Shelton and one of the other officers were about to leave the office with Teri, who was complaining that her arm might have been broken in the scuffle.

"Sorry, ma'am," the officer said. "That sort of thing can happen when you're trying to kill someone."

Outside the office door, Hubert surveyed the scene with a look of relief on his face. I stepped into the hall to speak with him. I had just opened my mouth when Teri was led out by the officers.

"You!" Teri said when she saw Hubert. "I should have known you would be right in the middle of all this!" She practically spat the words.

Hubert shrugged and looked away. I wondered if he realized how we'd all dodged a bullet with that woman—some of us quite literally.

Dusk was approaching, but a glance out the front of the shop revealed a flurry of activity. Police officers were posted at the front and back doors, and a patrol car had pulled up, probably waiting to take Teri to her new home, one she wouldn't be fighting over with her remaining sibling.

"I want to leave out the back," Teri said, glaring at the officers. "Don't parade me in front of this hick town. When I get out of jail, you people are going to have a lot to answer for."

Detective Shelton appeared unmoved by her request. "Take her out the front."

Carleen asked Hubert to get her some bottled water from the office mini refrigerator, and I tagged along behind the police officers as they escorted Teri from the shop. I wasn't at all surprised to see the photographer from the newspaper there, snapping away as Teri was placed in a patrol car. Where she was going, she would no longer need any emerald jewelry. She would have to get used to her new jewelry—a pair of handcuffs. At least the nice jumpsuit that awaited her would go well with her hair. It was a good thing she liked orange.

Jen was waiting by the front door of the shop. She looked worried, her brow furrowed as she tried to sneak a peek inside. Detective Shelton told her he had a crime scene to process and she couldn't enter.

"She might not be able to enter, but I can certainly leave," I said.

"Not until we interview you, Emma. You're a witness to an attempted murder."

"Witness? I was almost a victim, Detective. But please, give me a moment to let my friend know I'm okay."

He stared at me for a long second, as though he were wondering whether another fight was worth it. Apparently, it wasn't. "You can stick your head out the door and let her know you're okay, but please, let us get your statement before you go announcing this in the press, all right?"

I nodded at the detective then turned to the man next to me. "Say, Hubert." I patted him on the back. "Why'd it take so long for the officers to get here?"

Hubert jerked his thumb toward Detective Shelton, who was writing a few notes before he interviewed Carleen. "Turns out, Shelton here had been trailing Teri and knew she was in the shop with your friend. He had a perimeter set up around the building and was waiting for the right moment to head inside. Said it complicated things when you showed up. At that point, he had to make sure neither of you got killed."

I gulped. So the detective had actually discovered Teri was the killer before I had.

I turned around and saw that Detective Shelton had been listening to our conversation. I was pretty sure he could see guilt written all over my face. We made eye contact for a few seconds, then he gave me the slightest nod and returned to his interview with Carleen.

Outside the shop, Jen was fidgeting while she waited, probably to make sure I was unharmed. I stuck my head out the door, and she fired off the first question. "So it was the sister, eh?"

"Oh yes," I said. "Once you've had a gun stuck in your back, I think it's safe to suggest the woman holding it there just might have some violent tendencies."

"Why'd she kill her sister *here*, though?" Jen asked.

I winked and, in a low voice, confided, "Let's just say there was some sibling rivalry involved, over a man, and then she got enraged when Tina refused to hand over the necklace that morning. Tina grabbed a candelabra off Carleen's desk to protect herself, but Teri snatched it from her and eventually killed her with it. Teri claims she only meant to scare her away, but of course Tina was fatally injured.

And all that's not 'official' until I finish my interview with the police, of course."

"Of course." Jen grinned. "Got it. So when can we expect the 'official' statement from you?"

"Just as soon as they let me out of here, which I expect may be more than a few minutes. I'm fine, though, really. I'll call you the minute I'm done. Okay?"

"You'd better. They'll never forgive me if our paper isn't the one to break this story."

Before heading back to Carleen's office, I stopped to see how Hubert was doing.

"You think they'll put anything in the paper about me and Tina and Teri? I was kind of hoping to patch things up with Harriet, believe it or not. But if word of this gets out on the street..." He spread his hands in a helpless gesture. "I don't know how she'd react to that."

Oddly, flirty old Hubert was growing on me. "I don't see why it has to. Teri's... *infatuation* with you was unfortunate, but it's not the reason she killed her sister. That was just good old-fashioned greed, plain and simple."

Carleen had reapplied her lipstick and was placing an etched silver compact back in her desk drawer, a sure sign that she must be feeling better.

"And now it's your turn, Emma." Detective Shelton quietly gestured to a chair in the office. "I'm glad you're all right."

"I'm glad too. And I'm sorry to hear that I complicated things for you tonight. I had no idea..."

He held out his hand, and I shook it, even though it made me die a little inside to acknowledge that he had obviously been working on the case all along.

"Sure," he said. "But promise me one thing."

"What's that?"

"The next time there's a murder in this town, let us handle it, will you?"

I chose my words carefully. "Detective, I hope we won't have another murder in this town anytime soon, but I promise you that I won't go looking for trouble."

He nodded as if that answer satisfied him.

What I didn't say was that I hadn't gone *looking* for trouble this time. Trouble had found me. Besides, what were the chances I would ever be called on to help solve another murder? I lived in Roseland, for Pete's sake.

I joined Carleen in her office and gratefully accepted the bottle of cold water she offered. I gulped it down, surprised at how thirsty I was.

"So what will happen to this necklace now?" I asked Carleen as I looked at the brilliant emerald piece of jewelry on her desk.

"I asked Detective Shelton that same question. He seems to think that will be up to Tony LeMann unless some other family member has a claim on it. Teri apparently lied to us about inheriting her sister's estate. That hadn't been decided at all, and she certainly wasn't automatically going to get that necklace." She shuddered. "I wouldn't want the thing. I hear it's worth over fifty thousand dollars, but I don't care how valuable it is. It wasn't worth taking Tina's life."

That was the understatement of the year.

"For now, it's going into evidence," Carleen said, "so Detective Shelton asked me to leave it here until they can bag it in a few minutes."

I studied the necklace a final time. It truly was a gorgeous piece of emerald jewelry, nothing to kill someone over but exquisite nonetheless.

Considering all the unhappiness that had surrounded that lavish emerald necklace, I was suddenly grateful I designed simple costume jewelry. All I wanted to do was go home and spend the evening mindlessly sorting beads and buttons and charms without worrying about a killer roaming the streets of Roseland.

"I think I'm going to take the rest of the week off," Carleen said. "Do you think there would be anything wrong with putting up the Closed sign and staying away until Monday?"

"I'd question your sanity if you didn't."

I said goodbye to Carleen, gave her a tight hug, and walked out of the Silver Squirrel, breathing a great sigh of relief. I hardly knew what to do with myself now that the murder investigation was over. I knew one thing I had to do pronto—catch up on jewelry orders. But first, I wanted nothing more than a hot shower and a good night's sleep.

Chapter Twenty-Two

The next morning, the Cupcake Café was abuzz with news of the arrest in the Tina LeMann murder case. I had promised to meet Jen at the café for breakfast at nine o'clock, and I had just finishing giving Mavis my update on the previous evening's excitement when Jen walked in. She had a huge smile on her face.

"How did I beat you here?" I pushed the bud vase out of the way so I could see past the yellow silk daffodils.

"Some of us have a news operation to run, you know." Jen plopped her cross-body purse on the table along with a copy of the latest *Daily Tribune*.

"Nice article." I tapped the front page. "And please tell the photog I said thanks a lot for getting that great picture of my rear end along with the image of the perp walk."

Jen laughed. "Nobody even knows that's you."

"I do." I groaned. "And I'm going to have to get out to the park more often and get in shape."

"Maybe that will be easier to do now that you don't have to worry about a killer being on the loose. But before you go get in shape"—she pointed toward the baked goods—"what do you want to eat? My treat."

"Really? To what do I owe this honor?"

"Hey, do you know how many copies of the paper are flying off the racks today? If only we could have a murderer on the front page every day."

"Jen!"

"Oh, come on. You know I'm kidding. But I'm serious about breakfast. What'll it be?"

"Get me a caramel cappuccino and..."

"Yes?"

"Oh, shoot, one of those giant chocolate-fudge muffin things."

While Jen was at the counter, I checked my phone, which had been blowing up with messages all morning. So far, I needed to return calls to Savannah and Michele, and Carleen had texted to ask whether I'd be interested in joining her for a facial in the next day or two. She was taking that rest-and-recuperate business seriously. I couldn't wait to tell her that the Miriam Haskell brooch had just sold online for an astonishing seven hundred dollars!

"Here you go." Jen set a cappuccino and muffin before me, then she looked toward the counter. "Mine's on the way."

After delivering a large coffee and not one but two strawberry cupcakes to the spot in front of Jen, Mavis tapped my arm. "And you ladies let me know if you need anything else."

I wondered once again how Jen got away with eating so many sweets. Maybe all that deadline stress burned extra calories.

When Mavis walked away, Jen grinned conspiratorially. "Now then. Fess up. Wasn't it at least a little exciting to be held at gunpoint?"

"Exciting? No. Terrifying? Yes." I broke off a piece of muffin and savored the fudge flavor.

"Hey, all's well that ends well. Right? Teri's behind bars, and the downtown business owners are no longer spooked that a killer's on the prowl." Jen bit into one of her cupcakes.

"I'm thrilled that Teri's been caught, but it doesn't quite feel as if the situation is over and done with. Carleen's taking time off to recover, and I'm glad of that. Harriet apparently thought that Hubert was about to lose his life last night, and word is that she's open to reconciling with him now."

"So there's your silver lining. I guess." Jen smirked.

I had to laugh. Jen would never be one of Harriet's biggest fans. "I suppose you're right." I savored another rich bite of muffin and sipped my drink. "But I still have my concerns about those two. Savannah tells me that Hubert is set on opening that new consignment shop downtown, so it'll be interesting to see if it comes to pass."

"Downtown would be a great location for it." Jen had already polished off one cupcake and was peeling the wrapper off the second. "And what about you? What are you going to do now that you've helped catch a killer? Open your own detective agency?"

I scoffed. "Hardly. I hope I never land in the middle of anything like this again. And with Tina gone and her sister in jail, I'd say that about wraps it up."

Jen finished licking the strawberry icing off a cupcake. "But what about Brother of the Year? He didn't return any of our calls last night, so I'm wondering if he'll show up again."

"Doubtful." I crumpled my napkin and pushed my plate away. "Gail's husband told her that Tony LeMann is stirring the pot in Atlanta again, making life miserable for the legal community instead of Roseland, thank goodness."

"Huh." Jen leaned back in her chair. "So I guess everything really is wrapped up, then."

I clasped my hands. "And if things will just stay calm around here for two seconds, I can finally catch up on jewelry sales and custom jewelry designs. I had a good month, but I should have an even better one now that my attention is no longer focused on finding a killer. From now on, you're going to find me in my kitchen, nose to grindstone, slaving away at new jewelry designs and—"

"There you are, Emma!" A hyper Savannah rushed up to our table. "Hi, Jen. Sorry to interrupt you two, but Emma, you need to come with me. The mayor's mom is moving into a retirement home, and she let me come over last night and take a peek at her cast-offs before she sends them to the thrift store. She's got five jewelry boxes that are absolutely overflowing with old rhinestone jewelry, and she said if you can get there this morning before the donation truck comes by for a pickup..."

I looked at Jen and pointed at my plate.

"I've already told you, I've got it," she said. "I know what it's like when duty calls."

Duty or not, those five jewelry boxes were calling my name, and it would have been downright rude not to answer.

Rhinestones, here I come!

Recipes

Emma's Blueberry Tea Bread

1/4 CUP BUTTER, SOFTENED
    1/2 cup sugar
    1 large egg
    1/2 teaspoon lemon extract
    1 cup fresh blueberries
    1/4 cup plain Greek yogurt
    3/4 cup all-purpose flour
    1/2 teaspoon baking soda
    1/4 teaspoon salt
    2 tablespoons almonds, chopped
Preheat oven to 350 degrees. Combine ingredients in order listed, mixing well after each addition. Pour batter into 9 x 5 x 3-inch loaf pan prepared with cooking spray or lined with parchment paper. Bake for 50 minutes. Yields 1 loaf. Delicious served warm. Refrigerate any leftovers.

Carleen's Egg-Olive Sandwich Spread

4 BOILED EGGS
    4 ounces (half a large block) cream cheese

2 teaspoons mustard

20 green olives

1 teaspoon olive juice

1/4 teaspoon each of salt and pepper

Place all ingredients in food processor and pulse a few times, just until blended. If you like olives, you will love this spread! Cut out circles or other shapes in wheat bread, spread filling, then garnish with a slice of olive. Makes enough spread for 3 to 4 dozen small tea sandwiches.

Acknowledgments

Many friends and family members have encouraged me throughout my writing career, and I'm especially grateful for those who have supported me through the writing of my first novel. My critique partner, mystery writer Debbie Rasure, was an invaluable source of support, encouragement, and wisdom. My friend (and fellow tea lover) Joy Breedlove quickly volunteered to be a beta reader, and I so appreciate her constructive criticism and helpful comments.

At Red Adept Publishing, my editor, Neila Forssberg, was an absolute delight to work with and taught me so many things that not only made this book better but that will also, I suspect, improve the following ones. My Red Adept mentor, author Karissa Laurel, has been another voice of encouragement, although hers sounded, early on, like this: "Finish your book already!"

My biggest and best cheerleader is forever my husband, writer Alex McRae, who made some great suggestions to improve this book. I don't suppose most writers have a spouse who is a writer as well, but I'm so fortunate that the man I love is also a man who writes.

This book is dedicated to my firstborn niece, Madison Horton, and Emma Madison's last name honors her. Madison, please remember that when your mother occasionally tells you that you should have been my child, she means it as a compliment. I'm sure she does. Also: We are not bossy. We have leadership skills.

Finally, a little blog about teatime that I started in 2007 has grown into something much, much more, and today my Tea With

Friends readers remain a great source of support and encouragement. I hope they all will prepare a delicious cup of tea as they read the story of Emma and her friends, some of whom were inspired by some of them.

About the Author

Angela McRae began her writing career as a newspaper reporter, initially covering the police beat and then moving on to features. In a small local bookstore, Angela came across Laura Childs's *Death by Darjeeling*, a tea shop mystery set in Charleston, SC. As a longtime tea lover, she had to try it, and she's been hooked on cozy mysteries ever since.

Angela currently lives with her husband in Georgia. When she's not writing, she enjoys traveling, cooking, going to afternoon tea with family and friends, and "junkin'" at flea markets and antique malls, where she often finds inspiring artifacts that wind up in her stories. She also writes a monthly cooking column for a local publication, the *Coweta Shopper*, and enjoys connecting with readers who love to cook.

Read more at https://angelamcrae.com.

About the Publisher

Dear Reader,

We hope you enjoyed this book. Please consider leaving a review on your favorite book site.

Visit https://RedAdeptPublishing.com to see our entire catalogue.

Don't forget to subscribe to our monthly newsletter to be notified of future releases and special sales.

Made in the
USA
Lexington, KY